LOVE
TIMES
INFINITY

LOVE TIMES INFINITY

LANE CLARKE

Poppy

LITTLE, BROWN AND COMPANY

New York   Boston

Poppy
Hachette Book Group
1290 Avenue of the Americas, New York, NY 10104
Visit us at LBYR.com

First Edition: July 2022

Poppy is an imprint of Little, Brown and Company. The Poppy name and logo are trademarks of Hachette Book Group, Inc.

The publisher is not responsible for websites (or their content) that are not owned by the publisher.

Library of Congress Cataloging-in-Publication Data
Names: Clarke, Lane, author.
Title: Love times infinity / Lane Clarke.
Description: First edition. | New York : Little, Brown and Company, 2022. | Audience: Ages 12 & up. | Summary: As high school junior Michie plans for her future and explores a new relationship, she tries to reconcile with some uncomfortable truths about her life which becomes more complicated when she is contacted by her estranged mother.
Identifiers: LCCN 2021027526 | ISBN 9780759556706 (hardcover) | ISBN 9780759556713 (ebook)
Subjects: LCSH: African Americans—Juvenile fiction. | CYAC: African Americans—Fiction. | Mothers and daughters—Fiction. | Friendship—Fiction. | High schools—Fiction. | Schools—Fiction. | LCGFT: Novels.
Classification: LCC PZ7.1.C588 Lo 2022 | DDC [Fic]—dc23
LC record available at https://lccn.loc.gov/2021027526

ISBNs: 978-0-7595-5670-6 (hardcover), 978-0-7595-5671-3 (ebook)

Printed in the United States of America

LSC-C

Printing 1, 2022

For Grandma, who saved me

Que sera, sera

This book discusses the legacy of trauma, specifically sexual assault. While this trauma isn't directly experienced by the protagonist, it impacts character and plot. Additionally, this book closely examines anxiety and depression. Please consider while reading.

CHAPTER ONE

THE ILLUSTRIOUS AALIYAH, MAY SHE REST IN PEACE, ONCE said, *If at first you don't succeed, dust yourself off and try again, try again.* Well, no offense to Aaliyah, but I say, if at first you don't succeed, save yourself the heartache and give up. And if my good sis had been writing a scholarship essay for her dream college, I'm sure she would have agreed with me.

I glance at my blank computer screen. The cursor blinks steady and strong, like a healthy heart, knowing it can run in this race far longer than I can.

The mostly rotten wooden floors of our apartment creak under Grandma's feet. She tries to be quiet in the mornings, on account of the fact that I sleep like a wind chime, easily disturbed. But our apartment yawns loudly as it stretches beneath us.

She knocks twice on my bedroom door, entering before I respond. Typical. I'm still in my pajamas (read: ratty old clothes too comfortable to donate but too effed up to wear out in public).

I sleep with my head at the foot of the bed because it feels safer farther from the wall. This is due to the roaches, and the water bugs, which I would happily trade for more roaches. It drives Grandma mad, but she says nothing as she finds me in that position now, my feet up against the headboard.

"What are you working on this early?" she asks. She's already wearing her cerulean-blue scrubs and tie-dyed Crocs. Under-eye concealer that will smear off by midday hides the bags beneath her eyes. Grandma retired a long time ago but still works as a nurse's aide to keep our heads above water. She invites herself the rest of the way into my room until she's standing over me. From this angle, I can see the extra skin folded beneath her chin.

"Loads. Answering the questions of the universe. Why the chicken crossed the road. Who shot the deputy after Bob Marley shot the sheriff."

She stares at me with a blank expression that barely masks her exasperation. I read her thoughts between the lines in her face, typed out in bold by her frown: *Say less.*

"College essay about who I am and why they should give

me a truckload of money to grace them with my genius, blah, blah, blah."

"And what's hard about that? You know who you are?" She sits on the edge of the bed.

"I'm not sure *Dear Admissions, I am the kid who definitely shouldn't exist, but the world sucks and people suck more, so please let me into your world-renowned institution* is the wave."

She winces at my words. "You shouldn't be so hard on yourself. I thought group was helping."

"It is helping. It doesn't erase what I am, though."

Grandma put me in group therapy for children of sexual-abuse victims last summer, after a frightening downward spiral during Depressed Girl Summer earned me a 5150. My best friend, JoJo, deemed it The Incident. Basically, the hospital held me hostage so I wouldn't play with matches or sharp objects. We affectionately call group R.P.E.—Raised as a Product of Evil—pronounced *reap*, like the Grim. You know, since most of us were pretty close to being *on the other side* before we ever took our first breath, if you catch my drift. That might seem crass, but we get to take some creative liberties, all things considered.

"You're more than just one thing, Michie." Grandma taps a finger against my nose.

"You have to say that. Or you go to grandma jail or something."

She sucks her teeth before using both hands to push herself off the bed. Since her double-knee replacement, she's not as spry as she once was, though she is young for a grandma. My mother was only fifteen when I crash-landed, so it's not surprising.

"It'll get better. I promise." She begins to leave my room but then stops midway out the door. "And Michie, don't let me catch you with your feet up on the furniture again."

I drop my feet down in a blink.

"Lunch is in the fridge. Have a good day back," she calls, before the front door opens and closes with a thud.

My hands type out another jumble of word soup before I give up. I slam my finger down on the delete button. That damn cursor stares back at me, flash, flash, flashing and never getting anywhere. It begs for raw honesty, the kind of trauma porn that colleges love. But I'm not ready to be that vulnerable, because the irrevocable truth is that *who I am* is my mother's colossal mistake, big and bright like a super-nova. She hates me with every fiber of her being. And I'm not just being extra. She's told me so, which is pretty defini-tive proof. But also, she hasn't bothered to see me or even talk to me since my seventh birthday.

I pull up Brown's home page and stare at the smiling stu-dents (mostly white, with a token brown face here and there). It's very "I read a lot of books" status quo of me to want to go there for college, like every other boy and girl on BookTube. I'm not reinventing the obsessed-with-literature wheel here.

But Brown, with an English Lit program I would sell my soul for, would be scared away if they really knew me. Because I am for sure a walking liability in the whole *is this one most likely to crash spectacularly* analysis. And I can't scare away Brown. What began as a pit stop when visiting MIT with JoJo became the only thing I wanted. It was the first college campus I stepped foot on that felt like a fresh start. A place where I could reinvent myself. I'm not sure I deserve to be great, but if I do, there's only one place for me to do it. Brown.

If I can get in, and even then, if I can afford to go. A lifetime's supply of ifs.

I dig for my phone in the blankets and connect to the knockoff Bose speakers Grandma got me for Christmas. The opening beats of the playlist I put together from last year's *XXL* Freshman Class bounce against the walls. I slam my laptop lid closed with a sharp snap, wincing at the sound. This MacBook cost two years' worth of café money, and that was the secondhand eBay price. I'm dead if I break it.

I stumble to the bathroom in a rush, crashing into the old acoustic guitar I pilfered from my boss's donation pile. The getting-dressed part of my morning routine is painless because I always wear the same thing—jeans, Converses, V-neck tee shirt. Sometimes ironic. Sometimes not. But my hair is its own beast, as I struggle to tame the curls into something manageable before I give up and pull it into a messy bun. I race down the hallway and glance at the microwave clock. Three minutes until the bus leaves me behind.

I grab my winter coat, throwing the hood over my head, no arms, and fly out of the door. My backpack is hanging from one shoulder, open like a wound as loose papers bleed out. I shove everything back in like a wartime trauma surgeon. Dr. Owen Hunt–style. I cup my hands in front of my mouth, breathing into them for warmth. My Fitbit, a Christmas gift from JoJo, flashes the time. One minute to spare. Nailed it.

A large group stands by a stop sign on the opposite side of the street from my bus stop. In the not-so-distant past, I was friends with many of them, but not anymore. Most of them don't notice I'm here.

One smiles. Morgan Williams, a year older and the only one who acknowledges me with The Nod. I nod and smile back. She's cool people, even if she did kind of shun me along with the rest of the neighborhood kids. Around here, school is no escape, where you're greeted with old books and ceiling leaks. But I go to school in the suburbs, with new books and filtered water fountains and well-funded after-school activities. So I understand why I get treated like an outsider. We don't have the same struggles anymore.

Soon an empty school bus stops in front of me. The doors pop open, rubbery edges squeaking. I smile up at the bus driver. She's been picking me up since fourth grade, when I was first transferred out of district and enrolled in the gifted program.

"Morning, Ms. Turner," I say, climbing up the steep steps.

"Good morning, dear," she says, snapping the doors shut behind me.

I relax into the worn leather of my usual seat, starting

my audiobook from where I paused it yesterday. Mr. Darcy is mid-first-proposal. I close my eyes as the bus jiggles beneath me, listening to the sounds of Pemberley for the next hour and a half until we pull into the empty bus bay.

The fluorescent lights in the junior hall buzz overhead as I rush to my locker. As is typical, the bus got in just late enough to require a light jog to first period—AP US History, or APUSH. Everyone else moves in slow motion, sullen and zombielike. All courtesy of the March SAT in a couple of months. Thank God, I took it this past October for the first and last time.

"Boo," a voice clamors over my shoulder as I yank my locker open.

I yelp, almost slamming the door shut on my fingers. Joanna Kaplan, JoJo if you don't want to die, both brilliant and beautiful, leans onto the wall of metal lockers. It's like having a best friend who is equal parts Mila Kunis and Merriam-Webster.

"Jesus, Jo," I wheeze, holding my hand to my chest. "You almost gave me a coronary."

"You keep using that word. I do not think it means what you think it means," she deadpans, quoting one of our favorite films, *The Princess Bride*. "No one can give you a coronary. A coronary thrombosis, perhaps. Clogged arteries from too much red meat and few vegetables." She raises an eyebrow brimming with accusation.

I roll my eyes. "I eat plenty healthy."

"Candy corn is not a vegetable, Michie."

I give her the closed-mouth smile older white women give me when my hair is especially big and I look more Black and less racially ambiguous.

She waits for me to close my locker before looping her arm through mine and pulling me toward class. The history department has its own wing in the back of the building.

"Quiz me," she demands, squeezing my arm. JoJo is one of the juniors retaking the SAT in March. But while everyone else resembles *The Walking Dead* cast members, JoJo looks like one of those trophy girls at the Golden Globes— curled jet-black hair, contoured cheekbones, and winged liner that makes her green eyes pop. Though genetics have also dealt her a pretty stacked hand. Her mom was Miss Virginia when Persian women were still spit at. Not that they aren't still.

I groan but acquiesce, calling out a list of words like a drill sergeant. I stop as we get to our desks, JoJo seated in front of me.

"I've studied so much with you, I could slay the test myself," I tell her.

"Yes, you could." She meets my eyes. "A 1300 is not getting you into Brown."

She's not wrong. It's too low of a score for Brown but fine for most Virginia colleges, which is all that matters realistically, and financially. Especially if I can't write a single scholarship essay without banging my head against a wall.

"That's still the goal, right?" she asks.

I fiddle with the notebook in front of me, my notes from last night's quiz prep handwritten like type font. "Brown isn't even a real thing," I mumble.

"Of course it's real," she says. "You, me, tearing up the East Coast fifty miles apart. Whatever we need to do to make it happen, remember? You've got the grades; you just need the grit."

And the money. But I don't expect her to appreciate the height of that hurdle. JoJo is *toss out a full drink because it's too cold to carry to the car* rich. Oh, and schools have been throwing cash at her since she won an international collegiate robotics competition. When we were *fourteen*. She's pretty much had a guaranteed full-ride spot at MIT since we were prepubescent. She, quite literally, cannot relate.

"All right, everyone. Let's get started," Ms. Yancey says from the front of the room, passing out quizzes for us to hand back.

JoJo spins to face forward, the topic dropped. I wish it were that easy to put behind me too.

It isn't until I return to my locker at lunchtime that I realize my lunch is still sitting in the fridge at home. I forgot it in my rush out the door this morning. Damn it. My stomach growls mockingly as I mutter every swear word in the English language under my breath.

"Um, are you okay?"

I twist my head to find a small pixie-like blonde standing beside me with a can of Cherry Coke and a five-dollar bill in her hand.

"Sorry." I chuckle, the sound more of a breathless snort than a laugh. "Yeah. Forgot my lunch. Low, uh, blood sugar."

"You can buy lunch," she says, like it's obvious.

"Forgot my wallet," I reply, though I don't bring it to school on purpose in case I'm tempted to buy anything stupid, like six honey buns from the vending machines. Again.

She hands me the five dollars. By reflex, my fingers close around it.

"No, I don't—" I sputter over my words.

"Please," she responds, pulling her hand away like I'm a stray she wants to help but doesn't want to touch. "You clearly need it more than me." She glances down at my Converses, falling apart with frayed shoelaces.

She turns and I stare after her. I finally remember her name as she disappears out of sight. Brit. Short for Brita, like the water filter, she explained the first day of freshman year.

I push into the swinging cafeteria doors with a huff, the cacophony of noise bubbling out as the doors part open. I'm not sure how far five dollars goes, so I grab two bananas and a mini bottled water to be on the safe side. The woman standing behind the glass has an ice cream scooper in one hand, hovering over a platter of mashed potatoes. Each scoop makes a slurping sound, like water rushing down the pipes of an unclogged sink.

The cashier scans my school ID, waving me away with a flick of her hand. The money sits in my palm, limp. I don't move.

"You gettin' anythin' else?" she drawls, whistling through spaces that once held teeth.

"Oh," I mutter. "No. I didn't pay yet." I have never wanted anyone to take my money so badly.

"Free-lunch program," she responds, her tongue tripping over the *r* sounds. She taps the computer, where my student account is pulled up on the screen. *Balance due: N/A* flashes at me like a Times Square neon sign.

My cheeks grow warm at the blatant reminder of my financial inferiority here. I stare at the five dollars like it's venomous. The girl behind me in line drops her head down to hide a smile, or even worse, a laugh. Great, now I've made it a whole scene.

I retreat, crushing the bill into my pocket as if it were ticking. I'm itchy from embarrassment, ashamed that I feel ashamed. I have never considered myself free-lunch poor. And at Lee High, no one, and I mean no one, except I guess now me, gets free lunch. It's one of the most affluent public schools in the state.

I slump down into my empty seat at the end of our table. Across from me, Gwen is on a tirade about her latest save-the-world passion project—bee endangerment. I peel a banana in silence and ignore its price tag. Zero dollars in cash, but breaking the bank in dignity.

"Okay, so I checked, and there's a robotics tournament tonight at U of R," JoJo says as she bites into a mini carrot. "Pick you up after work?"

"You only want to go to check out the team," I grumble.

"I am done dating high schoolers. Amy Ferrara was a total nightmare. And Ben Haley turned me off of boys for two years and counting." She holds up two fingers for emphasis. "Plus, I'm an old soul."

"You just binge-watched *Doc McStuffins*."

Her hand slams over my mouth. "You promised!"

Gwen stops midlecture, noticing us for the first time. "Oh, hey, are y'all going to the assembly after school?"

"Is it about honey desserts or vegan Oreos?" I ask, licking the inside of JoJo's hand until she rips it away with a grimace.

"Oreos are already vegan," Gwen answers.

"Barely," JoJo says.

Gwen's eyes narrow. She simply refuses to accept the fact that Oreos live a fraudulently vegan life since they're cross-contacted with milk. The Scarlett Johanssen of the vegan community.

"That's a technicality," she responds. I don't point out the irony of her veganism relying more on her convenience than the cold hard facts. "Anyway, no, the college fair assembly. Lee's hosting this year, and we all get to enter a Hunger Games–esque, dog-eat-dog death match to get host assignments for each school. You work as some alum's personal attaché for a few hours, and boom, you've got yourself a straight-to-Go, collect $200 card to the school of your dreams. They pretty much have instant admissions power."

"Sounds awful. Pass." I crack the top on my mini water bottle and gulp half of it down.

"No pass," JoJo says. "Hosting is the Brown golden ticket. I can't believe I forgot about it. This is it, baby. The big leagues."

JoJo turns to Gwen, leaning forward with her elbows on the table. "We're in. Save us two seats." She glances at me with a raised eyebrow, challenging me.

"Fine." I roll my eyes, but caterpillars settle in my stomach and cocoon themselves. I hope they turn to butterflies and not moths. I hope they mean something promising. Something beautiful.

CHAPTER TWO

VOICES COME FROM EVERY DIRECTION AS JOJO AND I move through the students crowding the auditorium's middle aisle. Gwen waves with a large sweeping motion from the fourth row.

I apologize behind JoJo as we teeter-totter over everyone's laps to get to our seats, praying I don't pass gas in anyone's face. I think I've endured enough back-to-school embarrassment for one, or two, or even three lifetimes.

A large projection screen hangs in the center of the stage. 2022 RICHMOND COLLEGE FAIR sits in large letters in front of geometric shapes. *Robert E. Lee High School* (yeah, I know... welcome to Richmond, folks) is in script at the bottom. For such an allegedly fancy affair, the presentation is giving me clip art.

Principal Hamil approaches the podium, and the room falls into instant silence. A prim woman in a knee-length pencil skirt and a bun so tight she looks inquisitive sits in a plastic chair behind him. Her legs cross at the ankle just like Grandmère taught Mia Thermopolis.

Principal Hamil clears his throat. His black hair, combed to the side to cover his receding hairline, glows beneath the lights. I'm not sure if his hair or his forehead is shinier.

"Thank you all for coming to today's assembly detailing the process for hosting this year's citywide college fair." He scans the room for the impact of his words and receives nothing in return. Hamil's like a Will Ferrell movie—it would be a more enjoyable experience if the effort wasn't so strained. He clears his throat again.

"It's a great and unexpected honor for Lee to be chosen as this year's host."

It's actually *not* unexpected. Despite the fair being a city-wide event, the only schools ever chosen to host are in the suburbs, of which there are seven, even though the fair is held in the heart of the city. So the chances of Lee being chosen are pretty high because 1) money, money, money; and 2) there aren't enough brown kids here to make the Ivy League school representatives "uncomfortable." Which also means that the inner-city kids never get to host, and thus never get the instant in to their dream schools. A self-fulfilling shit prophecy. I'm not even sure I want any part of it. Or if I deserve to skip the line when my next-door neighbors don't get the same shot just because they go to school on the wrong side of the river.

But… Brown. JoJo is right. It feels selfish and dirty, but I want it. How broken must I be to want to take part in such a broken system?

"As I'm sure you are all aware," he explains, "the process is simple. The online application will open at the close of this assembly. You will have one week to submit your applications by answering a series of short-answer questions and ranking your top three choices."

I roll my eyes. Great, more essays when I'm doing so well on the ones I already have.

"After online submissions are evaluated, those selected will interview before a panel. Each panel will then write a report that the College Fair Board will use to make final decisions."

Hamil clicks through the presentation as he explains. The participating schools are on the last slide. MIT (for JoJo), Sarah Lawrence (for Gwen), and Brown (for me, hopefully).

"As you leave, please take a brochure of the application requirements, as I will not be repeating myself. Now a few words from a representative of the board." He nods in the woman's direction, and she stands, joining him at the podium.

"Good afternoon," she says, her voice quiet. "I'm Debbie Matthews, and I'll be your main liaison to the board. I know there are always rumors that hosting guarantees a spot at your school of choice. This is false." She gives us a tight smile. "We cannot make such guarantees, and the coincidence of hosts' admission into their host schools is beyond our control. But we on the board are thrilled for this journey with you all and wish you the best of luck."

She steps away and reclaims her seat.

"And with that," Principal Hamil says, "dismissed."

Sound erupts across the room. He looks pained at how excited we are to get out of there.

"You will definitely get MIT," I tell JoJo, passing her a brochure from the table by the auditorium doors.

"I don't know." She shrugs, flipping through the pages as we make our way to the parking lot.

"What do you mean you don't know? You and MIT are like a dream match. And they already want you."

"Exactly," she says. "They already want me. But hosting is your Hail Mary pass. I should pick a school I have to work for."

I stop in the middle of the lot, earning a honk from a Bronco attempting to pull out of its spot.

"You don't have to work for any school. You could get in anywhere comatose."

"Maybe."

She's being weird. We both know she's being weird. Tim Burton–movie weird.

"What school are you applying to, then?"

"I don't know yet. I have to read the brochure. Yale is still a reach. And University of Chicago."

UChicago. The school where her mom has been an assistant professor for three years and desperately wants to be tenured. The school that has kept JoJo's mom halfway across the country for ten months every year since eighth grade. If she gets in, JoJo will finally get the mother-daughter time she pretends she doesn't care about. But I don't mention any of this, because while our mom situations are different, they both suck big-time. So I pretend I don't know why her plans have suddenly changed.

"You want a ride to work?" she asks, holding up her keys.

"Is Cherry Garcia the superior Ben and Jerry's flavor?" I ask, opening the passenger door.

"No," she says. "It's Phish Food, but I'll allow you into my car anyway."

She laughs, and I laugh, and the tension releases like a popped balloon.

People think being best friends means being open and exposed all the time. I think it means being able to hide in a safe place.

Javier Navarrete's *Pan's Labyrinth* score floats over the room as I run a rag doused in Windex over the stained-glass window at the front of the café. The inset letters spelling SIP AND SERENDIPITY glisten in the dim lighting.

Then I straighten the pillows piled high in the reading nook and reorganize the bookshelves that Taran, the café owner, built herself. My fingers drag over the tapestries brought back from Taran's adventures abroad. I have traveled the world in this small corner.

I circle the room again and again, clearing tables of empty mugs. When the large coffee machine beeps twice, I pour its contents into a wide-lipped carafe marked *At Your Own Risk*.

The bell above the front door tinkles. The boy's hair glides against the top of the doorframe, spiraled curls falling in every direction. He looks like he's been drinking the sun from a firehose, he's so golden. He takes in the world that Taran has crafted. His eyes shift from overwhelmed to awed in the space of a breath as he approaches the counter. Someone so long shouldn't move with so much grace.

"Hi," he says, reaching up a hand to scratch an earlobe. Up close, he has dark freckles across the bridge of his nose. They're spread haphazardly, as if an artist flicked them over his face with a paintbrush.

"Hi," I say, my voice pitched too high. I clear my throat. "Welcome to Sip and Serendipity."

His eyes scan over the rows of books that line the walls. He reaches for the mystery shelf.

"You can take one," I suggest, watching as he reads each title. "They're free. Just bring another one back next time. Or that one if you don't like it." A take a penny, leave a penny, but with stories as the currency. "Or you can pass it on. Or even keep it if you want." I'm babbling, words tripping and stumbling over themselves to get out.

"Cool." He nods, folding a small book, *We Have Always Lived in the Castle*, in half and sliding it into his back pocket. I wince but say nothing.

He looks down at me now, and my breath hitches under the full power of his glance. His eyes are deep-set and a brown so dark they're nearly black, the pupils bleeding into the irises.

"So, what's good here?" he asks, leaning forward and gripping the edge of the counter with both hands.

I take a deep breath before rattling off a long list of drinks, from traditional options, like the iced mocha, to concoctions of my own creation. A hazelnut buttercream frozen latte, a peanut butter Americano, and on and on. When I'm done, he blinks at me in amazement.

"Can I get an iced coffee, black?" he asks.

"I…" He could have a peppermint latte with a dusting of cinnamon sugar, and he wants the bare minimum? "Okay."

He reads the disappointment on my face.

"Sorry." The left corner of his mouth turns up. "You sounded really excited. I didn't want to interrupt."

I scoop a plastic cup into the ice bin beneath the counter and fill it to the brim with hot coffee. The ice melts immediately, steam rising as I click a lid on top. I smooth my hand around its edges to ensure it's on tight.

"Anything else?" I hand him the cup and a straw.

"No, this is fine, thanks." He punches the straw through the lid and takes a large gulp before setting the cup back on the counter. Pulling a wallet from his jacket pocket, he slides out a twenty for his $1.59 coffee.

I hand him the change, and he dumps it into the tip jar. I stare into the jar in disbelief as he backs away.

"Oh," he says as I notice his coffee on the counter. We reach for it at the same time, his hand closing over mine. A jolt flies through my fingers.

"Sorry," I say, slipping my hand from beneath his. I tilt my head down so he can't see the blush spread over my face at the softness of his skin.

He leaves the café like a sudden breeze, the door swinging shut behind him.

Wally, a middle-aged writer who spends every Monday night here, catches my eye. He winks with a toothy grin. "That was fun," he says, his voice gruff from heavy smoking.

I look away to hide the warmth in my cheeks. But the boy sits at the front of my brain like an unwelcome guest for the rest of my shift.

CHAPTER THREE

I SHOULD BE FOCUSING ON TODAY'S LEWIS AND CLARK lecture, but my laptop is open to my college essay. Or at least the file that *should* be my essay, but is instead still a bone-white page. On the other half of the screen is the PDF version of the college fair's hosting application. I've completed the easy parts—name, age, address. The short-answer questions are still blank. Essays. Junior year is becoming nothing but essays.

I reread the first option: *What would make you a good host?* Honest answer: *I don't know; I have crippling anxiety but am sometimes a little funny.*

I move on to the next: *Describe a facet of your identity that is essential to who you are.* I either have to talk about my race, or the fact that I'm poor, or both. Or I can talk about Renee and being the result of her worst nightmare come to life. Either way, if I could answer it for the College Board, I wouldn't be suffering under the weight of my scholarship essay in the first place.

In fact, I have to turn in a draft of the scholarship essay a couple of weeks from now, and the idea of sharing it gives me hives. It won't be the happily-ever-afters my classmates have been working on all year. So far, I've kept it smothered like a gas fire. Never feed it; always choke it out.

A crumpled page of lined notebook paper bounces off my shoulder and hits my desk. The blue lines spiral like broken piano strings. I lift it off my notes, where I've scribbled only *purchased the Louisiana Territory* on the first line. I'm a little bummed I missed the lecture. Ms. Yancey teaches it as if Sacajawea were the first Captain America. Which she basically was, because she led the entire expedition with an infant attached to her hip and probably endured a lot of colonizer mansplaining. So, I have no choice but to stan.

JoJo huffs as the bell rings over Ms. Yancey's last words. I palm the ball of paper as I head out of the classroom, JoJo close on my heels.

"Do I need to read this, or are you going to save us both thirty seconds?" I ask, slowing down so she can fall in step beside me.

"I need you to appreciate the dramatic flair," she says, swinging her hair over her shoulder. The scent of tea tree oil is overwhelming.

"Hit me with the highlights."

"Do you think they're going to have proofs on the SAT? And do you want to go to Garrett's party Friday night after the game? And the mall? Before the game?"

She continues with her questions in a stream of consciousness. Her brain is the equivalent of those bullet trains in Japan.

"No to proofs. No to party. Yes to mall." I can't afford any shopping, but I want a cinnamon-sugar pretzel and a lemonade from Auntie Anne's.

"Boo. I don't want to go solo. And I know you aren't busy. Therapy is tonight, and you don't work Fridays."

It will never cease to amaze me how someone who studies so much also finds the time to both have a social life and memorize my schedule.

"You don't have to go solo. You have a million friends."

"But you're my favorite friend," she says with a large grin.

"Please." I toss the balled paper across the hall and into the metal trash can.

"Kobe!" a voice like jazz calls out above the noise of stampeding students. His voice cracks over the name. He's easy to pick out of a crowd, a head and shoulders above everyone else. My mouth drops open.

Iced coffee, black. *We Have Always Lived in the Castle*. JoJo reaches over and pushes on my chin to bring my lips back together.

Suddenly the hall feels way too warm. JoJo shuffles

me forward, both hands gripping my shoulders to lead me toward our classes. AP Chemistry for her and Spanish for me. I crane my neck backward to keep him in view, but he turns to face his locker.

"Wh-who," I sputter, letting JoJo push me around an automatic water fountain that I almost slam into hip-first. I flinch with phantom impact.

"Derek de la Rosa," she answers, her voice amused. She removes her hands, and I stand frozen in place, having lost all ability to use my legs. She pulls her phone from her back pocket, smiling at a passing teacher who pretends not to see it. She loops her arm in mine as she maneuvers us to second period, never looking up from her phone. She stops in front of her classroom, mine next door.

She turns the phone screen up, showing me the Instagram and Facebook pages she's found and followed in the last half minute. The Feds, I swear. "Just moved here from"—she scrolls through his profile—"San Francisco."

San Francisco, California, to Richmond, Virginia. The land of *Full House* and an ocean breeze to the land of, well, Monument Avenue. Talk about a culture shock.

"And guess what?" JoJo teases. She wiggles her eyebrows at me.

"What?" I'm scared to know what she's found. He has a girlfriend. He likes Starbucks better than Dunkin'. He wears seersucker.

She wraps an arm around my neck and places her chin into the mass of curls. She's eight inches taller in her heeled ankle boots and more often than not enjoys using me as her personal armrest.

"He responded *attending* to the party Friday night." She dangles the information in front of me like bait. Finding a brown face in these halls that isn't my reflection is like searching the ocean for that necklace Rose threw overboard. Finding a beautiful brown one? Miraculous.

"You lie." He's been here for five seconds.

"Bible," JoJo says, putting her hand up in Scout's honor. "The devil works hard, but Brit Forman works harder. He's some big-deal basketball player. Team's up his ass. All in a day's work of being the school's social coordinator."

Black-coffee-drinking, freakishly tall, honey-colored basketball star who reads classic mystery novels. Look at God.

"You're telling me Idris Elba and Salma Hayek's love child is running the halls of Lee High sans supervision?"

"Heads will roll. Panties will drop," she jokes. "Yours maybe?" She pokes me in the upper arm with a well-manicured finger.

I snort. The last boy to even look in my direction was Ronnie Taylor in sixth grade. He asked me to switch seats with him on our field trip to the National Gallery of Art in DC so he could sit next to his girlfriend of three days, Neomi Nwankwo. They broke up before we even got to our bagged bologna sandwiches.

I move around JoJo to get to my class. She grabs my backpack before I get too far away, pulling me back with a snap.

"You're going to the party," she says, emphasizing each word like it's a separate sentence. She releases me and turns into her classroom, sticking out her tongue as she slides into her desk.

I'm not, I mouth back. She waves her hand dismissively. *Yeah, yeah.*

I enter Spanish class as the bell rings, shoving my backpack under the desk and flashing Señora Cortez an apologetic smile. She rolls her eyes, taps the face of her watch, and lifts herself from a seated position on her desk. She claps her hands once to hush the murmur of whispers pulsing across the room.

"Buenos días," she says, her clasped hands bouncing with each syllable like a pacemaker.

"Tenemos un nuevo estudiante esta mañana," she continues.

Something, something, new student, something, I translate to English in my head.

"Por favor, por favor." Her hands move with excitement through the air like she's a conductor. But at least one person understands her, because a desk screeches across the tile as someone stands.

I glance over my shoulder to the back of the room and almost choke on my tongue. Derek de la Rosa stands with his hands in both pockets. He casts a smirk in my direction, letting me know I've been spotted. He rocks once on his toes.

"Preséntate, por favor," Señora Cortez urges. She sits back on the edge of her desk.

"Um, hola. Soy Derek, acabo de empezar hoy." I don't

catch anything but his name and the way his *r*'s roll over his tongue in a pirouette. "Me mudé de San Francisco por el trabajo de mi papá." His Spanish is smooth as melted butter. Warmth spreads deeper and deeper into my belly.

"Ah." Señora Cortez claps her hands. "¡Tu hablas español! ¡Bravo! Toma asiento, por favor." She smiles at him brightly.

Derek follows what I assume are her instructions and sits, all without removing the hands planted in his pockets.

For the next fifty minutes, Señora Cortez heaves us all through the rest of the class period. I keep my head angled, so that if I force my pupils all the way left, I can still see Derek out of one eye. He's leaning casually back in his seat, his feet resting on the chair legs in front of him. Even from here I notice the muscles below his skin flex with each movement. I try to focus on steady breathing.

Before the bell, Señora gives an exasperated sigh and shakes her head in sullen disappointment. "Ay, pueden irse." She waves us away like nagging fruit flies.

Everyone scrambles out of the room in a stampede toward an extra two minutes of freedom. Derek collects a stack of work from Señora's desk. He may already be her favorite, but no one escapes Killer Cortez's workload.

I'm halfway to the bathroom when heavy footsteps approach me from behind. I let out a hoarse croak as a large hand comes down on my shoulder. I pivot, and my neck strains backward as my eyes go up and up and up. One of Derek's hands is still raised where my shoulder had been. The other clutches a pile of workbooks and a printed syllabus.

"Sorry, sorry," he says. "I come in peace." His fingers move into the Vulcan salute, and he tips his head forward in a bow.

Oh my effing God. My heart stutters around an inaudible gasp.

"Don't run up on people like that," I scold, regaining my composure and moving a stray curl out of my face. "You run like a stomping baby buffalo."

"They're called calves," he corrects.

"Seriously?"

"Sorry, yeah, that was obnoxious," he agrees, tilting his head in a nod. "You're Michelle, right?" He points to the spot on my chest where my Sip and Serendipity name tag was the first time we met. He blushes with the realization of where his finger is hovering. "Uh…" He shuffles his feet and jabs a thumb behind him. "Señora Cortez said you would have good notes for this." He raises the stack of papers in the crook of his arm for clarification.

Because she knows I'm the only one who actually attempts the reading assignments.

"You want my notes on"—I twist my neck around to read the upside-down words on his syllabus—"the Spanish edition of Percy Jackson?"

"If you'd be so kind. Missed one day of class and I'm already buried."

"You know it's the same book in English, right? I don't think I can give you much more than you already know."

"And I'm supposed to know what exactly?" He stares down at me with a blank expression. "He's a wood nymph or something?"

"Oh my God," I squeal. "You've never read Percy Jackson?" It's a question and an accusation all tangled into one incredulous utterance. The excitement at meeting a beautiful nerd dissipates.

"I don't know. I watched half a movie once," he admits. "Everyone was super high at a Vegas casino."

"Okay, that was admittedly a god-awful movie. But the books at least? Rick Riordan's Twitter account? The trending topics?"

"I've been busy." An amused grin spreads, dimples I hadn't noticed before appearing in his cheeks. "Are you going to help me, or do I have to beg? Because I will."

The visual of him begging, on hand and knee, flickers, and I shake my head to clear it.

"Will I enlighten you on the greatest boy demigod"—I stress the words—"since Achilles? Certainly."

"Achilles?" He tilts his head to the side.

My mouth gapes in protest.

"Kidding."

I roll my eyes, but a chuckle spills through the cracks like a thief, stealing away my feigned antipathy. I grab the syllabus and place it in the front cover of my Spanish textbook. I'll pull the notes at lunch.

We stand silently for a few moments, until both of our

bodies jolt at the electric sound of the bell. There went my extra two minutes. The hall fills at a trickle and then in a rush.

"Well, I'll see you around," he says. "Michelle."

"Michie," I say.

"Michie." He repeats it with a smile. I decide I never want anyone else to say my name ever again if they can't make it sound like music.

He double-takes before waving and slipping into the crowd.

A deep breath blows through my pursed lips. God, I am in so much trouble.

CHAPTER FOUR

THE FIRST TIME I HEARD THE WORDS *GROUP THERAPY*, **I** imagined plastic chairs arranged in a circle, "Kumbaya" singing, and lots of crying. Safe to say that idea wasn't super appealing to me.

But the whole campfire confessions thing isn't Dr. Schwartz's style, and for that I'm grateful. All six of us, five kids and her, are scattered around her office. It's furnished with plush couches and a jumbo beanbag chair Han, who goes by his last name, asked for. I stare at it now, wishing I could sink into it like a hug, but Han has already dropped down into its squishy center.

"So," Dr. Schwartz says, settling down onto the floor. That's her thing. She says if we're going to look down on someone, it should be her and not ourselves. She's kind of cool, as far as super-white therapists who have never listened to Nipsey Hussle go. "How was everyone's holiday?"

We have group every other week. Most of us have separate individual sessions too. That's how R.P.E. got started, when she noticed that a lot of her kids had a similar background. For a month or two after The Incident last summer, I used to meet with her weekly too. But that was pretty short-lived. I hated talking about what happened. And I hated that she wouldn't let me forget it either. I still haven't found the words to mold into an apology to Grandma. The way she looked at me when she thought I was another person choosing to leave her behind haunts me. But it wasn't a choice. It never is, is it, to feel so lost in your own body? Like your life is an escape room with no solution.

But Grandma and JoJo convinced me that group therapy was a good alternative if single sessions made me uncomfortable. And as much as I'd never let them know it, they were right. Sometimes group is the only place where I take off the "I'm okay" mask.

Monica raises her hand even though we don't have to. We share popcorn-style.

"Yes, Monica," Dr. Schwartz says, putting all of her attention on the rotund girl who takes up as much space on the couch as I do. Cherry-red hair, courtesy of Kool-Aid powder, hangs over her shoulder in a long braid.

"They placed me in a new home right before Christmas," she says. Her voice is miniscule, like she's afraid for anyone to hear it. Monica is my closest friend here. The Big Girl Brigade we named ourselves when I joined R.P.E. last July.

"And how are you liking it?" Dr. Schwartz asks.

Monica has lived in fourteen, I guess fifteen now, foster homes. Two of those in the last six months that I've known her. There's this idea that if you're sweet and tolerable, you'll find a forever family early, and if you're a nightmare demon, you'll be passed around until you age out. None of that is true. Monica has the temperament of a firefly—she just wants to light up your life.

"I like it okay," she mutters. "The mom's nice. Made gingerbread houses on Christmas Eve. And they have a PS5 they let me use."

Oh, Monica's also one of the biggest gamer girls on the East Coast. BorderlensMonica02 would be YouTube famous by now, and super rich, if she had the equipment to record her gameplay. But she's usually stuck playing on the old consoles her social worker keeps in his office.

"That's wonderful," Dr. Schwartz coos. Her tone is chipper, but it carries the undertones of an unsaid *but*. But how does that make you feel? Typical shrink stuff. She prods. "A fresh start, yes?"

"I guess. I get to stay in the same school and stuff. So that's pretty good."

"We're all crossing our fingers that this one is it." Dr. Schwartz gives her a warm smile. She says this to Monica a lot. This one will be *the* one. She may actually be right this time. Monica turns eighteen in four months, and then she'll be on her own. The thought twists my stomach into knots.

"Well, Hanukkah bit," Peter says from his spot on the floor. His back leans against the couch beside me.

"And why is that?" Dr. Schwartz asks, glancing at Monica one last time to make sure she's done sharing. Monica gives an almost imperceptible nod.

"Scott's trying to be present and shit," he says. Scott is his father, but he doesn't call him Dad like I don't call Renee Mom. *Mom* never fit, no matter how hard I tried to bang it into place.

Peter has Scott's steel-gray eyes and lanky figure, but that's about it. I wonder what I have of my Scott.

Peter's parents were engaged when *it* happened. In reality, most sexual assaults are committed by people you know and trust, people you even love. Stranger danger? I mean sometimes, but not usually.

They broke up. Scott called Peter's mom a selfish whore. Peter's mom called Scott a rapist. And that word makes people real uncomfortable. *I did it one time*, they say. *That doesn't make me an* -ist. Once you're an *-ist*—rapist, racist, you know—there's no coming back from that. So when Peter's mom found out she was pregnant and decided to keep the baby, Scott punished her for that label the only way he knew how. He fought for his paternal rights, which men can do, by the way. It's sick. He wanted a new label—dad. Because rapists are cynical and heartless. They don't raise their children.

They don't love their quote-unquote *mistakes*. Which means *it* didn't happen. It is, to put it frankly, a load of horseshit.

Here's the thing that people don't talk about. When you're an R.P.E., it means you are one of the few who made it. And maybe we should be grateful for that. Here, kid, take your shit sandwich, and you better like it because it's a lot better than oblivion. But the fact that Scott gets to call himself a father, that Peter has court-mandated holidays and weekends with him, is, again, total horseshit.

"And that makes you unhappy," Dr. Schwartz says. It's not a question, because no duh. She wants him to vocalize it, because when you say it out loud, you keep it from clawing itself out in unhealthy ways. And Peter has a lot of unhealthy coping mechanisms. Drugs, piercings, more drugs.

"Yeah, Doc, it makes me unhappy," he says. His tone is condescending, but we all know Peter well enough by now to know when he's hurting. He runs his fingers through already messy hair. "Shit ain't fair."

"It's not," Dr. Schwartz agrees. She doesn't sugarcoat.

"Fuck him," Han calls from the beanbag. You can always trust Han to shoot straight.

Peter smiles. Han smiles. Dr. Schwartz smiles with a shake of her head at the language. I reach forward and squeeze Peter's shoulder.

"Yeah," Peter says. "Fuck him."

We all laugh. Sometimes you just have to.

"Who else?" Dr. Schwartz asks with a chuckle.

Lindell got into Berkeley's architecture program. He

tells us about his campus visit and how his mom, who raised him alone, took a metric ton of photos. We plan a going-away celebration for the end of the summer. He'll be the first R.P.E to move on.

Han, the youngest of the group at fourteen, is finally adjusting to high school after one rough semester. He never shares much, but he's the true storyteller of the bunch, weaving us a tale of winning his indoor track event. I went to one once, and the kid is fast. Like Naruto fast.

"A track star on our hands," Dr. Schwartz responds.

We clap and cheer. He pushes himself farther into the beanbag, but he gives us the biggest smile. He doesn't bring up his mom. Like me, he was raised by his grandparents, both physicians at VCU Medical Center. His mother left when he was three.

"And that leaves Michie, last but certainly not least." Dr. Schwartz turns to me, and I shrink under her penetrating stare.

"Well," I start, "our school is hosting the college fair this year. And I'm thinking about applying as a host."

"Oh, shit," Lindell says, catching a glance from Dr. Schwartz. "I mean, shoot. That's cool. I wanted to host for Berkeley, but they didn't pick our school."

Lindell lives near my apartment complex, but we never ride to group together. No matter how much I love Lindell when I'm in group, it's safer keeping him confined to this space. If he exists in my world outside of group, then the truth of why I'm here, or that I come here at all, will start leaking through the cracks of my life.

"Yeah," I say. "It's whatever." We both know why his school wasn't chosen. It becomes an elephant in the room that neither of us wants to acknowledge. "I think I'll go for Tech. Or maybe Brown."

"That's like saying maybe you'll eat microwaveable chicken nuggets or prime rib," Peter snorts.

"There's going to be tons of competition for the Brown spot."

"So?" Han says. "You're as good as those kids."

"Han, you don't even know *those kids*."

"I know that you're the best." He says it matter-of-factly, like it has no chance of being untrue. I wish I had as much faith in myself as he does in me.

"Thank you for the vote of confidence, Hanny." He grimaces at the nickname, his face contorting, and then he smiles.

"He's not wrong," Peter agrees.

"Do you want my thoughts?" Dr. Schwartz asks, folding her hands in her lap like she's about to go full Mr. Miyagi on me.

"I guess," I answer.

"If you want to host for Brown, it doesn't cause any harm to apply. Self-rejection isn't how you get anything in this life. And you miss one hundred percent of the shots you don't take."

"As said by Wayne Gretzky, as said by Michael Scott," Lindell provides.

"I don't want to waste anyone's time. They have to read

my application, interview me. Seems like a lot of work for something I don't have a real shot at."

"The only people whose time you're wasting is ours with all this naysaying," Peter says. "You wanna host for Brown? Go get it."

Monica reaches for my hand and squeezes it between her squishy palms. "You have to at least apply," she says. "Or Peter's going to kick your butt and violate his probation."

"Nah, I just can't drink any alcohol. Ass kicking is allowed." Peter pats my knee, ignoring Dr. Schwartz's language death glare. Usually, she doesn't even try. Peter swears like he breathes.

"Fine," I say, moving my knee stubbornly from beneath his hand. "I'll apply."

CHAPTER FIVE

THE LIBRARY IS COMPLETELY EMPTY WHEN I GET THERE
for Friday free period. The stress from the first week of
school has settled into my neck and shoulders. I'm already
looking forward to the weekend—two days off chowing
down on Johnny Rockets onion rings and finishing the
hosting application.

I pull out my copy of *The Lightning Thief* and set it on the
table. Neon pink and green tabs stick out from the pages. I
flick my fingers over them, trying to ignore the nerves buzzing beneath my skin. The tabs are such a good distraction
that I nearly jump out of my chair when the library doors
bang open.

Seeing Derek makes me feel like I'm standing on the edge of a cliff, one breath from teetering off the side. We've already met during free period three days this week, and what was supposed to be a hand-off of old notes became an agreement for full-blown study sessions. I don't understand how someone who speaks better Spanish than Señora needs so much help translating a book for eleven-year-olds, but I'm not complaining about it.

Derek's carrying a stack of books, with a thick black Sharpie between his teeth. He dumps the books on the table and drops his empty backpack to the floor. Ms. Wexler, the seventy-year-old librarian with a nest of gray hair and glasses on a beaded chain, glares at the sound.

"You know the purpose of a book bag is to be a bag…for your books, right?" I gesture at the stack on the table with my pen.

He lets the Sharpie fall from his mouth, catching it before dropping into his seat. "Or a *backpack* is a pack…for your back."

"That doesn't make any sense," I whisper-laugh, trying to stay silent so as not to get any further on Wexler's bad side. There aren't a lot of adults who scare the bejesus out of me, but she is definitely one.

"Or it makes perfect sense, Padawan." He stretches his legs until they graze mine beneath the table.

I roll my eyes and reach for the book on top, expecting to find *El Ladrón del Rayo*. Instead, I'm holding a battered library copy of *Great Expectations*. I raise my eyebrows at him.

"Pleasure reading?" I ask, tossing the book back and digging through the rest until I find the right one.

"No way," he says. "Required for World Lit. Dickens is a hard pass."

"Them's fighting words." I laugh. Dickens is one of the few old white men who wrote about classism and abolition before it was trendy to do so. Before it was cool to be a decent human being. "And the king of teachers, Mr. Milligan, would duel you to the death for that hot take."

"Dude was way too obsessed with poor people."

My stomach drops like an anchor, and a metallic taste spreads across my tongue. I've bitten clean into the side of my mouth.

"Too obsessed with poor people?" I ask. Heat rises up the back of my neck, and I pray that my face maintains its composure.

"It's a weird thing to harp on all the time. Pip, Oliver, all of them would've been a lot more interesting if dude had said, *Hey, these kids are poor, but here's a bunch of stuff they also care about that has nothing to do with that*."

"Pip wanted love," I argue. "Acceptance."

"Pip might've gotten his dream girl if the kid had a hobby."

I don't have any hobbies beyond reading, which I squeeze in during work shifts or on the morning bus. I don't have the time or the funds for anything extra because I work half the week and save every penny. It's easy to tell someone without money to worry about other things when you have it.

"Mmm," I grunt, yanking my notes from my binder. For the first time, the comfortable silence I've grown used to around him feels suffocating.

"Hey." He reaches across the table. His hand is inches away, and static leaps from his fingers to mine. "You good?"

I give a sharp nod and continue reading.

"Are you sure?" he asks. "You got super... I don't know, you seem kind of mad."

I study his face. His dimples disappear as a deep frown settles onto his lips.

"Why would I be mad at you?" I ask finally. "I barely know you. It wouldn't hurt you to check your privilege, though." And I'm not mad. Not at him. I'm upset that I can't defend Dickens without revealing too much about myself.

"You think I'm privileged?" His eyes widen in shock.

"I think you're talking out the side of your neck about income disparities you don't understand, yes."

"How so?" he asks, his tone challenging.

I stare back at him. How much am I willing to put out there just to win this argument? "Pip and Oliver are a little too busy wondering where their next meal is coming from to *get a hobby*. You have no idea what it's like to be hungry."

"Oh, and you do?" To be fair, no, I don't. We struggle, but we do well enough to not have to worry about starving. We're lucky. Or at least, I'm lucky because Grandma works her butt off to make that the case. But Derek doesn't know I'm not from here. He doesn't know my entire outfit is from Goodwill or that I cut my own split ends last night because Hair Cuttery is too expensive, much less a nice place that knows how to handle natural hair.

I lean back in my chair. "Does it matter? Poor people don't deserve condemnation for being too preoccupied to join a knitting circle."

His eye twitches, and I'm certain I've said too much. He's going to figure out the reality behind my words. But then his lips move into an already familiar smirk.

"Touché." He raises his hand in surrender. "My apologies. You're right." He leans forward and rests both forearms on the table. "I'm not privileged, though. My dad grew up in public housing. East End."

Where I'm from. Where I live.

"Your dad. Not you. You sure this is the hill you want to die on?"

"Absolutely not." He bristles. "We should change that, though."

I tap my pen onto his open book to redirect his focus. "Change what?"

"You *barely* knowing me," he says, moving the book aside. "Are you coming to Garrett's party tonight? You know, the one after that basketball game you're not going to?"

"I don't do parties." Which isn't completely true, because I do attend them under duress with JoJo.

"Too cool?"

I bark out a laugh, earning my own death glare from Wexler.

"Maybe you can make an exception." He gives me a wide smile. "This one time. For me."

"Do you tend to get everything you want?"

He rubs his chin. "Yes, usually. Until this one girl started giving me a hard time."

"Oh, the nerve of her." I again point to his book, but this time to distract him away from my smile. He drags the book back in front of him and drops his head dutifully to read. But his eyes drift up toward me again.

"You know you want to," he chides, with a poke to my forearm.

"Maybe," I mutter to shut him up.

"Well," he says, reaching for my unlocked phone on the table. "Let me know when you change your mind." He adds his name and number, saving the contact.

"If," I correct. "If I change my mind."

He raises both of his hands in front of him and gives himself a high five. "Take that, I will."

JoJo twists toward me as I get into the passenger seat of her Beamer. A creepy Jigsaw-like grin stretches from hoop earring to hoop earring.

"What?" I ask cautiously.

"Is your phone broken?" She drops her smile for a moment.

"Uh, no?"

"I figured it must be since you didn't tell your best friend that you got asked out by Derek freaking de la Rosa?" She hits the steering wheel with each word of his name, missing on *Rosa* and blaring the horn.

"I didn't get asked out by Derek freaking de la Rosa."

"What are you talking about? He asked you if you were going to the party tonight."

"Okay, and?" I pause. "Wait, how do you know that?" We were the only ones in the library. Except Ms. Wexler, and I don't think JoJo has her on the payroll.

"*And* that's a personal invitation. A partyposal, if you will. God, you don't know boyspeak at all." She turns forward. "And don't worry about it. I have my ways."

Okay, so maybe Wexler is in the JoJo-hive.

I roll my eyes and stuff my backpack beneath the glove compartment. "I'm helping him catch up in Spanish. He was being nice, like an *Any weekend plans?* inquiry. That's it."

"Michie, the boy is fluent. You only know how to sing 'Mi Burrito Sabanero,' and even that's horrendous." She presses her push-to-start. Her lead foot stomps down on the gas pedal, and we rocket forward, receiving irritated honks from the other cars.

I think about the way my legs feel like pool noodles whenever Derek's around. But we are so incompatible, it's laughable. Except for one thing.

"He's a Blerd, JoJo," I say, leaning against the headrest.

"A what?" She presses on her horn. "Come on!" she

screams out of her rolled-down window, despite the cold. "Get your head out of your ass. Anyway, a what?"

"A Blerd. You know, a Black nerd." I picture his Vulcan salute, hear his Yoda-isms.

"Your brand."

"Indeed."

"This is so exciting," she squeals. "You're like the Crisco of male attention. Nothing sticks to you, baby." She accelerates forward and then halts. My head bounces off the headrest. "And here you are, stupid in love."

"Okay," I say. "Let's not get ahead of ourselves. He is aesthetically pleasing and knows his phaser from his lightsaber. That's it."

She scoffs and taps her finger on the steering wheel.

I shake my head, but it's not worth arguing with her. When JoJo's made up her mind, there is no changing it.

Narrowly avoiding a head-on collision, she slams on the brake. My teeth grind.

"You're going to kill us," I whine, pulling my seat belt to lock it in place. I'm not Catholic, but I still move my hand in a cross over my chest.

"Ha," she screeches as she jolts in front of another car, and we make it out of the parking lot alive. She turns up the music now that it won't break her concentration. "Okay, so what are we wearing to the party?"

"I'm not going." And I *did* think about it. For a whole five minutes, just as I promised.

"Express? H&M?" she asks, ignoring me completely

while bobbing her head in time to the music. See, no changing her mind.

"Fashion Nova pop-up shop?" I add with sarcasm.

"Don't tease," she responds, staring off dreamily.

I groan but go through the options one by one in my head.

"Not H&M," I advise. "Their sizing sucks." And I'm trying to quit fast fashion.

"Cary?" The eclectic hub of the city.

"Hear, hear." I nod, even if that means no Auntie Anne's.

Fifteen minutes later, we're parallel parked in front of a cute boutique clothing store, one of the many that line Cary Street.

JoJo has a pile of clothes in her arms before we even make one loop around the small boutique. I grab a distressed pair of jeans, humming along to the Top 40 radio station playing over the speakers. The dressing room is small, and I have to keep my elbows tight to my sides as I shimmy the denim over my hips. They're a little long, but not too shabby. And they're on sale.

I take them back off and sit on the bench in my dressing room while JoJo tries on dress after dress until she lands on a silver iridescent slip dress. She emerges with the dress draped over her arm and rips the jeans out of my grip, stiff-arming me away as she pays.

"I hate you," I tell her, but I don't put up much of a fight.

"You love me."

I grab my bag with an eye roll.

As usual, JoJo's house is quiet and carries a resolute echo as our feet hit the hardwood. Her floors don't creak, but they tell as many stories as mine. Silent films in black and white, devoid of any color.

Both of her parents are away. Her dad, a banker, is at a conference in Charlotte. He pops in and out, but he's a ghost when he's home. Her mom, an ex–beauty queen turned political science professor, pretty much lives in Chicago now. I haven't seen either in months. Not even for Christmas, which JoJo spent at our house.

We grab drinks from the fridge, stocked by her dad's personal assistant, and carry our bags up to her room. The plush carpet squeezes through my toes.

JoJo layers a thick coat of foundation, concealer, contour, blush, and setting spray onto my face. By sorcery, she's straightened my hair in less than half a day. I look pretty, though not much like myself.

The game ended a few minutes ago, and my fingers twitch with nervous energy. Parties always put me a little on edge, but I end up at so many of them. It all started with Lacy Olsen's Lucky Thirteen party. When JoJo asked if she could bring me, Lacy actually laughed before saying no. So JoJo threw her own birthday party on the same night and invited the entire seventh grade, even though her birthday wasn't for another four months. It was deliciously spiteful and the moment I knew that JoJo was here to stay. So we're kind of a package deal.

"Alrighty," JoJo says, spritzing another layer of setting spray over the both of us. If I fall on my face tonight, it'll shatter like fresh pottery. I move my mouth in wide circles to stretch the skin. "Calling the Uber."

She has just enough time to zip up her thigh-high boots before the car pulls up to the curb. Our shoes crunch across frozen grass as we race to the waiting car.

CHAPTER SIX

I FEEL THE BASS THUMPING BEFORE WE EVEN TURN ONTO Garrett Kyle's street.

Garrett's parties are the stuff of legend. He lives in a River Road mini-mansion, where he throws weekly ragers because his parents are too scared to put their foot down mid-divorce.

JoJo's shoulders are already shimmying as we climb out of the Uber. The smells of weed and beer twist together around us. I don't mind the beer, but weed smells like skunk, and the odor is already coating my skin.

Noise explodes from the house like a bottle rocket when we open the front door, letting ourselves in. A few heads nod hello in our direction, eyes lingering on JoJo a bit longer.

Bodies gyrate on tables, on counters, on couches, on stairs. It's a blur of hips and legs and arms and hair. Red Solo cups are held close to chests to avoid spilling. In a few hours, no one will care, and the entire student body will make it home with the party's fingerprints all over them.

JoJo turns to me and raises her hand to her mouth in a drinking motion. I nod in response, and we elbow our way to the kitchen, where a keg stands tapped beside the oversized island. Open bottles of Jose Cuervo, 1800, and peach-flavored Cîroc sit scattered on the counters. Orange juice and Coke are dunked in a makeshift cooler in the farm sink, sunken down in the ice.

JoJo mixes two rum and cokes with a heavy pour and puts one into my waiting hand. After two sips, my chest fills with heat as the rum flows down like magma. I lift my hair up and over my shoulder so I don't sweat it out against my neck.

A meaty arm—attached to an even meatier body that reeks of cigarette smoke and tequila—circles around JoJo's shoulders. The collar of Garrett Kyle's too-small polo shirt presses into his neck like sausage binding as the fabric encases his belly. He's too young to have a beer gut, but here we are.

"Nice o' you t' show up, Jo'nna," he slurs, shouting her name into her ear. His arm drops from her shoulders to encircle her waist. I get warmer, heat now rising from my belly instead of down to it. There are few things that piss me off more than grody boys like Garrett who touch and take whatever they want. Grandma always says not to trust a man with two first names.

I step forward, but JoJo reaches over and holds my wrist with a firm grip as she glides out of his reach. His heavy and inebriated arm falls back to his body like a brick. He stumbles without her body for stability.

"Cheers," she shouts, thrusting her cup above her head. Distracted, Garrett whoops into the air, and the kitchen crowd cheers in unison, cups raised to the ceiling. Then he slurps the rest of his beer as he retreats into the living room of grinding skin.

JoJo mouths *wow* as she leans back against the counter.

"You could've let me get one gut punch in." I'd love to see him deflate like the Pillsbury Doughboy.

"Why bother when you can beat him with his own stupid?"

My stomach lurches at the thought of Garrett being on the loose for the rest of the night.

"Besides, you're busy." She stares over my shoulder, taking another gulp of her drink. A smirk settles onto her lips.

"What?" My eyes narrow as I cross my arms. She's not fazed enough about Garrett being a total Neanderthal. I need a greater sense of urgency here.

"You came," a familiar voice says from the other side of the island.

I turn to find Derek standing with a Coke in his hand. His curly hair shines damp, and I smell the scent of Dove soap from where I'm standing. He must have showered after the game. He's now wearing a *Call of Duty* shirt with a machine gun and the words *Drop it like a bot* across the front.

JoJo takes a lazy sip as she trains her eyes on him over the top of her cup. On our side of the island, below his line of sight, she pokes me in the ribs.

"Hi." My voice is hoarse with smoke and rum.

"You didn't text me." His grin spreads into his eyes.

JoJo places her cup in front of me on the countertop. "I have to pee," she announces. "Watch this." She darts from the kitchen surprisingly fast in her high-heeled boots. Subtle, JoJo. Real subtle.

Derek makes his way around the island and takes her place beside me, so close that his T-shirt grazes my arm. It's a soft cotton that sends goose bumps shooting from my elbow. He taps his can against my cup before bringing it to his lips. I note that he's not drinking, but I don't ask. I follow suit, but my cup is close to empty. Rum has settled at the bottom, and I wince at the taste.

"Having fun?" he asks, tipping his head as if he already knows the answer.

"Loads."

"Well, I'm happy you came." He scans my face like he's searching for something he lost. "Your hair's different."

I run my fingers through the straightened strands. It's already gone frizzy in the too-warm house, but it's still straight for the most part.

"Yeah," I laugh nervously. "Looks better than usual."

"Not necessarily."

I push my glasses back up the perspiring ridge of my nose.

"So what's up?" he asks. "Get that host application in?"

"No." I sigh, remembering our conversation from our first "tutoring" lesson.

"Isn't it due..." His eyes float toward the top of his head as he thinks.

"Monday," I finish for him with the last sip of my drink. It's way too strong, but a welcome distraction from the looming deadline. "Yeah. I don't think I'm going to send it in though."

"Why not?"

"Kind of feels like a waste of time."

"Never know if you don't try. Go, Hokie Cavaliers."

"That's blasphemous," I gasp. My tongue bitters at the Virginia schools shout-out. They're great options, but not what I want. What I want terrifies me, though.

"I prefer Tech, actually." He smiles. "My sister will roast you to the high heavens if you don't agree."

"Taste." I nod approvingly. His head's bent down toward me. "You have a sister?" I find myself leaning closer to him as well.

"Yeah." He nods. "Eleven and a total pain. But also kind of the best." A joyful smile overwhelms his face as he talks about her. "You remind me of her."

"I remind you of your sister?"

"Yeah...no!" He turns a deep scarlet. "Absolutely not." His free hand tugs on an earlobe. "You, uh, both like Tech but hate sports."

"Right."

"And like magic and stuff."

I nod, one eyebrow arching. That describes a large percentage of the population.

"To be clear, you in no way remind me of my little sister." He opens his mouth to continue but changes his mind and snaps it shut again. "What about you?" he asks finally. His body shifts in front of me as a group of girls storms through the kitchen. One slides the length of her body against his as she passes.

"What about me?"

"Siblings?"

"Oh, no, not really."

His head cocks in amusement. "Not really?"

Shit. Who says *not really* to a yes-or-no question? People with a defective family, that's who.

I turn my attention to my empty cup and pour the remains of JoJo's drink into it, gulping it down in heaves.

He reaches around me to grab another Coke from the sink.

"You're not drinking?" I ask. I wasn't going to, but now I'm desperate to change the topic.

"Nah." He looks uncomfortable. Perimeter breach noted.

A grunt spouts from his lips as he's shoved forward. His

56

free hand grazes my hip as it beelines for the countertop, trying to steady the rest of his body. I'm pinned between his chest and the island as a large group moves behind him, each person pushing him closer. I close my eyes and let his warmth sink into me.

"Do you want to go outside or something?" he asks. My eyes fly open. The words roll through his chest with a thrum.

I glance behind me. It's still early-January cold, but steam from the heated pool is rising in large clouds over the yard. Girls with bare legs huddle together, but my jeans should be fine.

"Okay."

Derek leads me out the back French doors and skirts us around the pool. He plops down onto a thick patch of grass, his back to the house. I hand him my cup before lowering myself down beside him, then place the cup in the space between my crisscrossed legs.

"So," he says when I'm settled, wasting no time, "not really?"

I groan. Are we back to this?

"So," I bargain. "Not drinking?" If he doesn't want to share, then I won't have to either. But if he does, then at least we've both surrendered something of ourselves.

He chuckles to himself, ripping up a patch of grass and shredding it with his fingers.

"You know, when I said we should get to know each other, I meant more like what's your favorite color or SpongeBob song. But okay, I'll play." He tosses the grass shrapnel back to the ground. "I don't drink."

"That's it?" I am not giving him the Cooper family saga for that.

He drags his palms over his face roughly. The tip of his nose is bright red when he pulls them away. It's the first time I've seen him wrinkled, fresh out of spin cycle. "My grandpa was an alcoholic," he explains, almost in a whisper.

"So he doesn't drink anymore? That's good, right?"

He tugs at his earlobe again.

"He died last year." He swallows around the words as they stick in his throat. "It's why we moved back. My grandmother didn't want to move to California, and Dad didn't want her here alone. So we told everyone he came back for work. I don't think anyone believed it though. Who comes to suburban Virginia for a job in"—he pauses—"for a job like his? But I guess it was the only way for him to feel like his family wasn't irreparably broken. Not sure it worked, though."

"No?"

"No." He stares off into the tree line. "Sometimes your family breaks in a way that can be glued back together. When you catch the damage before it festers. But we were broken for a long time. My grandpa was broken for a long time."

His stares blankly ahead as if he's left his body and I'm talking to the empty shell left behind.

"You were close," I say, presuming.

"When I was a kid, yeah." He shrugs. "He was the

greatest. I idolized him. But not lately, no. He became kind of an asshole. My dad couldn't face him, but he also couldn't let him go. And it had a trickle-down effect that made me resent all of them—my dad, my mom, my grandparents. Like, they were the adults; why wasn't anyone doing anything about it? So I…" He stops.

I'm not sure what to say. It's a pretty serious chat for someone I've known for less than a week.

"Anyway." He shakes off the grief like an old coat of skin. "Alcoholism can be genetic. The good memories growing up with him have been completely absorbed by all the shit he put our family through in the end. I don't want to get in too deep and only be remembered for the crap I catapult into the world. So I stay away from the stuff."

"And you moved clear across the country as a second-semester senior."

"Seems that way."

"That sucks."

"It does. There's a lot of shit here I'm not ready to confront." He shoots a glance at me. "It's getting better though."

We sit in silence for a moment, collecting our thoughts. I don't want to be remembered for the crap either. I want so desperately to be good, but can you ever be good if your mere existence came from something so vile?

He gives me a light shove with his shoulder. "Your turn."

"Well, my favorite color's periwinkle, and 'Sweet Victory' is objectively the best SpongeBob original."

"Michie," he chides.

"Can we say you win?"

"If bad life stuff was a contest, then sure. But it's not."

"It's just not a big deal. I should've said no." I wring my hands in my lap, cracking my knuckles subconsciously.

"But you didn't." He's moved closer, and I feel his breath on my cheek. My skin hums where our bodies touch.

"It's complicated."

"I've got time," he urges.

I pull air into my mouth, my cheeks puffed out, and release it slowly.

"I have two biological siblings, like from my...mother." I stumble over the unfamiliar word. "But I was raised by my grandmother and grew up pretty much as an only child. So I have siblings in the *yes, they exist* sense. But they're not like *sibling* siblings that I know stuff about. I don't even remember how old they are. Hence the *not really*."

"Sounds fucked." He doesn't ask about Renee or why I live with my grandmother. His eyes settle on me again. They're warm, but not pitying.

"You have no idea." I swallow the rest of my drink, needing the taste to distract me from Renee-related thoughts, and the way Derek's eyes brighten beneath the moonlight.

We sit in comfortable silence until the noise behind us is drowned out and I can hear only our breathing, deep and in sync. I glance over at him to find his eyes studying my face once again.

"Stop staring at me," I whisper, though I don't mean it.

He chuckles, looking down at his lap.

"Sorry, just taking it all in."

I straighten, pulling up my head last, loose and heavy on its hinges.

"Taking what in?"

"Everything." His eyes beam as our fingertips brush.

CHAPTER SEVEN

A FULL-CONCERTO HEADACHE, HEAVY ON THE PERCUS-sion, wakes me the next morning. Lightweight Cooper strikes again, leveled by a mere one and a half rum and cokes. My cheek is stuck to a wet drool spot on my pillow. JoJo, heavyweight champion of the Solo cup, is already awake beside me, her fingers tap-dancing across her MacBook keys. I lift my head and smoosh it back down into a dry spot.

She adds her electronic signature to the college fair host application and presses submit.

"Good morning, sunshine," she sings. "Finally."

The covers fly off my body as she snatches them away.

"Jesus Christ," I yelp, pulling myself even more into the

fetal position. The headache has slithered from the top of my skull to right behind both eyes.

She slaps me on the butt several times. "I don't think so. It's a new day, baby." She places her head on the pillow, touching her nose to mine. She must be in the drool spot, but she doesn't notice or care.

I glare at her. She blows a puff of air into my face before rolling on top of me. She goes limp like a corpse.

"You're the worst." I try to move from under her. For someone so tiny, she's very dense, like a Boston terrier or a French bulldog.

She pokes me, and my stomach clenches as it twists inside out.

"I will throw up on you," I threaten.

She pauses for a moment before resuming her poking, now in my ribs instead of my stomach as a precaution.

"How was keeping Garrett in his place?" I ask, diverting her attention. It still fills my mouth with acid. He should know as a theoretically intelligent life-form how to not be a total ass.

"He passed out five minutes after the whole thing." Groping, but I don't correct her. It was her experience, and it's not my place to characterize it differently for her. "Mac dragged him upstairs and flipped him over so he didn't choke on his own tongue or something." She shrugs. Years of friendship and I still can't tell what she buries and what genuinely doesn't bother her.

Or maybe I'm overreacting for my own reasons. I don't know.

"But if you think you're going to squirm out of telling me what happened last night, you have another think coming. I left you for ten minutes and came back to find y'all canoodling in your own little world."

"We were not canoodling," I object. "We were talking."

"Okay, *talking*." She sits up and forms her fingers into quotation marks.

I pull a pillow from beneath me and toss it at her head.

"Next time I ask you to make me a drink, don't." Last night is her fault. "The rum disconnected the wiring between my brain and my mouth and short-circuited errant thoughts all over the place." I lift myself up into a seated position so that we're on the same eye level. "Detailing the sorry excuse that is my life to Derek de la Rosa is not my idea of a good time."

"Your life isn't sorry. Stop being a scaredy-cat. This isn't last summer." She looks at me meaningfully.

Before my depression went full *Girl, Interrupted*, I had put on a brave face for everyone, especially Grandma and JoJo. JoJo saw the cracks a little sooner because she spends a truly obnoxious amount of time with me. If she's not worried, part of me wants to rely on her judgment that I really am okay. But if I tell her why my essays are giving me so much trouble or why Brown and Derek and the future seem so out of reach, she will see the cracks I've tried so hard to plaster over.

"I'm not scared."

But I am. If I lived a life without fear, I'd be submitting my host application along with her. I'd be finishing up my college essay to my dream school. I'd be more than just friends with Derek. I swallowed Renee's rejection, and now I'm bloated with it. I can't handle any more.

"If you weren't afraid, your tongue would've been drilling burr holes into the back of his throat."

"That is a terrible visual." I grimace. Even I know that can't be the preferred technique, not that I've ever tried any technique.

She rolls her eyes. "I searched that whole damn house for you, and you want to know how I finally found you?"

My eyebrows arch up to my forehead.

"There was a big ol' sexual-tension cloud looming over y'all like the Eye of Sauron."

I throw another pillow, but she catches this one with a laugh.

"I'm serious. I don't understand how you didn't jump his bones. That house has like twenty-three bedrooms."

It's not that I don't feel it. In fact, I feel way too much of it. But I know that I shouldn't. I'm like a grenade. If you stand too close, you'll end up splattered on the walls. It's why even JoJo doesn't know the whole truth. How could she keep loving me if she knew where I came from? How could he start?

My tongue runs over dehydrated and cracked lips, trying to wet them with saliva I don't have.

JoJo leaps out of the bed, padding to her en suite bathroom. The water tap runs, and she returns with a tall glass filled to the brim. Bless her.

"I'll allow"—she glances at the clock on her nightstand—"four more minutes of feeling sorry for yourself."

I take a sip, testing my stomach. She had dropped in an Alka-Seltzer that fizzes down my throat and settles my stomach. Bless her twice. I continue drinking for as long as possible until I'm too full to take a deep breath.

"You're deflecting."

"Don't psychoanalyze me." I place the near-empty glass on her nightstand coaster shaped like a miniature flying carpet.

Her shoulders rise and fall in an exasperated sigh. "If you don't at least see where this goes, you'll regret it. And I won't blow smoke up your ass and say this guy is your soul mate or that this won't possibly end terribly." Comforting. "But he's hot, you're hot, and you're both obsessed with each other. Let the math math."

Her eyes brighten and I finally laugh.

"You're being ridiculous. It's been a week."

"My dad proposed after a month," she says.

I glance at her with a blank stare.

"Okay, bad example. All I'm saying is don't make me Cupid your asses. Because I will."

"It's too early in the morning for reason." A loud growl sounds from my stomach in agreement. I could use a bagel.

Or French toast sticks. Or a bagel and French toast sticks. I glance at the clock. We may still be able to catch breakfast.

She continues to stare me down, smug, knowing she's planted a seed deep enough to make me reconsider if avoiding Derek-feelings is the best plan. The path of least resistance is always straight through. She gets up from the edge of the bed and tosses me my phone from my heap of discarded clothes on the floor.

"Breakfast?" She slides her feet into a pair of fuzzy slippers, wiggling her toes.

I check the time on my phone: 10:12.

"French toast sticks?" I ask, turning the screen toward her. The time stands out against a photo of her, Grandma, and me from Christmas when we went to see *Elf* at the Byrd Theatre.

"Eighteen minutes? Child's play."

We exit the Burger King drive-thru at 10:28 and inhale two three-piece cartons each in the parking lot, crumbs coating the laps of our pajamas.

CHAPTER EIGHT

DURING A SLOW SHIFT SUNDAY AFTERNOON, I TAKE another stab at the short-answer portion of the hosting application. I've written and rewritten the responses umpteen times, and I can't tell if each try is getting better or worse. Peter sits at the counter, alphabetizing the business cards in our free-gift-card fishbowl.

The *Addams Family Reunion* tune travels across the café. Peter's tongue moves over the silver piercing in his bottom lip while he works in a precise and methodological fashion. Peter seems all over the place to anyone who doesn't know him, but he's a total perfectionist.

"Smells like Christmas in here," he says absentmindedly, noticing the pine tree and gingerbread scents for the first time.

"Is that a bad thing?" I reach behind me for the coffee-pot, pouring him a cup in the largest mug we have.

"Well, I'm Jewish, so I don't do the Christmas vibes, but no," he says, licking his lips. "Even though fall has a more pleasant aroma."

"Didn't think you had such strong opinions on this very serious issue." I close my laptop. *If* I turn in the application, these will have to do.

"I contain multitudes." He drops the business cards back in the bowl, ruining his work. His black-painted nails knock sharply against the glass.

"So, to what do I owe the pleasure?" We had each worked in silence for about a half hour, but I can tell he's here for a reason. Peter lives across town, and I can't imagine that he was in the neighborhood. I don't want to say it's strange seeing him in daylight hours because he kind of resembles a vampire. But it's strange seeing him in daylight hours because he kind of resembles a vampire.

"Avoiding the old man," he says. Right, Scott lives about half a mile away, and it's his weekend. "I did have a question, though, and I thought, why not ask the smartest person I know?"

"That's a stretch, but okay."

"Well, I couldn't ask myself, so I'm coming to you." He ducks as I swing a dish towel at him, laughing. "Do you think Monica's into skinny, like Skeletor-skinny, dudes?"

"Do I—" I have no idea. But he's looking at me with so much hope. "I'm sure she is. I mean, I don't see why not. Mo isn't judgy."

I place the coffeepot back on the heater and skirt around the counter, pulling out a stool to sit beside him.

"So I assume you have a thing for Monica?" Which, when I think about it, is pretty sweet. Both of them with their similar baggage packed in different ways. I like the idea of it.

"Maybe."

I smile, reaching to squeeze his shoulder like I do in group when he's starting to shut down. Despite us being the same age, Peter has always felt like more of a little brother. He's wild and raw, and the only reason most of R.P.E. has kept any sanity is because we couldn't implode around a live grenade. Sometimes you don't need calm to keep you centered; you need a storm even more destructive than you are.

"You should tell her," I say.

He looks at me like I know a secret. "Did she say something to you?"

"Not exactly." Not at all. Shit, I don't want to get his hopes up. He stares down at his hands. "But I know you and I know her, and I think it would be good."

"She's older."

"By less than two years."

"She's smarter."

"You're pretty smart."

He shrugs, but I see the hint of a smile. Peter is adorable when his anger isn't a living, breathing thing that consumes him.

Taran comes like a strong wind from the back of the café, her long robe swinging around her as she moves. She's carrying a new stack of ceramic plates she brought back from her recent trip to Jamaica.

"Why, Peter," she sings, because she never forgets a name or a face, though Peter's is hard to shake from memory. "I haven't seen you since, well, I guess pre-piercing." She taps his chin with a long finger. "How's your dad?"

Peter flinches like he's been shot. Most people don't know the full truth. It's not something we go around broadcasting. Because even though it says so much more about *him*, we fear what it says about us too. So people say innocuous things like that, unaware of their impact.

"He's fine," he answers, but he retreats into himself, shadows forming in the deep circles beneath his eyes. He chews on his lip so hard I'm scared he's going to bite his piercing right out.

"Tell him I say hello." She smiles, oblivious. Peter nods but stays silent.

"Actually," I say, cutting through the building tension, "I was trying to convince Peter here that he should ask out a girl he likes." I elbow him lightly and he shoos me away.

"Oh?" Taran's ears perk up. She loves love. "Well, tell us. What do you like about her?" She sits down on his other side and brushes her bronze-blonde bangs from her forehead.

He thinks about her question, measuring it. "Everything, I guess."

Taran nods, urging him to continue.

"I dunno. She takes all the bad shit that happens and makes it not so bad. I can't explain it."

Taran and I look at each other above his head. He's not eloquent, but we both get it.

"Do you know how I met my wife?" Taran asks.

"You got a wife?" he asks.

"I do." She nods. "She named this place. A creative spirit, even if she is just a lawyer." She winks. "I saw her on a train platform when I was still trying to be an artiste in New York City. I looked right at her in her little pantsuit and thought *her*. No rhyme or reason, but I knew it deep in here." She presses onto her heart. "And, you know, in New York strangers don't talk to each other. It's not cool. But I marched right on over and introduced myself. And now we're married."

"Cool." Peter nods. "You weren't, like, scared or nothin'?"

"Oh, I was scared shitless," she says. "So scared I almost let her get away. And where would I be now if I had? Sometimes when you can't describe it, that's how you know it's real."

Homework lies scattered on my bedroom floor as I sit in the eye of the mess. My cursor hovers over the host application's submit button. Grandma is playing smooth jazz on her old stereo, and the saxophone reverberates through the air vents.

My phone vibrates under my thigh, where I stashed it so it wouldn't distract me. So much for that.

DEREK DE LA ROSA AT 10:14 P.M.: I hope you're not twiddling your thumbs about that application.

I read the message twice. I uncross my legs and stretch them out as far as they will go, flexing my ankles in a circle. It's like he's here, watching me be paranoid. He hasn't known me long enough to perceive me like this. It's dangerous, like exposed wire in a thunderstorm.

MICHIE COOPER AT 10:17 P.M.: i dont recall

His response comes immediately.

DEREK DE LA ROSA AT 10:17 P.M.: Decide on schools?

You pick only three, ranked in order of preference. Virginia Tech was an easy choice, but would have the most competition with UVA, which I'm not interested in but seemed silly not to rank. That leaves one more option. I'm still deciding between playing it safe(r) with William & Mary or gunning it and choosing Brown.

MICHIE COOPER AT 10:21 P.M.: UC Sunnydale and Hillman College. Waffling between South Harmon Institute of Technology or Yale.
DEREK DE LA ROSA AT 10:23 P.M.: 🤭 Gotta go with SHIT. Think about the merch.

My fingers dance over the screen as a laugh escapes my lips. We could keep it light, we *should* keep it light, but I follow JoJo's advice and open up a little bit.

> **MICHIE COOPER AT 10:25 P.M.:** i'm scared
>
> **DEREK DE LA ROSA AT 10:28 P.M.:** Worst case they say no and you're no worse off.
>
> **MICHIE COOPER AT 10:25 P.M.:** i guess
>
> **DEREK DE LA ROSA AT 10:28 P.M.:** You gotta tell me what you choose though so I can plan out my route. You know, for when I visit you.
>
> **MICHIE COOPER AT 10:29 P.M.:** so you're trying to stalk me?
>
> **DEREK DE LA ROSA AT 10:30 P.M.:** Only a little.

A grin spreads over my face and I scroll to the top of the chain, rereading our conversation.

> **DEREK DE LA ROSA AT 10:32 P.M.:** Calling you.

"What?" I sputter out loud, stricken with horror. I do not have a good phone voice. It's straight out of the Alvin and the Chipmunks classic Christmas album, but way less charming. Before I can respond with an adamant no, a Face-Time request flashes across my screen. My hand hovers over the red *X* to decline. I mean, seriously? This is a major breach of decorum. I already put my bonnet on, for goodness' sake.

I press the green check mark before I can talk myself out of it and pull my hood over my silk-wrapped hair. There's a delay after the call connects, and his face fills the screen one pixel at a time.

His curly hair is slightly mussed, as if he's been lying down. His constellation of freckles are even more pronounced in the low light of his room.

"Do you know how rude it is to FaceTime someone without permission?" I grumble.

"No ruder than you saying no if I'd asked first." He smirks into the camera.

"Fair."

The reflection of his television is a small blue square in his irises.

"So I've been thinking about what you said on Friday," he starts.

"I said a lot of things." I cross my toes that he's referring to any number of things but one.

"I was thinking about San Francisco. How everyone always seemed so perfect but had all this shit brewing under the surface. And no one was ever honest about it, like a continuous loop episode of *Full House* or something. So I thought my family was the only one messed up. The only Black family around and dysfunctional as hell."

"And now there's another Black family dysfunctional as hell?"

"Yeah." He nods. "Well, no. I mean all of them are dysfunctional. It's how families are, I guess. This group of people allowed to cause you trauma because, you know, blood or whatever. I don't know. But I hated everyone for a long time because I thought they were making my life shittier than everyone else's. I pushed a lot of people away for silly reasons I regret."

He's so in tune with his feelings. Even in therapy, I'm not this honest with myself, much less with other people. Maybe when you know you're loved, it's easier to be kind to yourself. Like confirmation bias.

"Anyway, I was mad a lot. Lost a lot of friends being an angry jackass, so I guess I didn't even need alcohol to sling shit. I wanted to be pissed when Dad said we were moving here because, what the fuck, I'm a second-semester senior with a basketball scholarship. But to be honest, I had burned down everything I had there. And this is a new start. All to say, thank you for being honest."

I swallow thickly. By some combination of too much rum and momentary insanity, I had been vulnerable and told the truth. And it didn't scare him away. It even helped him.

"I mean, I can tell it's not something you really…" He considers his next word carefully. "Share."

"Uh, no. I don't." Which means he'll keep it to himself. "But I'm glad my chaos could lead you on this spiritual journey."

He chuckles, rearranging himself on his bed. I gulp as my brain enters a wormhole thinking about him on his bed. At eleven at night. Alone. Shake it off, Michie.

"I guess this is a convoluted way of saying I see you." His eyes glisten as they zero in on mine. A shiver raises the hair on my arms. It's like he's in my room, lounging on my full-sized bed with his long limbs and ever-present smile.

"Homework," I blurt, my self-preservation codes triggering. I feel the tug to let myself fall with no safety net. I scratch my nose with my free hand, giving it something to do other than tremor.

"Yeah, me too." He takes my sudden end to the conversation in stride. Endless patience, this one. "Night."

Where do they even make Dereks?

He waves and hangs up. I'm left staring at a blank screen.

I turn back to the application. It's due tomorrow, but I want to get it over with. I hover over Brown, click the box until a thick black check mark appears, rank it as my first choice, and press submit. The page twirls on the screen before a whooshing sound indicates it's beyond my reach.

My phone vibrates again as I close my laptop.

DEREK DE LA ROSA AT 11:16 P.M.: I'm not afraid of a little chaos.

CHAPTER NINE

GRANDMA IS FILLING IN A CROSSWORD PUZZLE WHEN I get home from work Sunday night, a week after submitting my host application.

She tilts her head up as I come into the living room and plop on the sofa next to her. "Good shift?" she asks.

"As long as my checks clear."

I watch her as she works on her puzzle silently. Sometimes I feel bad about complaining about life so much. She's had it way, way harder than me, and I don't even know the half of it.

Grandma drops her pen (she does her crosswords in pen because she's a badass) and reaches for my bouncing knee, holding it still. "You're making me nervous. What's going on?"

"Waiting to hear back from the college-fair people. I probably won't get it. I don't know why I'm stressing about it."

With a deep breath, she closes her eyes as she folds the book closed. "Why would you say that?"

"Every junior applied. And who isn't applying to Tech and UVA?"

"What was your third choice?"

I scratch the back of my neck. Grandma and I have talked about Brown before in the way one talks about going to the moon—it would be cool but never going to happen. We can't afford it, so I don't bring it up. She already works hard enough; the last thing I want is to make her feel like I want something she can't give me.

"Michie, what school did you pick?"

"I picked Brown," I answer. "But as a throwaway because I couldn't decide."

She looks at me like I'm full of shit. Because I am. And we both know it.

"And why do you think you can't get Brown?"

"Um, because it's Brown, Grandma. Every smart kid in school is applying."

"Who cares who is applying where? This is about hosting, and everyone could only pick three schools. Who's to say there aren't only five or ten of you? Those are good odds."

"No, they're not." It comes out in a snapping tone that I instantly regret. It's not her fault. But just thinking about Brown is starting to upset me. Even if by some miracle I got in, how would we make it happen? I'd rather not get in at all than get in and have to walk away because I can't afford to go.

"Michie," she sighs. "You have to stop counting yourself out. You're smart, and you're special, and schools will see that."

"I don't see why. No one else does."

She jerks back like I've slapped her. She isn't no one. She's the biggest someone I have.

"You should go to bed, clear your head." She opens her crossword book silently, hurt carved into her wrinkles.

"I love you," I say, kissing her on the forehead before I leave. My way of apologizing because words have abandoned me.

She holds my hand as I move past her. "Times infinity."

I don't have the energy to shower, so I undress out of my outside clothes and huddle beneath the comforter. I check my emails for the last time tonight.

From: 2022 Richmond College Fair Hosting Program Selection Committee

My fingers tremble as I open the email. I've been chosen to interview for only one school, but its name sits in the middle of the screen, bold and beautiful and mine.

Brown University.

I want to go back in the living room and shout the good

news, celebrate, but I feel guilty from our conversation. I text JoJo a million exclamation points and send a screenshot to both her and Derek.

JOJO KAPLAN AT 11:19 P.M.: BITCHHHHHHH
MICHIE COOPER AT 11:20 P.M.: what'd you get
JOJO KAPLAN AT 11:20 P.M.: MIT and UChicago.

We still need to discuss the UChicago thing. But not tonight. Tonight is for celebrating.

MICHIE COOPER AT 11:22 P.M.: BITCHHHHH!!!!!
DEREK DE LA ROSA AT 11:23 P.M.: Alright alright alright.
Remember me when you're big ballin.

I fall back into bed, a smile plastered across my face. There's still a lot to do and an interview I have to crush, but for one brief moment, it feels like I've won.

CHAPTER TEN

GRANDMA IS WRAPPED UP IN AUDIOVISUAL CORDS WHEN I make my way downstairs the morning of MLK Day. Ever since Taran's advice to Peter, I can't help but internalize it myself. Every moment spent with Derek feels like coming home after a long day. Maybe that's the point, and I'm playing myself trying to pretend something isn't happening.

A stack of old VCR tapes sits on the coffee table, covered in a layer of dust. The tape on top is a stripped-together recording of Martin Luther King Jr.'s speeches. Our MLK Day tradition. It's both frightening and comforting that the words he spoke so long ago still resonate.

The stack has grown over the years. *King: A Filmed*

Record…Montgomery to Memphis was added, and then *February One* and Spike Lee's *4 Little Girls*. *Soundtrack for a Revolution* because Grandma loves her music. And *Zora Neale Hurston: Jump at the Sun*. Then we added the fictional films starring our favorites. First came Denzel's *Malcolm X*. Grandma loves her some Denzel. Followed by *A Raisin in the Sun*. More recently, *Selma* and *Loving*. Last year I added *Fruitvale Station* and *Judas and the Black Messiah*, both always leaving me with a simmering rage.

Our very own Black history lesson, since they don't bother at school.

"You know these movies are online, right?" I reach to grab the wires from her hand and insert them.

"On that tiny computer screen? How you supposed to feel the spirit of Dr. King on that thing? Save it for your little Netbox."

"It's Netflix, Grandma."

"It's silly." She waves her hand and points at the stack of tapes and DVDs on the floor. I slide the first tape, the speeches, from its case and push it into the VCR. I might be one of the last teenagers alive who still knows how to use one, or better yet, who's seen one in person.

She hands me the large bowl of popcorn with M&M's scattered throughout. I settle onto the couch beside her.

"This is the good part," she says, pointing at the screen. She'll say it a hundred more times before the day is over, because to her, all of it is the good part.

"Why'd we start doing this, anyway?" I ask, pulling out an especially buttery and chocolate-coated kernel from the bowl.

She grabs a handful and shoves half of it in her mouth, speaking around her chews unintelligibly.

"What?" I ask, moving the bowl away as she reaches again.

She sighs. "Renee," she says. "She used to love this stuff. History, politics. Wanted to be a congresswoman." If I hadn't happened. I gulp and turn back to the screen, barely hearing Dr. King's words. "She made this one, actually. Spent months finding the footage and recording over some old exercise video. We used to read the speeches off little flash cards, but she wanted to modernize it for you." She picks up the empty cardboard case, already obsolete.

"Why would she care about any of this?"

"Because she loved it and she wanted to share it with you. Wanted you to know your history."

"But why?"

"Everyone should know where they come from, Michie."

But it takes more than learning Black history to know who you are. It takes the coming together of generations, the passing on of stories and lessons over time. We don't have any of that. Our little family begins and ends with Grandma and me.

"I mean…" I take a deep breath and compose my words into something coherent. "Why would she care about sharing anything? She couldn't even share a life."

"Michie," she says, reaching for my hand, but I pull it away.

"No." My fight or flight is activating, and I'm a millisecond from noping right out of this conversation. "She disappears for ten years and, what, this is supposed to make me feel better? What's the point of knowing your history when you don't even know your own..." I hug the bowl closer as if it can protect me. My chest tightens.

Grandma turns to me, her eyes seeing through me until she's latched onto every nerve ending. "Listen to me. I know you're hurting. You get to be angry. What she did wasn't fair. Not to you, not to me, not to herself. But people aren't perfect, Michie. And most of us are doing our best. She tried her best for a long time."

My eyes narrow in response. "Are you kidding me?" I don't recognize the voice spilling from my lips. "Her best? Why are you defending her?" Grandma used to be on *my* side. Us versus Renee. Us versus the whole damn world. And now, this. "Why are you telling me this?"

"Because you asked," she answers, in a patronizingly calm tone. It grates against my skin.

"God, lie to me or something."

"I'm not going to lie to you about your mother."

I flinch at the word, right there, like it should belong to me. *Your* mother. Like I could claim it if I wanted to. But I can't.

"Michie, this isn't healthy. You deserve to be a happy kid in high school, dating, and getting in trouble, and excited about what's next. But you're not, because of nonsense in your head. Renee doesn't hate you." She pulls the popcorn bowl from my lap and sets it on the floor, taking both of my hands in hers. "If you got the chance to talk to her, you would see that none of the things you convince yourself of are true."

"That's never going to happen." It's hard to believe what she's saying, because if Renee doesn't hate me, then why would she leave? Sometimes the hate is easier to swallow, because I understand it.

Grandma looks at me as if she's thinking of a solution to an impossible math problem, before she pulls me into her and holds me. We focus back on the screen. Dr. King is at the Lincoln Memorial in front of 250,000 people.

"Grandma?"

"Hmm," she hums, squeezing me closer.

"Do you think she'd have been a congresswoman?"

"I don't know," she answers.

"Do you think she'd be happier if I—" An overwhelming blanket of grief wraps around me, nearly as tight as Grandma's hug.

She sighs again. "I don't know," she says. "But I know I wouldn't be."

We grow silent again as we listen to Dr. King attempt to move mountains with nothing but his words.

"Do you think he was ever tired? Fighting against hate? Being told he didn't matter?"

"Exhausted," Grandma says. "But Dr. King kept going,

never stopped. Because he knew where you start isn't as important as where you're going."

His speech rings out over the living room, crackling over the shoddy recording. *With this faith, we will be able to hew out of the mountain of despair a stone of hope.*

Faith. Hope. I could use some of that.

CHAPTER ELEVEN

THE JOY FROM GETTING AN INTERVIEW QUICKLY WEARS off and is replaced, once again, by crippling self-doubt. Grandma, JoJo, and Derek are all excited, but I can only think about embarrassing myself in front of a panel of Ivy Leaguers. So I focus on the one thing I can maybe have some success at—getting Peter and Monica together.

"I need your help," I say at Tuesday's study session. I drop my books onto the library table, earning myself a hiss from Ms. Wexler.

Derek looks up from the Switch hidden behind his copy of *Los Tres Mosqueteros*. He's in the middle of terraforming his island on *Animal Crossing*. "Moi?"

"I think you mean *mí*." I sit across from him and place my elbows on the tabletop.

"I'm trying to be trilingual. Increase my chances of working for the CIA."

"Well, I'm trying not to choke you," I say with a huff.

He puts down the game and crosses his arms. "Promises, promises."

My eyes widen, and I look away as a knowing smirk settles onto his lips. "Anyway." I breathe slowly through my nose to regain composure. "I have a question."

He laughs, knowing he's made me the good kind of uncomfortable. "Shoot."

"If you knew a girl for forever, and y'all were friends, and you wanted to leave said friendzone, what would you do?"

A range of emotions flit across his face. "Are you messing with me right now?"

"No. It's a serious question."

"You come to me on the day of our tutoring session to ask me how a guy, presumably, gets out of the friendzone? Me?" He leans forward.

"Are you going to answer me or not?"

"Here's the thing, Cooper. I'm not sure I can answer your question."

"Why not?"

"Because I have no idea how to get out of the friendzone." His eyes brighten conspiratorially. This is the friendzone, right here. We are in it. Whoops.

"Okay, well, pretend you're an awkward boy named Peter and you like a powerhouse of a girl named Monica who is very smart and very cool and whoops ass in *Overwatch*."

Derek gives a low whistle, which earns him only a glance and a smile from the Wex. I mean, the absolute injustice of it all.

"Dude's got a tough climb," he says. "Not impossible, though, just needs a little confidence and a game plan. Who is this guy?"

"He's—" I pause. Is admitting I go to therapy going to be a red flag? Whatever. It shouldn't be. "We share a therapist."

"Mm." Derek nods, taking it in stride because of course he does. "Well, like I said, it's all about the confidence. If he's respectful about it and acts like a guy who deserves her, then his chances increase tenfold. Still may get shut down, though, so I wouldn't push it unless you think he can handle that outcome. For the friendzone is dark and full of terrors."

"You are so annoying," I laugh, pulling out my notebooks to get started.

"Y me vuelves loca," he responds with a smile.

"Why are we even doing this?" I point at his book. "You speak perfect Spanish. You don't need my help. You could test out of Spanish II if you wanted to."

"Eh, it has its perks. Plus, I do need your help," he objects.

"With what exactly?" Not that I'm complaining about spending time with him. It's pretty much the highlight of my day. But with work and R.P.E. after school, I could use free period to get other things done. Like testing JoJo on a Quizlet of flash cards for the verbal section of the SAT. Who knew that after you finished the test, you lived in SAT purgatory forever?

"Estamos aqui porque parece que no puedo alejarme de ti, Michie Cooper," he responds with a sigh.

"I don't know what that means."

He laughs and flips to his bookmark. "It means you keep me motivated." He smiles. "Michie Cooper."

I narrow my eyes, because I might not know what he said, but I know it wasn't that. "Liar."

"No." He smirks. "Just an omission."

"I want to try something different this week," Dr. Schwartz says as she hands out a stack of unlined note cards and gel pens. "We talk a lot about grief, loss, mourning for the relationships you never got to have." She squats down on the floor. "But today I want to talk about guilt." She crosses her legs in front of her. "None of you did anything wrong, and yet the one emotion you express to me every session, no matter the topic, is guilt. Guilt for being alive, guilt for being a reminder, guilt for being unable to reverse time even if doing so would mean erasing yourselves entirely.

"So," she says, holding up a blank card. "I want you to write down the things making you feel guilty. Guilt is like drowning in shallow water. You could breathe if only you could lift your head up. I'll give you ten minutes."

No one moves. We're used to her shaping our feelings into sense, naming them with words we can't reach on our own. *Sorrow. Regret.* She's written the glossary of our lives.

Han begins writing first. The rest of us follow his lead, the sound of pens scraping across note card paper.

I start with a solitary bullet. *Existing.* A little melodramatic, but I don't know how else to put it. If I hadn't been born, Renee could have lived out her dreams the way she imagined them. College. Congresswoman. The dreams I don't even know about but wish I did.

The next bullet point is *Grandma.* If she wasn't stuck with me, she could retire for real, relax, play bingo on weekends or something. She and Renee would have a relationship if I hadn't made that choice so long ago, the decision of a five-year-old who didn't understand consequences.

Then *JoJo.* I know everything there is to know about her life—her parents, her empty home, the chemistry test she cheated on last year during a mono outbreak. And in return, I hide everything meaningful from her. She knows how many times I've read *Atonement*, which rapper is my current favorite, the small stuff. But she can't tell you why happy-ending movies bring me to tears (the idea is so foreign) or how many letters I've written and left unsent at the bottom of my sock drawer (a lot). That's not how friendships are supposed to work, with one person giving half of themselves.

"Okay," Dr. Schwartz says. Her words are hushed.

Everyone is thinking in whispers, while my thoughts are screams I can't lull to sleep. "How about we all share one thing?"

I don't hear most of the rest of the session. Peter taps his pencil on the table in front of him. *Tap, tap, tap-tap, tap*, like a heartbeat with a murmur.

There's a gentle tap on my shoulder. The room slams back into focus. All eyes are on me.

"Do you have one you'd like to share?" Dr. Schwartz asks me. "You don't have to."

"Um." I look down at my list. Sharing Renee slash general existence feels like overkill. I mean, duh, that's why we're all here. Sharing Grandma is too personal. I don't want to speak aloud all the ways her life would be better without me. Which leaves only one choice. "I feel guilty that I'm keeping all of this"—I gesture around the room—"from my best friend. I hate that I can't tell her."

"Why can't you?" Dr. Schwartz asks.

My foot taps against the carpet. The downbeats to Peter's pencil taps. The sound finally smooths into a pulse. *Tap, bum, tap, bum.* The rhythm urges my words out.

"We shouldn't be here. Life of the mother, incest, rape, get rid of it, right?" I look her straight in the eye. "My best friend in the world is one of those people, and deep down she believes the world would be better off without me. Because that would mean a woman didn't have to carry her rapist's baby. But she's a good person, a great person, and she would feel awful if she knew that truth applied to me. Pity would be involved. And I don't want that. I want the good, uncomplicated things to stay the way they are."

"What if nothing changed at all?" Dr. Schwartz asks. "What if you told her and life went on as normal?"

"It wouldn't." Because if it did, it would mean I've been hiding things for no reason, and that's worse. That would mean a lifetime of wasted moments.

"Do you trust her?" Han asks from his beanbag chair.

"With my life," I respond.

"Then I don't get it," he says.

"Do you think you're doing your friend a disservice by assuming she will respond poorly?" Dr. Schwartz asks. "Do you think you're projecting how you feel about yourself onto her?"

JoJo's never given me any reason to believe she would ever reject me. But there's a nagging self-doubt that I shouldn't be here—and if JoJo, of all people, believes that, then what shot do I have at anyone else accepting me?

I lean back into the couch cushions, exhausted. It's so quiet I can hear Peter knock his lip piercing against his teeth.

"Okay," Dr. Schwartz finally says. "Well, here's my challenge to you all. Take one of those guilts on your note card and scratch it out in your real life. I want you all to stand up and breathe, so that you can live." Her eyes never waver from mine. "See you in two weeks."

Monica catches me on our way out of group, with a hand wrapped around my elbow.

"Hungry?" she asks.

"Starving." I studied for an English exam during lunch to free up free period for Derek's "study session," and now my stomach is devouring itself.

"Sushi?" She leads me out of the front doors of the tall office building. Lindell waves goodbye as he unlocks his bike from the rack. I try to catch Peter's eye as he takes off on his skateboard, but he turns his head away so fast he probably gave himself whiplash. All right, guess I'll have to play a one-sided game of matchmaker today.

"Yeah, I—" I start to say, but collide with another body. Breath releases from my chest in a grunt.

A maroon hoodie hangs low over the person's head, hiding most of their face. The end of a long brunette ponytail sticks out. They bring their head up, startled.

"I'm so sorry," they mutter. Big, storm-blue eyes stare back at me. I recognize them in an instant. Trish Peterson. Another junior at Lee High who I haven't seen since sophomore year. The events of her summer blew through the rumor mill like a cannonball. I glance down at her stomach subconsciously. There's nothing there to see. Not anymore.

"That's fine," I say, stepping out of her way.

She studies my face. I'm not popular, no surprise there, but when you're the only Black girl in any of your classes, people remember you. I catch the recognition in her eyes.

Words are sticky on my lips. A tangle of *are you okay*s and *how could you*s. She says nothing as she darts around me, hurrying into the building.

"You ready?" Monica asks from beside me.

I watch Trish's retreating form as I raise my backpack higher on my back. "Yeah. Thought she looked familiar." The doors snap shut behind her.

Monica and I start walking toward the sushi buffet on Broad Street. It's happy hour, which means the sushi is only fifty cents per piece, and I've got a crisp twenty in my pocket from café tips.

"So, how's the new living situation?" I ask, kicking an errant rock.

"Surprisingly good," she responds, her tone cautious. "But I don't want to jinx it. Last time I said a foster home was good, an electrical fire burned it to the ground."

Okay, so new topic. I don't need that on my conscience.

"Dating anyone?" Subtle transition.

She snorts. "That's a joke, right?"

"Thinking about dating anyone, then?"

"Right, because high school boys want a foster kid with truckloads of trauma."

I hum, thinking about one boy in particular.

"Ever think about anyone in group? I mean, who better equipped to deal with our particular brand of trauma."

"Okay, but who? Lindell is 1) gay and 2) leaving, Han is a baby, and Peter..." She pauses.

"Peter is?" I ask, perking up at the direction of the conversation.

"Way too cool."

"Peter is not cool," I object. "The kid sings 'Baby Shark' unironically."

She laughs. The sound is so rare.

"And remember those TikTok dances he tried to learn over Thanksgiving break? But if you like him," I say, as if the idea has just come to me, "you should talk to him." It's an echo of JoJo's advice to me. If only it were as easy to take advice as to give it.

"I talk to him all the time."

"I mean *talk to him* talk to him."

"No thank you." She shakes her head. "I'm good."

"You should let yourself be happy, Mo." It's like JoJo is speaking through me.

Her eyebrow raises in indignation. I grab her hand as she reaches for the door to the buffet.

"I will pay for your sushi if you talk to Peter. Really talk to him." Which means I'll have to use my emergency card instead for this excursion, but whatever. It's worth it. This is an emergency of the heart.

She stares down at my hand. "And you care about this because?"

I release her. "You two's goth aesthetic would be a thing of beauty."

She laughs even louder now and pulls open the door. "Whatever gets me free sashimi."

I give a silent cheer in my head. At least some of the R.P.E. kids are doing all right.

∞

I drape myself across my bed, flash cards scattered over the comforter.

"JoJo, please. My crops are dying," I moan into a pillow. We have been going over vocabulary words for the past two hours. JoJo can do the math portion of the SAT in her sleep, but apparently the verbal section kicks her ass. The thing is, it kicks my ass too, so I really don't want to spend my night like this.

"Five more minutes," she says, gathering the cards back into a pile.

"I'm kicking you out of my house effective immediately. I rescind your invitation."

"Okay, Elena Gilbert," she snorts. "Interview prep, then."

"Oh my God." Doesn't she want to chill? Doesn't she want to relax and watch *The Crown*?

"Our interviews are in a month, and neither of us is prepared."

"We're prepared. All they're going to ask us about is our life, our hopes, blah, blah, blah." I mean, it kind of is hard for me, but I figure I'll BS my way through. Why waste time on something that's such a long shot?

"Oh, my sweet summer child, no. They're going to go full Laurence Fishburne in *Akeelah and the Bee*, throwing questions like Ping-Pong balls. They will find a weakness and prey on it. UChicago is going to hound me on MIT clearly being the school I was destined for and why I'm all of a sudden changing my mind. They want commitment."

"Why *are* you changing your mind?" I ask.

"I'm not changing my mind," she explains. "I'm weighing my options like any reasonable person."

"Chicago, though, Jo? You cried in New York because it was so cold your fingers were practically frostbitten. You hate winter, and it's winter *all the time* there."

"It's not any worse than Cambridge. I am going to suffer either way."

"Or there's another reason?" I sit up and poke her foot with mine. "An *m-o-m* reason?"

"Don't be stupid," she scoffs. "I'm not picking a school based on where my mom is teaching. She could move at a moment's notice. That would be foolish. MIT is closer to my dad. It's just an opportunity."

My eyebrow raises of its own accord. "JoJo, you don't give a damn about your dad. And MIT is still ten hours away. It's closer in, like, dog years."

JoJo doesn't dislike her dad; he's just been way more blatant than her mom about his disinterest in her life. Mrs. Kaplan is so career-focused that her family takes the back seat. If I'm being generous, it's not for lack of love that she's not around. But Mr. Kaplan is a forty-year-old frat boy who still measures his value by how many women he sleeps with and what other dudes think about him. It's an open secret, but as long as he pays for Mrs. Kaplan's Chicago apartment and keeps JoJo in designer clothing, everyone seems happy to proceed as normal.

"Whatever." She averts her eyes.

"Okay." I shrug, feigning indifference. If there's one thing JoJo hates, it's moving on from a topic before she's said her piece. Pretending I don't care is the best way to get her to spill.

"It would, of course, be nice to spend time with her. Maybe have dinners every once in a while, depending on how our schedules work out. I wouldn't give up any freshman-year shenanigans to hang out with my mother, of course."

"Mm, no, of course."

She flicks the flash cards in her hands absentmindedly.

"You know, Jo, it's okay to admit you want to spend time with your mom. And it's okay to pick a school because of that."

She nods, letting the words sink in.

"Plus, if you changed your mind, MIT would die to have you. You could always transfer."

She looks up at me, finally, her eyes flashing bright. "I could always transfer," she repeats.

"You could always transfer."

She smiles and takes a deep breath. Like her lungs are clear and her body is more buoyant and easier to inflate. Her brow furrows. "*Loquacious* means..."

CHAPTER TWELVE

"I HEARD HER PARENTS KICKED HER OUT OF THE HOUSE. It's devastating," Gwen whispers to the rest of the lunch table, her eyes stricken wide.

I pause while taking my usual seat. They're in the middle of a conversation I am certain I don't want to be a part of.

"Gross." JoJo grimaces. "But I get it."

Gwen narrows her eyes, scandalized. "You *get* her parents being total monsters?"

"They're super Catholic, aren't they? If that's something they believe in, then I get it, yeah. I'm not saying I agree with them."

"Well, I don't get it," Gwen scoffs. "She's their daughter."

"If parents accepted everything about their kids, a lot would be handled better. But they don't. So here we are."

"Do I want to know?" I ask.

Derek smiles from across the table. Instead of being in third-period lunch with the seniors, he eats with the juniors because he needed third period for the only open Calculus II slot. He joined our table a week ago. The juniors on the basketball team hold court in the center of the cafeteria. But he chose us. Chose me.

"Trish Peterson's parents found out about her little DC trip to Planned Parenthood last summer," Gwen explains.

A *little* trip, like a *little* fire, before it burns your home down.

The shadows of Trish's face when we collided the other day flash across my vision. I wonder if she had already been kicked out. JoJo's words—*I don't agree with them*—feel like a slap. Does she mean tossing Trish away like garbage or their stance on abortion? If the latter, would she think me a monster too if she knew maybe I agree with them? Or am at least unsure?

I remember when I found out about Trish over the summer. It was a scandal that blazed out, literally, when Connor Alvarez set fire to the chemistry lab in a senior prank gone wrong. But Trish's story stuck with me, a phantom pain that left me shaken. I had come so close to the same fate; how could I say we don't all deserve the chance at life? It took months for Dr. Schwartz to get me to connect that feeling of indispensability with The Incident.

I want the conversation to end, want to think about anything else, but my mind grips onto the subject with an iron fist. Would Trish have hated what her baby would take from her? Or would she have loved it in spite of that? If I could have spoken for myself, would I have asked for a life of resentment, but a life nonetheless, or would I have wished for Renee's peace? What was either of our pain worth?

Was the look in Trish's eye remorse or relief?

I don't engage as their argument flares around me. I bite down on my tongue. If I open my mouth, I'm afraid of what might spill out.

Derek's eyes drip with concern. He taps my foot with his beneath the table, and I shake my head. Everything around me is moving at once as I slide deeper into a panic. Derek taps my foot harder, but it feels like it's happening to another body, like watching someone poke at a numb limb.

Derek's voice cracks through like thunder after lightning.

"Can you show me where the art wing is?"

I blink, not understanding. His head cocks.

"You don't take art," JoJo interjects. She knows he's asking for something else. He is, but not the something she thinks.

"I'm considering it." His eyes never leave mine. "You took Mr. Mbale's class last year, right?"

He nods and I mimic him.

"Great." He stands, circling the table to lift me by the elbow. I manage to find my feet beneath me. JoJo opens her mouth to object, but then casts us a conspiratorial smile. He leads me through the cafeteria, his grip light but commanding.

The second we're in the hallway, the noise left behind in the cafeteria, sweat explodes from my pores. I turn my back to him and lean my forehead against the cold metal of a locker. In through the nose, out through the mouth, I breathe, my chest rising and falling rhythmically. In. Out. In. Out.

Derek doesn't touch me, but he moves closer.

"Are you okay? You were a little green in there."

"I'm fine," I mumble, taking in everything around me. Cold metal, hard floor. I flex each finger until I get to ten. I feel dangerously close to how I felt last summer. The loss of control. The spiral. I push against it, like my nurses taught me my first night under observation.

"Are you sure?" He reaches for my shoulder, but I flinch away.

"I said I'm fine," I snap.

"Okay." His eyes look distressed, and I kick myself for taking it out on him. My fault. Always my fault.

I fold the skin of my nose between my fingers and pinch down, massaging the bone. He stands close but maintains a few inches of distance.

"I'm sorry," I apologize. "A little anxiety." I nod back toward the cafeteria doors.

"No offense, but that wasn't a little anxiety. It was a full-blown panic attack."

I nod, not arguing the point. He's right. I haven't had one this bad in months. The off-brand Zoloft (because we can't afford the real stuff) I stubbornly tucked away in the back corner of my medicine cabinet taunts me. I wouldn't be so against bringing it to school if I didn't have to register it with the nurse. I don't want to be *that girl* to the administration.

My heart rate starts to speed up again.

"Let's get some air." He reaches for me again, and this time I let him. He drapes his arm over my shoulders, and his warmth sinks through my sweater.

Through the doors, the cold late-January breeze slaps us in the face, sharp and unrelenting. My eyes both water and dry out in an instant. Only now do I remember my coat is still in my locker and I'm wearing nothing but a light sweater. I fold myself farther into him and his muscles tighten around me, pulling me closer. He smells of cinnamon and a scent I can't place. He leads us through the parking lot to a silver Audi.

"Um." We both have free periods after lunch, and we're supposed to stay on campus. But the last thing I want to do is go back into school.

"Stop thinking so loud," he says, his teeth chattering.

The car alarm beeps as the locks pop up.

"Get in." He slides into the driver's seat. The motor purrs as he rolls the passenger side window, leaning across the center console. "The longer you stand there, the less time we have to live on the wild side."

"It's th-the suburbs," I stutter, shivering. I climb into the passenger seat and buckle myself in. Why the hell not? "There is no wild side."

"Ah, but you're wrong, young grasshopper." He backs the car out of its space.

A defiant smile settles onto my lips. John Legend croons through the speakers, and the music weaves around us. I close my eyes and let my muscles melt into the seat. I turn my head toward him, peeking through my eyelashes at his blurry profile. Unlike me, with my resting bitch face, he has lips that settle into a slight upward tilt so he's always smiling. It's been only a few minutes, and already my panic attack is a distant memory. His effect on me is scary, how much I already need him in order to stay grounded.

Apparently, the wild side of the Richmond suburbs is 7-Eleven.

"Seriously?" I ask as we get out of the car.

"Hey," he scolds. "Have some respect. This is the home of the taquito."

"On behalf of your Mexican ancestors, I'm going to take offense."

"Fun taquito fact," he says, holding the door open for me. "They didn't even originate in Mexico."

"Wait, really?" I stop midway through the door and he slams into my back, grabbing my waist. He snatches his hands away like he's put them on a stove-top burner and rubs an earlobe between his fingers.

"Really." His voice hitches. "A Mexican American culinary masterpiece."

We stock up on Life Savers neon gummies and extra-large Slurpees. I get cherry with a hint of blue raspberry. Derek gets half and half, Coke and cherry. We walk down each aisle, grabbing a plethora of snacks along the way. Flamin' Hot Cheetos: check. Little Debbie Zebra Cakes: check. Taquitos, obviously: check.

We dump our spoils onto the counter in a heap. It's enough to feed a small army. Derek attempts to put his credit card in the reader, but I swat him away.

"My meltdown, my money," I chide. Enough people spend money on me already. Grandma, JoJo. Not him too. And I still have the twenty I didn't use for sushi. I slam it on the counter with a little too much force.

"Okay, Hulk." He collects the bags in a bear hug as the cashier fills my palm with the change. I stuff it into my pocket before grabbing the Slurpees. They're already half-empty from our slow perusal of the aisles.

He opens my car door and dumps our haul on the floor. I duck beneath his arm and navigate my feet through the bags as I sit.

There are still twenty minutes left of lunch period when Derek pulls back into his spot. He puts the car in park but keeps it running, the heat circulating at full blast. He double-checks the time before scrolling through pages of apps on his phone to find Disney+.

"Very organized," I laugh. It's so different from my carefully curated masterpiece, in which my streaming apps (JoJo's streaming apps) are in a folder titled United Procrasti-Nations.

From his Continue Watching tab, he chooses *Black Panther*, and I'm already emotional when Chadwick pops up on the screen. Derek drags his thumb across the time bar to fast-forward, stopping at Shuri driving around the streets of South Korea from her lab's sand table. He holds the phone out so we can both see, the audio playing through the aux cord. The background music thumps around us, like our bodies are inside a pair of fancy headphones.

"Oh, best part," I mutter as I bite into a hot Cheeto.

"Big facts," he agrees, splitting an extra-large Zebra Cake straight down the middle. He leans back in his seat and switches his phone to the other hand, reaching with his now free one to the Cheetos bag in my lap. His knuckles drag across my stomach and I clench my legs together, popping the plastic top off the Slurpee cup squeezed between my knees. A popped cherry Slurpee. I laugh to myself.

"What?" he asks.

I cough into my hand and shake my head.

With three minutes to spare, we stash all the snacks we didn't get to in his glove compartment. We collect the empty bags and dump them in the outdoor trash bins.

"When Okoye throws her spear through the car, I want to scream," I say, fangirling while rubbing my hands up and down the length of my arms for warmth.

"If Black Widow gets her own movie, Okoye definitely deserves one," he replies.

I stop at the front doors and inhale until my lungs reach capacity.

"Ready?" His shoulders are hunched so far up they're almost earmuffs as he fends off the cold.

"Yeah." I nod and exhale. "I'm ready."

He opens the door and I walk in front of him. His palm finds my lower back, his thumb brushing the small space of skin exposed from my raised sweater. It sets my skin on fire as he ushers me through the doors. The halls are filled with the normal hustle and bustle, as if nothing has happened. You can fall apart, and the world will keep spinning. His hand falls away and I miss it instantly.

Derek walks me all the way to English. My backpack, left behind at the lunch table, is sitting in my seat. Gwen catches my eye and waves. *Thank you*, I mouth.

Derek and I hover by the door. Even for my favorite class of the day, I'm bummed I have to go.

"So," I start. "Thanks. For the rescue." I motion my hand in the vague direction of the parking lot.

"Anytime." He leans down, his mouth dropping to my ear. "Though I don't think you need rescuing."

I smile up at him as Mr. Milligan, my English teacher, squeezes between us, muttering an apology even though we're the ones in the way. He's a short and round man, with only a few wisps of hair left on the top of his head.

Derek bends down even closer. "Is this your king?" he whispers, pointing his chin to Mr. Milligan, who I've gushed to him is my favorite teacher during too many of our library sessions to count.

I laugh and shove him away. He waves before heading to his own class. Somehow, I forget about every bitter part of the last hour and store away each minute with him so that I can hold on to them.

CHAPTER THIRTEEN

AFTER SCHOOL, I TAKE GRANDMA DINNER FOR HER DOU-
ble shift. The doctor's office smells like hydrogen perox-
ide and latex. Patients sit along the walls in varying states
of misery—some waiting for an annual checkup and some
with paper masks over their hacking mouths. A chorus of
coughs sing a ballad around the room, the altos wet and the
baritones dry.

I hold the paper Panera bag up to Sylvia, sitting behind
the reception desk. She doesn't look up as she presses a button by her computer screen. The door to the patient rooms
buzzes. I make my way through the winding halls to a
massive room lined with exam tables and curtain dividers.

Grandma sits on a low couch in her scrubs, a clipboard in her lap.

I drop the bag on the arm of the couch and fall heavily onto the other end, a file folder crinkling under my butt. She scowls at me before pulling it from beneath me and dropping it to the floor with a splat.

"Bacon turkey bravo with swiss." I nod to the bag.

"My love," she exclaims. She could be talking about me or the sandwich. She hands me the pumpkin muffie on top and devours half the sandwich before coming back up for air. "How was school?"

"Same old, same old. Ate most of my lunch by second period. Señora Cortez yelled at me for butchering her beautiful language. Skipped free period."

Grandma stares at me, the sandwich held halfway to her mouth. "Excuse me?"

"I had a good reason."

"I doubt it."

I tell her about lunch, and needing to escape, and 7-Eleven. Her eyebrows pitch upward at the mention of Derek, who I've never brought up to her before. Oops. But she lets me finish without interruption.

"Michie, you can't run away when things get uncomfortable. I'm sure your friends would've talked about something else if you'd asked."

"You don't know Gwen," I say. "She'd scold me for not being interested in female body autonomy or something. It would've been a whole thing." My desire to change the subject would have been interpreted as indifference, not self-care.

"Well, I'm sure no one was trying to be hurtful," she suggests.

"I'm sure they weren't. Doesn't make it hurt any less, knowing my friends would be disgusted."

"When are you going to learn that the only person who cares about where you came from is you? Your friends love you."

"I already have a therapist, thanks."

"I'm going to let you feel what you're feeling, but watch your tone, Michelle Cooper."

I mumble an apology.

"How's the essay going?" she asks around a mouthful of turkey as she bites into her sandwich again.

"I have a couple months until I need a finalized version to send out to schools." There are a few private scholarships with due dates in early summer, but I still haven't been able to get down a single coherent sentence. I pulled the raised-by-a-single-grandparent card for the host application, but I doubt that's good enough for Brown. Plus, I've been focusing on the, apparent, death-match interview. I would love a break from work my entire future hinges on. "Mr. Milligan is looking at our most recent drafts now. Mine was pretty polished," I lie. I had written the entire thing on the bus the morning it was due. It wasn't my best work, but I think it was passable.

Her gaze is penetrating as she chews. Her eyes are

slightly crossed behind the thick lenses of her glasses. Just another thing we have in common.

"Or I can take a year off," I suggest, somewhat serious. "Hike El Camino, start a travel blog."

She snorts. Not a single person in my family went to college, and yet I don't even get a choice. But college will be as much her victory as mine. There's no way I'd have gotten this far without her. So I let her push and prod, because she deserves this win too.

"My SATs could be better," I say.

"Your SATs are fine."

"You don't even know what they are," I proclaim.

"But I know they're fine. It's you." At least one of us has unyielding confidence in my abilities.

"They're not top-school fine."

"As long as they get you in somewhere you'd be happy, anything else is a bonus, no?"

"Yeah." I swallow. "As long as I get in somewhere."

"Good. Then it'll all work itself out." She says it without a hint of doubt.

Sometimes I forget how lucky I am to have her, even when everything else is a dumpster fire.

I slap my hands on my thighs. "Well, this has been fun, but speaking of essays, I'm going to go work on mine." I give her a cheeky grin.

"Wait," she says, suddenly finding great interest in her sandwich wrapper. "I have some things to talk to you about."

"What things?"

She wipes her mouth methodically with her napkin, like it's the most important thing she will ever do.

"Not right now. I'll be home late tonight, so we'll talk when you get home tomorrow. It's nothing serious."

"Okay, Ms. Cryptic." I'm tired anyway, and I do actually need to go work on my essay.

Pumpkin muffie crumbs fall to the floor as I stand and grab the balled-up bag.

"I'm going to sleep in a little tomorrow," she tells me. "Take the chicken out of the freezer in the morning and put it in some cold water."

"Aye, aye, Captain." I salute.

"Michie," she says, catching me at the door.

"Hmm?"

"Please remember the chicken."

"Gosh, it's like you don't trust me or something," I say with a laugh.

Famous last words.

I'm in fifth period the next day, my brain drunk on a famous authors from the nineteenth century Powerpoint projected on the pull-down screen, when I remember the chicken.

"Shit," I mumble under my breath. I scoot my phone from beneath my copy of the most offensive book ever written, *Heart of Darkness*, and stealthily type out a quick text to Grandma.

MICHIE COOPER AT 11:15 A.M.: forgot chicken! sorry!

The read receipt comes back in seconds.

GRANDMOTHER-DEAREST AT 11:16 A.M.: Yes.... I noticed

Whoops.

I have three text messages I missed on Do Not Disturb. One is from MAC Cosmetics, announcing the release date for a collaboration with a not-Jackie-Aina YouTube star I couldn't care less about. Two are from JoJo. A screenshot of her BuzzFeed results for a "Which Disney Villain Are You?" quiz and her aggrieved reaction.

JOJO KAPLAN AT 11:01 A.M.: Maleficent?! Is this a joke?
MICHIE COOPER AT 11:17 A.M.: this is the most accurate thing I have ever seen
MICHIE COOPER AT 11:17 A.M.: plus cheekbones
She responds while I'm still typing.
JOJO KAPLAN AT 11:17 A.M.: The correct answer is obviously Cruella. Make it fashion.

I put my fist over my mouth to muffle a laugh. Gwen, sitting in front of me, casts me a quick glance over her shoulder.

JoJo sends me the link to take the quiz, but it'll have to wait until after class. I'm not *that* stealthy.

JOJO KAPLAN AT 11:21 A.M.: Derek got Gaston

JoJo's in nearly all senior classes because she's a certified genius. The only reason she's still in high school is because her mom thought it would stunt JoJo's development to be way younger than her peers. I guess she was right, since JoJo is now a large fish in a miniscule pond.

But I forgot she has World Lit with Derek. An unreasonable pang of jealousy spreads down my spine. Though I guess now his wrong opinion on Dickens makes sense, since it seems he spends English class comparing his Myers-Briggs personality to tree species.

> **MICHIE COOPER AT 11:23 A.M.:** because of the muscles?
> **JOJO KAPLAN AT 11:24 A.M.:** DEAD. Definitely the brawn. And the quads.

Another text pings simultaneously in a different thread.

> **DEREK DE LA ROSA AT 11:24 A.M.:** Yes because of the muscles thanks for noticing.

I gag. Is she showing him these? I scroll back up to make sure I haven't said anything embarrassing. Just muscles. That's not so bad. It's an objectively true observation.

My phone vibrates again before I put it down. I'm not even pretending to pay attention to the slideshow on the screen anymore.

I've been added to a group chat named #thiccneckGaston by JoJo. Odd, since she is very much anti–group chat.

> **JOJO KAPLAN AT 11:26 A.M.:** Did we just become best friends?

She adds a GIF from *Step Brothers*, Will Ferrell mouthing the words in a continuous loop.

> **DEREK DE LA ROSA AT 11:27 A.M.:** Are these those threeways the team keeps talking about?
>
> **JOJO KAPLAN AT 11:28 A.M.:** Vomming. Please keep sexcapades of bball heathens to strict minimum under the chat rules.

A laugh forces its way out through my clenched lips. Mr. Milligan raises his eyebrows at me before returning to his lecture.

> **JOJO KAPLAN AT 11:30 A.M.:** But I'm just the chaperone

JoJo and Derek are working their way through a series of other quizzes. JoJo is brie cheese—hard on the outside but soft in the middle. Derek is American cheese—simple, dependable, and adorably packaged. They both were not smarter than a fifth grader, to which JoJo took personal offense. JoJo is Iron Man—smart, cocky, and would die for you. Derek is Ant-Man—kind of clueless but always wanting to do what's right. It's a little bit scary how accurate they are.

As soon as Mr. Milligan dismisses us, I race to finish every quiz.

Villain: Yzma—eccentric with no attention to detail. I'll take it, because she was voiced by Eartha Kitt, an icon.

Cheese: Bleu—shouldn't work but does. If that ain't the truth.

Avenger: Thor—outwardly stoic but multidimensional to close friends. Fair.

I post screenshots of each one in the chat.

DEREK DE LA ROSA AT 11:37 A.M.: Pull the lever Kronk!

MICHIE COOPER AT 11:38 A.M.: wrong lever!

DEREK DE LA ROSA AT 11:38 A.M.: Why do we even have that lever?

JoJo sends me a text separate from the chat, between just the two of us.

JOJO KAPLAN AT 11:39 A.M.: Make out already.

CHAPTER FOURTEEN

JOJO CATCHES UP TO ME ON MY WAY TO THE BUS AFTER school.

"Why, Maleficent," I laugh, "lovely to see you this afternoon."

Normally, she would laugh. But she doesn't. Instead, she climbs the steps behind me without a word. I don't ask, because I know what's going on. Only one thing moves Joanna Kaplan to total silence. Her parents must be home. At the same time. She can usually handle one or the other, preferably her dad because he leaves her alone. But when they're both home, it's like World War III.

"It's been a while," Ms. Turner says to JoJo as she snaps the doors shut behind us.

JoJo fist-bumps her as we make our way to my seat.

I slide all the way to the window and JoJo sits beside me, her legs stretching into the aisle. The bus is empty, but we always share a seat when she rides home with me. The one exception being the mysterious twenty-four-hour bug I'd caught in ninth grade. She'd sat one seat over, hovering her hand over my chest to make sure I was still breathing.

"Your car?" I ask, pulling out my earphones and handing her one earbud.

"It'll still be here tomorrow." We won't have space in our visitor parking, anyway. And I don't want her Beamer sitting in our lot overnight. Not if we ever want to see it again.

I try to think of a conversation that won't make her feel worse. "Do you think Monica would be offended if I offered her a makeover?"

"Who is Monica?" she asks with a sigh, accepting my need to fill the silence.

"Monica," I say. "From group."

"Right." She nods. "Why does she need a makeover? Also"—and now she laughs—"what in the world makes you think you're qualified for such an endeavor? You don't even own mascara."

"For your information, I do own mascara. Ulta gave me a baby one for free on my birthday."

"Oh my God," she groans.

"And since I am Monica and Peter's—also from group," I answer preemptively from the raise of her eyebrows, "personal Cher Horowitz, I am uniquely qualified."

"What the hell are you talking about?" She laughs again.

"I'm pairing up Mo and Peter. Romantically."

She snorts. "And when did this project start?"

"A couple of weeks ago, Peter told me he liked Monica, and I have an inkling Monica likes Peter, but both of them are so stubborn...."

"Imagine," JoJo scoffs.

I narrow my eyes at her. "Anyway, they are perfect for each other, and it's my mission for them to end up together and get married and have beautiful gamer vampire-esque babies."

"Wow." JoJo nods. "Becoming the Black Emma Woodhouse is certainly a new look for you. Do you think Monica needs a makeover?"

"No," I decide. "But it comes with the package."

"Well, Cher and Dionne didn't really help Tai out when they did her makeover. Skater Boy liked her already."

"Fair point," I agree.

"Wait, am I Dionne in this scenario?"

"Aesthetically, I'm Dionne. But practically, yes."

"I'll allow it."

The bus pulls up to the stop in my apartment complex. JoJo's the only person I have ever brought to my apartment, and the first time was by her own invitation. It was a day like today, in fifth grade. We had barely spoken prior, but that morning I found her crying in the girls' bathroom, the first of only two times I've seen it happen. A permission slip for Williamsburg, the most anticipated trip of elementary school, was wrinkled in her hands. Her parents had forgotten to sign it. I sat on the bathroom floor and shared my basically-Oreos with her. By then, I knew the sting of being disappointed by parents. And when Ms. Brown collected our slips, I took one look at JoJo, the only person left behind, and threw mine away.

The substitute teacher let us watch episodes of *Bill Nye* and *The Magic School Bus* instead of making us do any work. We shared my Happy-O's and her Fruit Roll-Up. And when everyone got back from the field trip, JoJo got on the bus home with me. Grandma called her parents to tell them where she was, but they hadn't even noticed she never came home.

We weren't best friends yet, but we've been family ever since. I told Derek I don't really have siblings, but that isn't true. I have a sister.

The apartment smells like spaghetti when we walk in, the scent of chopped peppers and garlic in the air. A quick dinner choice to replace the chicken I forgot to thaw.

Grandma's surprised to see her, but as usual, she takes it in stride.

"We need to talk before bed," Grandma says quietly to me while JoJo removes her boots. "Don't let me forget."

I respond with a nod before loading up my plate.

JoJo and I sit with our filled paper plates in our laps, garlic bread piled upon layers of napkins. We binge-watch the old, and only, season of *Next in Fashion*. Grandma and I never watch our usual weekday programming when JoJo's here, because she's a very competitive *Jeopardy!* player and a sore loser. So Grandma banned it.

As JoJo goes to take a shower first, I knock on Grandma's door. She waves me in and I collapse on her bed. She pulls up tonight's contraband episode of the *Jeopardy!* Teen Tournament from the DVR. One of the contestants cracks open the John Hughes category right out of the gate.

"Let's go," I cheer. I am the '80s movie queen, having seen every John Hughes movie at least one hundred times.

"So what'd you wanna talk about?" I ask Grandma during the commercial. I listen to make sure the shower is still running. This is clearly not a conversation Grandma wants to have in front of JoJo.

Grandma stares at me with bated breath. "Your mother called."

"What?" I must have misheard her.

"Your mom," she repeats, "called."

"I don't understand. Renee?"

"Renee," she confirms, nodding. She looks at everything in the room but me.

"Why?" I can't conjure up a single reason. "I mean, why now?" Was there some kind of cosmic event that brought mothers back into their kids' lives, or were JoJo and I soul mates in bad mom vibes and breakfast menus?

"She wants to see you." Grandma shrugs as if she's

telling me the weather forecast. Cloudy with a chance of are you fucking kidding me?

"When'd you talk to her? How'd you talk to her?" I didn't even think she had our number.

"She called me at work yesterday. She's always been resourceful."

"I'll say," I snort. She's great at finding a place to discard the things she doesn't want.

"Look, you don't have to see her. But she asked me to tell you, so I'm telling you. Who knows, talking to her might help."

"Help with what?" I take a deep breath, like I don't have enough going on already. A college essay kicking my butt, my interview in a couple of weeks, Derek, group. "It's not a casual request." Renee lives in Houston, a place I haven't been since Grandma and I moved away when I was five. It's not a quick trip around the block.

"Maybe talking to her will help you figure out what you want to do about your essay. And give you some confidence for your interview."

"Trust me, Renee is not boosting my confidence. Period."

"Up to you," she says. She unmutes the television, ending the conversation.

It's not that I don't want to see Renee. Okay, it's at least 88 percent because I don't want to. Our relationship is not great, which is the understatement of the century. I consider it a collateral consequence of being the living and breathing reminder of the single most terrible moment of her life. But I still wonder if I could ever hate my little girl. How can you hate someone who shared your heartbeat?

"Is she dying or something?" I ask.

"Not to my knowledge." She's unfazed by the entire ordeal. I'd be more upset if it wasn't because she's been burned by Renee so many times that she's grown dragon scales for skin. She is impenetrable.

I was seven the last time I heard Renee's voice. Her last words to me putter around like a pinball. Sometimes I think I imagined them. But how could a dull seven-year-old conjure words so sharp?

I should have killed you when I had the chance.

Whatever her reasons, I don't know how to not let her hurt me if I let her in.

"I don't want to see her." My belly and mind tighten into unyielding fists.

"Okay," she says.

"Okay."

But her eyes stay on me, willing me to make a different choice.

I go back to my room in a zombie state, exhausted.

"So," JoJo says, bouncing onto her side of the bed, pulling the quilt up her lap. "What was your grandma being all shiesty about?"

JoJo is what I call *concernosy*—nosiness that stems from concern. Of course she noticed.

Her wet hair is pulled into a bun at the top of her head, and for some strange reason, it annoys me. My pillows will get wet, even though I've never cared before. Her hair will be perfect in the morning, while mine would be a rat's nest if I did that. That's not her fault either, but my mind is gearing up for a fight, latching onto every indiscretion.

"It's serious best-friend-talk time."

"When is it not serious best-friend-talk time with you?" It's sharper than I intended, whetted by my anxiety moving through me like a riptide.

She moves my favorite stuffed animal, a white tiger, out of the way and pats my side of the bed. I sit, pulling my legs beneath me. I drag a pillow onto my lap. The bed is so soft. I could lie down. If I could just lie down.

"Derek," she says, shooting me a penetrating stare.

"Derek," I repeat. The word is drowsy and slow, like I'm drunk. Or drugged. I remember the drugs. In a little paper cup. The way they helped me sleep. God, I want to lie down.

"I'm serious," she persists. "That boy is one smitten kitten. He practically manhandled me into making that group chat. And you know my feelings about group chats." I do. She finds them annoying, which is why I was shocked when she created one.

As much as I attempt to neutralize my face, a small smile creeps onto it, the corners of my mouth twitching.

"Ha," she shrieks, pointing her finger at my face. "I knew it."

I drag my hand over my face like water on clay, smoothing it plain. But the smile is stubborn.

"I don't know what you're talking about," I mutter, but I can't say it with a straight face. "We're just friends."

"You are a piss-poor liar. Never go into politics."

"It's true. Have you seen him?" The relentless smile finally flickers out. The sadness rushes back, sucking me down like quicksand. Can sadness kill you? I don't know why I wonder. I know it can.

"What's that supposed to mean?" Her brows knit together in the center.

"It means he's beautiful, and I am…" I wave my hand over my body. "Not."

Her eyes narrow. If looks could kill, I'd be a cadaver. Though there are worse things than one's final thoughts being about Derek de la Rosa. Better than Renee. Shit, think about Derek, think about Derek, think about Derek. You can't die thinking about Renee. Shit. Derek. Derek. Derek.

"Why do you do that?"

"What?"

"Talk about yourself like you don't matter. Even if you weren't hot, you wouldn't be unworthy of him or something. But you *are* hot. So stop it."

I snort, and her eyes flash as her temper flares.

"I'm serious," she says. "If you talk down about yourself one more time, I'm breaking your face, and then you can be ugly for real. And have you ever considered that you're being a little hot and cold? You spend every day tutoring him when he doesn't need your help. He talks my ear off about you. The eye sex at lunch is hotter than the Sahara. In his mind, y'all are already on, like, kid number three in your white-picket-fenced yard and you're *just friends*–ing him. The poor kid doesn't know which way is up.

"I get the whole emotionally guarded thing. I do," she continues. "But…just because your mom treats you like crap doesn't mean you have to expect crap from everyone else."

"Hey," I cry. "You don't know shit about my mom."

"Okay, so tell me."

JoJo is the smartest and most perceptive person I know. Why can't she hear the screaming? It's so goddamn loud in my head. I could tell her what Grandma said. I should tell her everything. But I don't. She waits and waits and waits. She'll be waiting forever.

"Tell me about yours," I challenge. I know she won't. And she doesn't. "You entered a whole contest just to get your mom to eat cold pizza with you. At least I know when I'm not wanted. So worry about your own shitty mom for once." It's spiteful and mean and petty, and I'm ashamed before it even leaves my lips. But for a moment I want her to hurt enough to leave me alone. That's what I do. I hurt people until they leave me.

"Nice," she says, but she doesn't look angry or hurt. She looks disappointed. Disappointed that I don't trust her. Disappointed that I would stoop so low.

I wish she hated me. Disappointment is so much worse.

She lowers herself into the blankets and flips over to

her side, her back a wall between us. She clicks off the lamp without another word, casting us in thick darkness.

Tears sting the backs of my eyes, but I refuse to let them fall. I should apologize—I know I should—before she falls asleep. But I'm so resentful. Her mom might be gone a lot, but she always comes back. She's home right now, in fact, and JoJo chose to be here instead. She gets that choice.

But aren't I doing the same thing? Renee is right there, reaching out, and I said no. How can I be angry with JoJo for struggling with the same decision? Is it because she seems better off overall? Is it because I'm jealous she can hate her mom without having to hate herself too?

I have to tell her. I have to. I pull my stuffed tiger closer to me for strength.

"Jo," I whisper. She doesn't respond.

I listen to her breath even out beside me, already asleep. The pit in my stomach grows. I'm like a tornado, indiscriminately hopping around and destroying everything in my path.

I reach for her in the dark, finding her arm beneath the blankets. In her sleep, or maybe she's awake and not ready to talk, she grasps my hand.

"I'm sorry," I whisper. I squeeze tight, and before my eyes close into restless sleep, she squeezes back.

I wake up extra early the next morning to get the coffeepot filled with hazelnut coffee, JoJo's favorite. Grandma makes my sandwich, scraping off most of the mayonnaise, enough to know it's there but not enough to be tasted. I mimic her, except I use mustard for JoJo.

Grandma watches me with suspicion, surprised that I'm awake and ready so early in the morning.

"I kind of snapped on JoJo about her mom." I fold under her gaze. Grandma's the only person I know who can get you to answer her questions without asking any. She twists the top back on the Hellmann's jar when she's done with it.

"Because?" Grandma asks.

"Because," I offer, trying and failing to sort out my feelings. "I don't know." How do you explain that you wish you had someone's crappy family situation because it seems slightly less crappy than yours? How do you explain that you're jealous of someone else's different kind of pain? "Sometimes I think she's lucky, you know. At least she has a mom she gets to fight with."

Grandma lines up the edges of the bread, smooshing both sides together. "Pain isn't a competition." I remember Derek saying something similar. Bad life stuff, he called it. She drops the sandwiches into plastic baggies and places them in brown-paper bags. Then she reaches to tuck a stray curl behind my ear. "Besides," she adds, "you have someone you get to fight with too."

JoJo has a mom she never gets to see, and I have Grandma, who's here all the time. Now I feel even worse for what I said. The guilt spreads like disease in my chest.

I'm smearing a blueberry bagel with dairy-free cream

cheese when JoJo traipses into the kitchen and hugs Grandma before she leaves for work.

I shove the bagel in front of JoJo's face.

"What's this for?" she asks, biting into it while it's still in my hand.

"This is an I'm-a-shitty-friend breakfast."

She nods, grabbing it and taking another large bite.

"And is that an I-couldn't-even-resist-stealing-all-the-blankets-after-crushing-your-spirit coffee?" She points at the thermos waiting for her on the counter.

I pick it up and shake it. The coffee sloshes against the aluminum.

"Blessings," she whispers, grabbing it even more hungrily than the bagel.

"I'm sorry," I repeat from last night, meaning it even more now. "I was a huge jerk."

I pick up the second bagged lunch and hand it to her before dropping mine on top of the books in my backpack, zipping it in.

"Huge, monumental," she agrees. "Wanna tell me where Monster Bitch came from?"

"Yeah, about that." Fear crawls up my back, but a small gleam of courage crawls faster. "Snapping at you last night, it wasn't—it wasn't about you. Renee and I don't have the greatest relationship."

"I mean, duh. But that was shitty of me too. I shouldn't have brought up your mom. It was way out of line."

The truth coats my tongue, rising from my stomach like bile. If I don't let it out, I'll asphyxiate on it.

"Yeah, well, there's a reason she's not around. And it's not because she's a terrible person." She opens her mouth to object, but I raise my hand to stop her. "This isn't me being insecure, I swear. She's not around because she kind of can't be."

She cocks her head to the side, and I hear the word she doesn't say. *Bullshit.*

The more time that passes, the more the fear begins to overpower any bravery I built up. I have to just get it out. Now, before it retreats into the corners of my mind where I can't reach it. "Do you remember the other day in the cafeteria when Gwen was talking about Trish Peterson?"

"You mean when you and Derek went to get it on in the art studio?"

"No. I mean, yes, that day. But we weren't." I groan, attempting not to get sidetracked. "I was having a panic attack, and he bailed me out."

"A panic attack? Why?" She straightens, worried now. In Michie Land, panic attacks are nothing to play with.

"About Trish Peterson."

"You don't even know Trish Peterson."

"Not about Trish per se. About her situation. The baby. The abortion."

"Why?" She uncrosses her arms. Her eyes are unflinching.

"Because the whole topic, abortion, it makes me uncomfortable."

"It makes lots of people uncomfortable," she says. "That's why it's nice to not talk about that stuff in public. Gwen's... Gwen."

"No, I mean it makes me *really* uncomfortable." I'm hoping that this will be one of those times she gets what I'm saying without me actually having to say it. But this is new territory where we don't have a shared language. "I mean, *I* was almost Trish Peterson's baby."

"I don't understand."

I close my eyes and reach up to pinch the bridge of my nose. "Renee was," I start. Rip off the Band-Aid, Michie. "Renee was raped. And that's, that's how I'm, how I got here." My face feels too warm, and I'm sweating beneath her scrutiny as her eyes bore into mine. "Except I almost didn't get here, is what I'm saying. And that's why I freaked out at lunch. And that's why I'm so sketchy all the time about, you know, mom stuff. Because it's—it's not her fault that she doesn't want to be my mom."

"Oh, Michie," she whispers. "I'm so sorry." She turns her head to stare at a spot on the wall. "Wow, I'm such a bitch."

"You're not a bitch."

"No, I am. You're dealing with all of this, and I've been up your ass about everything."

"You didn't know," I reason.

"I shouldn't have to know to be a decent person."

"JoJo, you are the *best* person. That's why I never told you. I didn't want you to feel sorry for me or think I'm some kind of devil spawn."

"How could you ever think that?"

How *could* I think that? About JoJo, who has been a ride-or-die best friend for as long as I've known her? Does Renee have this much control over me still?

"It doesn't matter. You're telling me now," she says.

"I owed you the truth." At least part of the truth. I consider telling her that Renee is back, but I'm not ready to acknowledge that yet. Plus, it doesn't matter. Grandma will tell Renee I said no, and it will cease to be a *thing* I have to obsess over.

"You don't owe anyone anything." Her head jerks with realization. "You know no one would judge you if they knew, right? Is that why you're trying to keep it a secret? I mean, what your..." She pauses. "What happened doesn't have anything to do with you. You're not, as you so eloquently put it, devil spawn."

"I don't know. Sometimes I feel like an accomplice to a crime. Maybe her life could have gone back to normal if it weren't for me. She could have tried to heal, but here I am, a constant reminder, rubbing salt in open wounds. Whatever he started, it feels like I finished it. Like he robbed the bank, but I drove the getaway car."

She sighs. "That's going to need some therapy-worthy unpacking that I am not equipped for, other than a blanket *Stop beating yourself up for things you didn't do*. But I love you," she says, pulling me in for a hug. "So, if you thought this would scare me away, that's tough cookies."

I'm dwarfed by her tall frame. It's safe here.

She lets go and retrieves her bagel. I follow her and pick

up my backpack from the floor before we leave the house. She drapes her arm over my shoulders as we walk to the bus stop, the bagel in her free hand.

"Hey," she says.

"Hmm?"

"I mean it, Mich. I love you."

"I love you too."

The truth is out there now. I feel empty—a good kind of weightlessness.

CHAPTER FIFTEEN

WHEN MR. MILLIGAN RETURNS OUR GRADED ESSAYS, I'M not at all surprised by the big red *See me* written across the top. It's hard to write an essay on a quivering school bus at 6:30 in the morning. And now after the Renee news, and the brief but earth-destabilizing fight with JoJo, the essay, and the host interview, feel so unimportant. Shouldn't I be grateful for what I've been given and stop thinking I deserve more?

I try to sneak out when the bell rings, but I'm as stealthy as a circus elephant.

"Michie, a word," Mr. Milligan calls, catching me at the door. He reaches for the draft I've folded in half. "Mind telling me what this is?"

"It's a draft of my scholarship essay," I answer.

"No, no, I don't think it is," he responds. He removes the small reading glasses from his jacket pocket and slips them onto the tip of his nose. *"My name is Michelle Cooper, Michie for short, and if there's one important thing about me it's that I love literature. From* Gulliver's Travels *to* Beloved, *I have a deep appreciation for the written word and how it shapes my view of the world."* He stops reading and raises an eyebrow at me. "You don't think this is what colleges want to know, do you? That you can read?"

He's officially not my favorite teacher anymore. That was excellent book taste.

"Not that I *can* read. That I *love* to. And its impact on me." I try to smile, but the pure disdain settled on his face withers it away. My shoulders slump forward. It may not be my best work, but this was finally a version of the essay I wasn't completely embarrassed about.

"I don't mean to be hard on you, Michie. But you're better than this." He hands me the paper, and I fold it in half again. "Do you know why I make you all start this a year early?"

To torture us longer. But he won't appreciate that response.

"Because I know it's hard. Summing up the messiest years of your life in two hundred words. It's absurd. But that's the test. I want you to make two hundred words read like one hundred thousand. Depth, truth."

"Everything in this is honest."

"I don't care if it's honest. Honesty is not truth. Truth is honesty plus heart. Your work on the loneliness and isolation of Tennyson's 'The Lady of Shalott' was truth, insightful. One of the best student papers I've read in thirty years. This"—he points at the paper in my hand—"might as well be a corpse. No pulse. No passion. No heart. You need to stand out in a sea of students just like you, with good grades and part-time jobs. Some will have even more—extracurriculars, legacy status. You need to get uncomfortable, tell them something real. I hate to say it, but scholarships are transactional. If you want them to open the coffers, you need to make them say, *This kid will make everyone around her better, and this is how much we value that.*"

I swallow down the lump lodged in my throat. All I hear is: Sell your trauma. And what if I don't make everyone better? What if I only make them worse?

"I want a new essay."

"Okay." I nod. "Um, when?"

"Let's say the end of March. I'm giving a few people another shot, and I'd prefer to get them in after this SAT and college-fair business is over with."

"I can do that."

"I know you can."

I reread my essay as I walk to my locker. It actually is terrible. Brown, and college generally, is slipping through my fingers like loose sand. Serves me right. It's laughable to think I'd be the first Cooper to get there. The least deserving one of all.

"Hey," Derek says, grabbing my elbow. "You good?"

"No. But I have Trig, so my burn-this-place down energy has to wait. And I'm starving, so that doesn't help."

"I'm not sure about the arson, but I have an idea for the starving." He tilts his head toward the front doors of the school.

"Are you forgetting that we have class?" I follow him anyway.

"You're sick. It's not skipping when you're sick," he says, pushing the doors open with his back.

"But I'm not sick."

"You said your stomach hurts."

"I said I was hungry." I cross my arms over my chest.

"Same difference." He shrugs.

"And your history class? Basketball practice?"

"Eh, they'll live." He grabs one edge of my open coat and tugs.

I scoff, but my legs move of their own volition as he leads me to the parking lot. JoJo is parked two spots over and leaning on her driver-side door, probably plotting what she wants to do for her free period. She straightens as we approach.

"What's this?" she sings, meeting us with a smirk by his trunk, where he dumps our bags.

"Michie's sick," he explains.

"What?" Concern crosses her face as she slams a palm to my forehead. I duck away.

"I said I was *hungry*," I repeat.

"Oh, same difference." She shrugs. "You are a little clammy, though."

"What?" Derek puts his hand on my forehead next, turning to nod at JoJo in agreement.

"Are y'all done?" I back away from his outstretched hand. It's just my luck that I would surround myself with two of the same person. Unbelievable.

"Oh! Gwen and I are getting Thai for our free period. You two should come," she says, retreating to her car. Speaking of the devil, Gwen stalks to JoJo's car and waves before slipping into the passenger seat.

"I'll AirDrop the address," JoJo says, climbing into her car.

"Or we could," I begin, but she closes her door. "Follow you."

Except JoJo drives like a NASCAR wannabe, and Derek gives up following her within minutes.

"It's in the shopping center on Three Chopt. By the university," I direct, staring down at Google Maps.

JoJo and Gwen are already seated at a booth when we get there. I sit across from them, and Derek sits beside me. Derek wraps his arm around the back of our booth, and I catch a small smile in the corner of JoJo's mouth. I scan the menu, searching for the cheapest options.

"Ready?" the waitress asks when she returns with the drinks—threes sodas, water for me.

"I'll have the duck curry," JoJo orders. "And can we get two orders of the dumplings for the table?"

"May I get the..." I point at the tom yum gai soup, not wanting to butcher the words. The waitress nods as she writes it down.

JoJo eyes me with a grimace. "That's all you want?"

I give her a tight smile and hand my menu to the waitress.

The food comes out quickly and the soup is pretty filling, though I might swing a sandwich when I get home. Gwen and Derek spend half the meal discussing *Monday Night Raw*, which is not a fandom I expected Gwen to partake in, what with the misogyny and frequent concussions.

"Oh, are you guys coming to Open Mic Night tonight?" I ask the table.

"Since you volunteered me for lifetime setup duty, yes." Derek laughs, recalling the deal we made a week into our study sessions. I tutor him if he drags tables around at my request.

"I would, but we have a sit-in planned at the history museum," Gwen offers, taking a big bite out of a dumpling.

"And what cause are you protesting this time?"

"Theft," Gwen says, like it's obvious. "Museums are nothing but theft. Imagine charging people to see items you stole from other civilizations."

JoJo shakes her head with a laugh. "Never change, Gwenny."

The waitress drops off the check, and Gwen says my least favorite sentence in the English language. My laugh screeches to a halt.

"Split evenly?" she asks, taking out her card.

I take in the appetizers on the table. Their drinks and meat-filled dishes. My six-dollar meal is suddenly a gold bar.

I try to catch JoJo's eye, but she's digging in the bottomless pit of her purse for her own card.

"Um," I start.

JoJo finally looks up and assesses the situation, her eyes widening. "We should pay for our own," she suggests.

"I have a good calculator," I add. "It does tips too."

"This is easier," Gwen says. "I don't care paying a little extra." Of course she doesn't.

Oh, God. This is why I don't eat out.

Derek tosses his card on the pile. "I got mine and Michie's."

My head snaps over. "What? No." So apparently there is something worse than not being able to afford a simple meal. It's the guy you like recognizing you can't afford a simple meal. My stomach turns, and we're all about to see that soup again.

"I still owe you for 7-Eleven. Jumbo Slurpees and Zebra Cakes ain't cheap."

"That was like eight bucks," I say.

"So was that." He points to the empty bowl in front of me.

I want to refuse. I *need* to refuse. JoJo kicks me under the table. Her eyes scream in italics. *Take the out.*

And it is an out. A big one. Splitting would be way, way over my budget. So I bite my tongue. As Grandma says, don't look a gift horse in the mouth. Even when it makes you feel gross.

I sit in silence as we wait for their cards and they chat around me. Derek pokes me in the thigh, and I turn away. We are not the same. I can't give him any more of myself, because when he's gone, he'll take too much of me with him.

CHAPTER SIXTEEN

DEREK HELPS ME DRAG THE ROUND TABLETOPS TO THE back wall of the café and set up the chairs in straight lines. As rain batters the windows, I expect a smaller group than usual for Open Mic Night. I press my ear against the stained glass, listening to the rain's echo. Each drop tinkles like fairy dust on the pavement.

Taran sets up a stool and a mic on the raised platform she built from scratch last year. She does a mic check with the small speaker she bought from a university student who DJ'ed parties for his fraternity.

Peter slams through the door, the storming wind ripping through the room. Paper menus scatter. "Yo, yo, yo," he says. "Let the party begin."

Derek raises an eyebrow as Peter loops his arm around my neck.

"Where are the goods?" Peter asks.

I laugh and duck from beneath his skinny arm. "Taran just made a fresh pot."

He taps two fingers to his forehead in a salute and bounces toward the counter, where Taran pours him a cup.

Derek comes to stand beside me as people trickle in. The sign-up sheet I taped to the inside of the door fills with names.

"Okay," Peter says, rejoining us. His cup is cradled in his hands. "What's the dealio for tonight?"

"Hi, Peter; lovely to see you, Peter," I say. "And yes, Monica is coming tonight."

"Who said anything about Monica?"

I give him a devilish grin.

"Chill." His eyes land on Derek. "Damn, Michie. Manners? Thought you was classy." He releases one hand from the cup and elbows me. "'Sup man, Peter."

"Oh," I yelp. "Peter, this is Derek. Derek, this is Peter."

They do that handshake-hug thing guys do, like hugging it out will get their man cards revoked or something.

"Peter." Derek puts the pieces together from my friend-zone hypothetical.

"I got something in my teeth or sum'n?" Peter asks, digging a too-long fingernail between his teeth.

Derek laughs while I grimace. "Please, Peter, I beg."

How am I supposed to play matchmaker if that's what I've got to work with?

Taran taps on the mic, eliciting a loud shriek that has the entire room covering their ears. "Thank you for joining us this rainy evening." She goes into the instructions for the night. Snap after each performance instead of clapping. Try to save bathroom breaks and coffee refills for between acts. Silence your cell phones. *Breaking Bad*'s DBAA—don't be an asshole.

The first performer, a poet, stands up as a cold breeze sends a shiver down my spine. Monica raises her hands in apology as she darts through the front door. Peter's back straightens as she scribbles her name at the bottom of the sign-up sheet.

"Sorry I'm late," she whispers, joining us by the window. "What'd I miss?"

"Right on time, actually," I tell her, pushing closer to Derek to make space for her between me and Peter.

"Hi, Monica," Peter says, a little too loud, earning a *shh* from Taran, seated in the last row.

"Hi, Peter," she whispers with a smile.

It's happening. The *spark*.

"What's the new piece?" I ask, nodding at the folded paper she's worrying between her fingers.

"Just a song about the new living situation." She stays vague, eyeing Derek with skepticism.

"That bad, huh?" Usually Monica writes about her pain. She prefers to keep the happy bits bottled up inside.

"Not bad at all. I wish I'd found them when I had time for it to matter." Her birthday is in less than four months. It sucks that the system finally works when it's too late. Couldn't they have gotten it right the first time? Or by the sixth time?

"That's great." I smile, but she's not looking at me. She's watching Peter as he focuses on the current performer. The girl's about our age, singing an original country song about heartbreak. "I'm happy for you." I lean in so the words wrap around her.

"Right," she says, turning back to me. "I wanted to know if you'd accompany, though."

"Me?"

Derek perks up, interested.

"Yeah, you were great on the guitar that one time. I only need a chord or two I can work with."

Great is a vast overstatement. When I say I don't play well, ya girl is not being humble. It'll be Elizabeth bullied by Lady Catherine in this joint. I accompanied Monica once before, and it hadn't gone well. Not that I could expect much from the stolen minutes I practiced on the café's guitar before it got rehomed to my bedroom, where it remains untouched because again: I. Don't. Know. How. To. Play.

"Monica, I know two chords."

"Please?" she begs. "Play anything and I'll sort it out. I don't want to do this one alone."

I open my mouth in objection, but she's still watching

Peter. And Peter's watching some girl sing off-key. And Derek's watching me. And we would all be better off watching less and doing more, so I nod in agreement. "Fine."

"Thank you," she squeals, pulling me into a side hug.

I go over the chords I know in my head. An A, a C, maybe a D. The less I have to move my fingers around, the better. Derek pulls up a YouTube instructional video and plays it on mute so I can study the hand movements. I practice on an imaginary guitar neck.

Monica's turn comes all too soon. My heart is already racing as she steps on the stage and introduces herself.

"You'll do great," Derek says, as I untie my apron and drop it into his waiting hand. I give him a whimpering pout. He spins me around and nudges me forward.

I squint in the bright lights Taran has pointed at the stage. The only thing brighter is Peter's smile, so big the room can barely contain it. I hope Monica notices, so she can see that other girl meant nothing more to him than a nice melody.

I drop the guitar strap over my shoulder and move to the back of the stage. This is Monica's show.

I play a shaky A and Monica takes it away. To minimize mistakes, I stick with the maybe-A and strum on a four-count. One, two, three, strum. One, two, three, strum. I'm no Jimi Hendrix, but it works.

I risk a glance at the audience, and they're enraptured. Monica's paper is already forgotten on the floor as she sings from memory. She's amazing. I search the back of the café.

Peter has floated closer to the stage, absorbed by her, and I can't imagine love wearing any other face.

My eyes push past him, finding Derek. He holds up the back of a disposable menu he's written on in his chicken scratch with the Sharpie in my apron. *Guitarist's Groupie*. It's so cheesy I could die. But that doesn't stop the ridiculous grin that spreads across my face or the feeling of flying that spreads through my bones.

Monica finishes, and the audience explodes in applause, snaps be damned. I find Peter and Derek once more. Their faces fall side by side, matching looks carved into their expressions, an identical glint of light in their eyes.

Derek wipes down the last of the tables and sets up three chairs at each one.

"You didn't have to stay," I say, grabbing the dirtied rag from him. The café is closed and we're the last ones here.

"And miss hanging with Richmond's newest guitarist phenom?" he says with a chuckle. "Besides, I was doing my duty as your matchmaking wingman. Though the kid's doing pretty well on his own. Monica's into him."

"It's so obvious, right?" I say. "And if you lost any hearing in your left ear from my guitar playing, be patient. It'll return in a few days."

"Nah, I did all the damage I could holding those dog whistles up so I could hear them."

I stop. "You're kidding."

"I wish." He sits in one of the chairs as I toss the rag bucket beneath the counter and start refilling the straw container. "So, Peter. He's cool."

"Oh yeah, he's great," I respond.

"You two ever…" He pauses, moving his head side to side like a pendulum.

"Ever what?"

"Ever, you know, date?" He drops his head and looks up at me through long lashes.

A laugh bubbles up and spills from my lips like a broken gumball machine. "Me and Peter? Oh, God, no. No. Peter? He's like a brother. And in love with Monica, remember?"

"Yeah. I don't know why I asked. You guys just seemed so comfortable."

"We know each other really well. Like I said, he's like a brother."

His shoulders untense and he relaxes into the chair.

A small buzz starts in my stomach, almost imperceptible were it not for the effect it's having on my bones. The idea that Derek could be jealous makes me vibrate with the kind of hope I should be snuffing out right now. But I let myself enjoy it for a moment.

He turns to the wall of books, most pulled from their shelves after the performances ended. "Do we need to put these back?" He gets up, gathering them into his arms to organize.

"I'll do it next shift," I say, letting him off the hook.

He catches my eye before refocusing on the scattered books. "Or I can do it now."

I take the books from his arms one by one, placing them back on the shelf. He reaches for the last book, and I move it away. "Go home, Derek."

His usually happy face crumbles, a sad expression melting into his features like warm candle wax. His eyes shiver, like he's trying to catch one scene from a film on fast-forward. They still, settled but uneasy.

"Are you okay?"

He doesn't answer, his eyes and mind somewhere else. I approach him slowly, placing my hand on his arm. His bare skin, exposed by rolled-up sleeves, sends a shock through my fingertips. "Derek, are you okay?"

"What?" His eyes drift out of focus.

"Are you okay?"

He shakes his head, as if trying to wake himself up. His eyes are glassy, too wet.

"It's so hot in here," he says, stepping away from me. "I'm going to get some fresh air."

Before I know what's happening, he's across the café and out of the door, the metal frame slamming shut behind him. He leans on the glass outside, beneath the awning. His curls sag under the weight of rainwater.

I watch him, unsure what to do. He's normally so happy, so full of light. I'm out of my depth. But I can't leave him out there alone, begging for pneumonia. I pull on my rain jacket and grab his coat, draped over one of the bar stools. It's freezing when I get outside, and my ears fill with the sound of my chattering teeth.

"Derek," I yell over the wind, but he either doesn't hear me or ignores me completely. I stand on the tips of my toes and wrap his coat over his shoulders. Rain is dripping from his hair and into his eyelashes. Droplets track down his cheeks, some of which I suspect are tears. I don't say anything as I grab his hand, pulling him back toward the door. He doesn't budge, his feet staying firmly in place.

"Talk to me," I yell. I'm starting to freak out a little bit. Thunder creeps closer in the distance.

He gives a sharp shake of his head.

"Please?" I tug again and he relents.

My ears ring from the storm in the café's silence. I don't release his hand, pulling him down into a chair. He shivers, his shirt soaked through. I grab blankets from the reading nook, wrapping one around his shoulders and the other across his lap. I find a clean rag under the counter and move it through his hair, scrunching as I go.

It's strange seeing him so uncomposed. So much of who he is in my head is built upon his perfection. But he's not perfect, and I guess it's not right to expect him to be because of the pedestal I've placed him on. I mean, he's having a panic attack in my arms right now. Maybe this is why he knew how to help me the other day. Maybe we are more alike than we are different.

"Are you okay?" I ask again.

He nods sullenly. His eyes follow my hands as I move them from his hair and drag a chair in front of him.

"Okay then, want to explain why you went out into that weather?"

He looks away. I reach forward and grab his chin, turning his head back toward me. He sighs and pulls his chin from my hand.

"It's nothing. You said something that reminded me of"—he swallows—"of my grandfather."

I search my brain for everything I've said tonight, landing on nothing significant.

"What did I say?"

He gulps, remaining silent.

"What did I say?" I lean forward in my chair, trying to ignore the frustration. If this is how JoJo feels when I don't open up, I have to apologize to her because it sucks. "Tell me. Trust me."

"Go home, Derek," he whispers.

I twist the words in my mind. I try on different tones, searching for the trigger for this kind of meltdown. He reads the confusion on my face.

"It was the last thing he said to me. Before he died." His chest rises with a deep breath he holds inside. Finally, he releases it. "I wasn't completely honest with you before, about my family." His voice shakes.

"About your grandfather?"

"Yeah, and my dad. And me. He and my grandpa, they were inseparable when my dad was a kid. He thought

Grandpa was a superhero, you know. When he started drinking, Dad was in complete denial it was a problem." His shoulders continue to shake, and not from the cold.

"But then it started getting worse. I hated my dad for letting it get so out of control. For not doing anything about it. So, I came here myself to tell him he was hurting us. He was my grandpa; I thought he would listen to me. I thought he would care. But he was so far gone. I think my dad knew that already.

"So, I snapped. I told him that if he wanted to drink himself to death there were easier ways to die that wouldn't drag the family down with him. And when I was done, when I had screamed myself hoarse, he said, *Go home, Derek.*" His voice cracks in a hiccup. "He wasn't even upset. Just…tired."

I put my hand on his bouncing knee and squeeze. He places his over mine, and even shivering, he burns hot.

"I didn't mean any of it," he whispers, trapped in a memory. "That night, he drank half a bottle of bourbon and then drove into the median on I-64."

An audible gasp escapes my lips. His hand trembles over mine.

"I never told any of them about the things I said to him. They all thought my visit was just bad timing. They consoled me. He was so drunk all the time, they said it was bound to happen, that it was *lucky* I got to see him one last time. And maybe it would've happened eventually. But it wouldn't have been that night if it weren't for me."

"No," I utter. This was not his fault. He has to know that. "Your grandpa was sick."

"He was. But I told him to kill himself, and he did."

"You did not tell him to kill himself, Derek."

"I didn't go to the funeral," he says in a pained moan. "I've never been to his grave. He died because of me, and I couldn't even give him a proper goodbye."

"Derek…"

But there's nothing I can say that will make him feel better. I know the steadiness of guilt.

He pulls his hands from mine, dropping his head into them. I pull him forward until his hair rests against my chest. His sodden curls soak through my thin jacket. My fingers wrap around the back of his neck as his shoulders shudder.

"It was beyond your control," I tell him. Feelings wash over me like riptides. First, a protective guttural reaction so fierce I gasp around it. And then there's something dirtier, more shameful, like the feeling I had ripping into JoJo about her mom. The jealousy of never having the chance to tell someone how you feel. A small voice pricks at the back of my neck. *But you have the chance.*

"It wasn't your fault," I say, again and again. I repeat the words until they're an incantation that locks itself around us, taking two incredible burdens and making them light enough to carry.

CHAPTER SEVENTEEN

THE ROGUE FEBRUARY SUNSHINE REQUIRES LUNCH ON the quad and my favorite stone bench. I plan to get some essay writing done, but I tilt my head to the sun instead, soaking it up for longer than intended. That's how Derek finds me when he sits on a sliver of bench where I haven't scattered my work. Things have been different since Open Mic Night last Wednesday, but my one lone brain cell is still clinging to our *just friendship*.

"Have you heard of Coco and Hazel?" Derek asks, swinging his leg over the bench. It's warm for the first day of February so he's wearing only a pullover quarter-zip over his T-shirt.

"The ice cream place?" It's a new shop by the university

known for its milkshakes, which in my food pyramid, make up the largest box at the bottom.

"Yeah. Some of the guys on the team go after practice." Derek pulls on his earlobe, and I straighten. It's a gesture I now recognize as nervousness. I remember watching him knead his feelings out on Wednesday, his fingers flexing as he pulled. He clears his throat. "Do you want to come?"

"To get ice cream?" I ask.

"Yes."

"With the basketball team?"

"Well, yes, they'll be there." His nerves have been painted over with a second coat of exasperation.

"Why?" I ask.

"It's a team thing, so they'll be there," he explains. "We could go *not* with the team, if that's what you want to do." I convince myself the light that flashes like a shooting star in his eyes isn't hope.

He fiddles with the basketball in front of him, rolling it sideways from hand to hand. Another nervous tic. I grab the basketball from his hands and place it behind my feet so it won't roll away.

"I meant why are you asking me to get ice cream with you and the basketball team?"

He starts cracking his knuckles, and it fills the silence between us. As per usual, I'm distracted by his long fingers as they move.

"Because Mac invited me, and I was told to bring my

girl. I assume he means you because you're one of two people I spend all my time with."

"Did you correct him?"

"Should I have?"

I like the sound of it. *His girl.* But I narrow my eyes at him to maintain my cover.

"It's noted without objection that you're not my girl," he says. "Yet. But since I don't officially have one of those, I'm asking you because I don't want to be the eleventh wheel. And you are *a* girl."

"Thank you for noticing," I deadpan. I file the *yet* and the *officially* away to obsess over later.

A *yes* dances on the tip of my tongue, but as much as I want to spend time with him, doing it with the rest of the basketball team is my worst nightmare.

"Ask JoJo. That's more her scene."

"She's busy," he responds.

Of course he's asked her already. Why would I be his first choice for something like this? He's not as oblivious to how incompatible we are as I thought.

"One hour," I offer, holding up a finger for emphasis. "One. And you are paying for my ice cream and extra toppings." It's not a date, but I *am* providing a service right now.

He pulls me into his chest before I can finish listing my requirements. His breath warms the part of my ear peeking out from beneath my beanie.

"All the ice cream you want," he exclaims. Before I have time to change my mind, he kneels down and reaches between my legs to pull the basketball from behind my feet. He bounds back into school, a bounce to his step.

Gathering my work off the bench, I head to English. I catch JoJo in the hallway on my way to class. She's chatting with a tall blonde who looks like Brie Larson.

"Traitor," I whisper into her ear before skirting around her.

She reaches for my forearm and squeezes, my bones whining under the pressure of her death grip. She smiles at Blondie before loosening her grip enough for me to wiggle myself free. We're close to my English class, so I disappear into the room, only to find her following behind me.

She's not in this class, but she sits in the empty seat next to mine. Her World Lit omnibus, for the class she should actually be in right now, is beneath her elbow on the desk.

"Would you care to enlighten me what's got your panties in a bind this time?" she asks.

"What could you be doing tonight that's better than free ice cream?"

She stares at me as if I'm speaking another language. "Can I buy a vowel or something?"

A throat clears from above us, and as I turn toward my periphery, I catch a plaid button-up shirt at eye-level. At the top is a patch of red hair sprouting in every direction. He points to the seat JoJo is occupying. She gives him the same smile she gave Blondie and holds up a finger, commanding him away from his own desk. Class starts in less than two minutes, but he concedes and wanders to the back of the room. He drops into an empty seat by the window, looking starstruck. JoJo's impact.

She snaps her fingers by my ear to draw back my attention, the sound like butterfly wings in flight. "Explain," she insists.

"Why can't you go to Coco and Hazel tonight?" I glance up at the clock. Mr. Milligan will be here any second, not that he'll care if he finds JoJo here. Teachers love her.

"Why would I go to Coco and Hazel? It's Tuesday." JoJo's lactose intolerant, but on weekends when she doesn't have plans to leave the house, she pigs out on pizza and ice cream. Apparently, it's worth the bubble guts if you only do it once a week. I'm pretty sure I'd disagree if it were me, but no one has ever tried to take the ability to dip cubed cheese into fondue cheese away from me, so I don't judge.

"So your excuse to Derek was, sorry, it'll give me the runs?" I ask. "And he bought it?"

"First," she says, "it wouldn't have been an excuse if I'd used it, because it's true. And second, what?"

"You're submitting me to social ostracism by a bunch of knuckleheads who only watch *American Dad!*, and their model girlfriends."

Mr. Milligan walks into the room without noticing her.

"You love *American Dad!*" This is true, but it doesn't dispute the fact that they're knuckleheads. "And last, I still have no clue what…" Her eyes dart back and forth as if she can see equations unfolding in her mind. She turns her head to me, a smug expression on her face. "You know what?" she

161

says, grabbing her book and getting up. "I'm going to let you figure this one out for yourself."

She sneaks out of the room as Mr. Milligan turns to start the lesson. He opens his mouth to begin, wiping a chalk-covered palm on his dark blue pants leg, but pauses. "Jason," he inquires at the redhead JoJo displaced, now slumped down in his temporary desk. "Why aren't you in your seat?"

Coco and Hazel is a small shop on Ridge Road. It has mint-colored walls that would be Joanna Gaines–approved. It's cool and hip, and I'm obsessed the second we walk through the swinging door. It would be the best place for a date.

"I should tell Peter about this," I tell Derek.

"Ice cream fan?" he asks.

"For a date," I answer. "With Monica. It's cute, right?"

He looks up from the ice cream containers and stares at me with an expression that makes me shiver. His head shakes, a bemused smile spreading slowly. "Yeah, Michie. Cute for a date."

I slip my phone from my pocket to shoot Peter a quick text about the parlor. He responds with a thumbs-up reaction and a series of emojis that don't make sense together but probably mean something inappropriate. Behind me, Tom, the shooting guard, advises me on the various ice cream flavor and toppings combinations.

"The salted caramel is great for something a little savory, but the cookie dough has huge clusters of dough *and* chocolate chips," he says. "The toffee is my personal favorite."

"I was thinking strawberry cheesecake with some marshmallow and graham crackers?" I say, pointing out each component of the concoction.

He rubs his chin with two fingers. "Not bad, Cooper." He nods with approval. To my surprise, I like the guys. They're rowdy and too large, but kind of funny and pretty nice.

Derek laughs as I close my eyes and suck as hard as possible to pull my milkshake through a paper straw. My brainchild tastes like a strawberry shortcake s'more, and it's the best thing I've ever consumed.

I'm squeezed between Derek and Tom. Brit, five-bucks lender and Tom's girlfriend, sits across from me. I wonder if she remembers the money. I'm so squished that there's little room for my limbs, so I'm half sitting on Derek's lap, my legs draped over his to make space for Tom's beneath the table. Derek lowers his arm until his hand rests on my knee. The heat from his fingers melts through the denim.

His other hand clasps a traditional chocolate scoop in a waffle cone. It drips into a spare bowl because he's already bitten the tip end of the cone off and is eating it bottom up. I'm spending half my time and all my concentration trying not to gawk at the side of his mouth as he eats.

The team's bromance is endearing. One month at the school, and Derek's already beloved. He's the point guard, which, none of them can stress enough, is a very big deal.

"Anyone apply for a hosting gig?" one of the girls farther down the table asks.

"Aw, little juniors," Tom jokes, reaching across the table to pinch Brit's cheek. It earns him a sharp smack to the back of his hand. "Applying to colleges, uwu."

I laugh at his pronunciation of the facial expression *oowoo*.

"Sorry, not all of us can free throw our way into college, Mr. Syracuse," Brit says. "Have fun freezing your balls off while I'm sunbathing in Florida."

"Do you have an interview?" I ask.

She looks at me as if she's noticing me for the first time. Then she smiles.

"Yeah, both of my parents are alumnae, so fingers crossed I crush the interview." She crosses her fingers and waves them by her face. "What'd you get?"

I stall, uncomfortable. I don't want them to laugh at me for being so far out my league. I clear my throat but no words come out.

"She's interviewing for Brown," Derek says, more pride infused in his voice than I thought could be possible.

Mac, the little forward or whatever, whistles, and a series of approving nods spread over the table. "Damn, De la Rosa, how'd you get this one?"

Brit taps Mac on the forearm with the back of her hand while Derek chuckles beside me.

"What?" Tom says, defending his friend against his girlfriend's mild assault. "That's badass."

Derek gives me a wide smile as the table jumps to the

next topic. They cover a lot of ground in a short span of time. His eyes sparkle as he laughs. Our foreheads are almost touching. If I leaned a little further forward...

"Hey," Brit interjects, snapping me out of my mind's tangled inner commentary so suddenly that my kneecap jerks into the underside of the table. A yelp rips through my teeth.

Her milkshake is empty, and she's now working away at Tom's. I'm not sure where she puts it all, but I respect it. I grant her a smile that is more of a grimace, my knee throbbing. Derek's hand gives it a gentle squeeze. My stomach pools down as I sink my teeth into my tongue to stop a groan of pain or a moan...of something else.

"Are you coming to the game Thursday?" she asks.

"Um, I wasn't planning on it." I check to see if Derek's listening, or if he's noticed my skin turning to custard beneath his fingers, but he's deep in an argument with Mac about the best sports movie of all time. The correct answer is obviously *Love & Basketball*, but Derek is sticking to his guns with *Cool Runnings*. Mac has dug in with *D2: The Mighty Ducks*, which is underappreciated, but still the wrong answer.

Brit's face pinches.

I shift under her gaze, the movement pressing my legs into Derek's lap. He squeezes my knee hard to hold it in place but continues unencumbered in the argument unfolding. Tom joins over my shoulder with his addition of *Bend It Like Beckham*, but I can't tell if he's serious and neither can they. Mac rejects it, denouncing the film for being too chickenshit to make Jess and Jules endgame.

"I have to work," I say, which won't be a lie when I ask Taran if I can pick up Thursday's shift. "And I don't like sports."

Brit stares at me, contemplating. She hums an assent. "Me either." She pulls the milkshake closer to her. "But let me know if you change your mind. I have an extra pass, and the games are fun if you ignore the whole playing part."

She smiles again, genuine.

I release a breath, relieved. Some people are kind if you give them the chance.

Derek's arm moves from my knee and finds its way around the booth, his thumb tracing circles on my shoulder. The buzzing in my stomach comes back, flickering like lightning bugs in summer. We are more skin-to-skin than the other couples, even though we're the least *together*. We could fool anyone though, even ourselves. I should disentangle my legs from his, my body from his, my mind from his. But I settle into the crook of his arm instead, deciding to face reality later.

CHAPTER EIGHTEEN

DESPITE MY ADAMANT REFUSALS, DEREK INSISTS ON DRIV-ing me home. The hour I agreed to for ice cream turned into three, and he wouldn't let me take the bus, even though I often get home from work much later than this. It's a half hour out of his way, but he's afraid of JoJo peeling off his skin and wearing it like a cloak if I disappear. His words, not mine.

Derek never turns on the radio. Every few minutes I hold my breath so I can hear his more distinctly. It's almost imperceptible, so I have to clear my head to focus on it. It's nice to be full of only this one sound, and not the constant screaming in my head.

But my anxiety peaks as we leave the suburbs, the

manicured lawns fading away in neighborhoods the city's forgotten. His shoulders tense up, and his grip on the steering wheel tightens. It's unintentional, but his discomfort hurts. We pass several bus stops along the way, and I want to ask him to let me out, but I know he won't.

His fingers unclench and drum on the steering wheel as we wait at a red light. "Tonight was fun," he says, looking at me out of the corner of his eye.

"It was," I agree. "Everyone was super nice."

"You sound surprised."

"I guess I am." It's on me for judging before knowing them. "They're kind of obsessed with you," I joke. "It's cute."

"The new car smell hasn't worn off yet," he replies.

"No," I disagree. "They're really in awe of you. You must be good at the whole balls thing you do." I wince at my phrasing. Please don't think about balls. Please don't think about balls. Please don't think about balls.

He snorts. "You'd know if you came to a game once in a while," he teases. "But it's good that you don't."

"Yeah, I'd do something embarrassing, and you'd never hear the end of it," I say.

"No, I mean I'd be way too distracted with you in the room."

Oh. I stuff my hands between my legs so he won't see them shaking.

"But if you want to"—he shrugs—"Thursday's game should be pretty good. St. Joseph's is ranked first in the state, so if we beat them, it'll be huge for our program."

He hits his blinker and turns into my apartment complex. A raccoon bolts across the street.

"I'll think about it," I answer, code for *probably not*.

He's silent while he navigates the speed bumps. I point at my building and he stops, changing gears to park. "Or we could do something else sometime. Just us."

I sigh and turn my head toward him.

"Why?"

"Why not?"

I reach over and push down on his shoulders, still tensed. "That's why. Look around you. We're from completely different planets."

"I don't think that's important."

I scoff. "Of course you don't. You're all sunshine and rainbows." Except when he's not. I flash back to Open Mic Night and shrug the memory away. "But in the real world, it matters."

"Not to me."

"Derek, why are you doing this? Why are you always so...perfect all the time? So nice?"

"That's your problem, Michie. You think you don't deserve people being kind to you, and I don't know why, but you're wrong."

"I just..." I think back to all he's told me. About not wanting to be remembered for hurting people. About his last conversation with his grandfather. "Wait, is this about your grandpa?"

He stills. "Excuse me?" His eyes narrow.

"Are you nice to me because you think I'm so messed up that if you say one bad thing to me, I'll..."

"You'll what?"

"Forget it," I say.

"No, you're doing well; you should keep going." His words are razor sharp. It fits him wrong, but that doesn't stop their sting.

"That I'll walk into traffic or..."

"Into a median on I-64?" He stares at me like I'm a stranger and then turns forward, twisting his hands on the steering wheel like he can rub the skin of his palms right off.

"For you to say that...you *are* messed up. You're so messed up, Michie. I spend hours every day with you, and I still had to beg you to come tonight. Actually, I had to lie to you. I never asked JoJo. But you're so goddamned impossible all the time, I had to come up with something ridiculous. Do you realize how hard it is to get a shred of your attention? If it's not about books or movies. The second it's about you, you run for the hills. And to be honest, it's exhausting trying to make this into something that, I don't know, it might never be. I think about you all the time, and you don't think about me at all. Oh, except when you're considering if I'm narcissistic enough to believe I could make you want to die. I mean, what the fuck?"

If only he knew how much space he took up in my mind. But he doesn't see how far the gap is between us. He doesn't know how far we'd both have to reach just to graze each other's fingers. He's angry now, but at least he's not broken. Not yet.

He stares at me, waiting for me to answer him. He sighs with aggravation.

"I'm not nice to you because I think you'll walk into traffic if I'm not. I'm nice because I want to spend time with you. Because I..." He stops, his head shaking and eyes wide. "Screw it. It doesn't matter."

Emotions flicker across his face like an old-time movie. "Derek." My voice cracks and, right now, I hate him for making me weak. This is the consequence of letting people in. They make you vulnerable. I gulp and reach for the door, desperate to escape this metal trauma box on wheels. I feel trapped inside this car, inside this mind, inside this life. I want out.

But I don't open the door. I don't take off my seat belt. I just sit, and sit, and sit.

"I'm sorry." He sighs after minutes have passed. And he's back. Sweet Derek, the one I don't deserve. The one I'm hurting just by being around him.

"You don't want to be with me," I whisper.

"Don't tell me what I want," he says back, the words pained, brittle.

"You don't. I promise. When I told you about my family, you said it sounded fucked. And it is. It's so, so fucked. I'm a mess."

He reaches for me, but his hand stops halfway. I want him to touch me, like he did at the ice cream shop, but I can't tell him that. I find his eyes in the dark, bright and sweet and full of a life free from the kind of pain I know so intimately. We're not even together, and I've hurt him. That's what I do. I make life harder for everyone around me. It's cruel to make him think he can love me.

Even if I already love him.

"You have to trust me. I don't want to lose you, and I can only do that as your friend. I'm not capable of more than that, and I don't want to hurt you. We need to step back, spend less time together."

He flinches as if I've slapped him. He takes several breaths before he speaks again. "Okay." He looks like he wants to vomit. I hate myself.

I squeeze my eyes shut. And then I remember that I'm home. I can end this.

I push the door open and climb out. My skin itches with dread. I don't know if he'll ever talk to me again.

"Hey," he says, before I shut the door behind me. I pause and look back. His Adam's apple moves as he swallows. "I'll—I'll see you tomorrow." He tries to smile and fails.

I close the door and speed walk up the walkway.

He doesn't back out of his spot until I'm inside my building and turn on my kitchen light, visible from the street. I peer out the window, watching until his brake lights disappear around the corner.

He is so pure. And I am not. But he's promised me tomorrow, and it's more than I deserve.

CHAPTER NINETEEN

DESPITE THE PROMISE OF TOMORROW, I HAVEN'T SPOKEN to Derek in days. Every time I see him, he goes in the opposite direction, even skipping lunch and our study sessions. He so quickly became a pivotal part of my life that not having him around has put me in the most rotten of moods. And worse, my Brown host interview is today and I'm unprepared. I rip down the blazer hanging from my closet door, sending the wooden hanger bouncing off the door with a hollow ping.

Grandma sticks her head into my room. She's off today for the first time in forever, and I'm surprised she's not taking the opportunity to sleep the day away. But she's holding my lunch bag in her hand.

"You okay in here?" she asks, sitting on the edge of my bed with my lunch in her lap.

"I'm fine." I pause in the middle of pulling the blazer up my arms. I'm much closer to crying than is acceptable. "I just don't know why I'm doing this."

My interview, *the* interview that may decide my fate, is scheduled for lunch period. I'm already anxious about keeping my suit, picked up last weekend from Ross, clean and unwrinkled. Nightmares of getting bird poop on it have kept me up every night this week.

"You're doing this because you were selected, and you deserve a chance like anyone else." She stands and straightens my collar, flattening the lapels. "You've practiced, prepared, and want this. Now all they have to see is how excellent you are."

"I thought you wanted me to go to a state school," I say, reflattening the lapel. I'm pretty sure it's already becoming a nervous tick.

"I want you to do whatever makes you happy," she says, grabbing my face and pulling me toward her. She kisses my forehead and releases me. "I want you to stop holding yourself back. JoJo's picking you up today, right?"

JoJo has one interview at eight, so she gets to skip first period. But she's picking me up so we can do our hype routine usually reserved for her bot tournaments or my, well, I don't typically have anything to get hyped up for.

"Yup," I say, grabbing the lunch she left on the bed and

stuffing it into my backpack. "She should be here s—" A loud knock on the door interrupts me. "Now."

"Finish getting ready," Grandma says, straightening the Bath & Body Works spray bottles on my dresser. "I'll get her."

I stare into my mirror one last time. JoJo's heels click against the kitchen tile. My skirt is too tight around my thighs, which won't be a problem until I have to get on the bus after school. My "skin-colored" tights are an ashy-beige color that makes me look like a store mannequin.

"Damn, Michie, you look like a young Kamala," JoJo says, leaning against my doorframe with a mug of coffee in her hand. "Gonna have to start calling you Michelle, put some respect on your name."

"Please don't," I say, lifting my backpack by the handle. Putting it on my back will wrinkle my jacket, and we're going for perfection here.

I follow her out of the apartment. "Love you," I call to Grandma, who's probably already back in bed now that she's seen me off for the big day.

"You excited?" JoJo asks, turning the heat on full blast. Sweat is already starting to coat my underarms. I should've put on extra deodorant, the men's kind I use when I can't take any chances.

"Absolutely not." I lean my head back against the headrest. "Wait, are you?"

"Sure," she says. Of course she is. JoJo is a total alpha.

She thrives on the things that spark fear in us mere mortals. "It's just a competition, like any other."

"Yeah, but you're good at winning," I tell her.

"And you're good at not losing," she responds.

"Only because I don't enter in the first place." I pull my portfolio from my backpack. It's a fancy brown leather, a relic from Grandma's days working in an office. For some reason I find it reassuring, like she's doing this with me. It's filled now with a million copies of my résumé and notes about each interviewer. Their colleges, their law/med/business schools, where they live, and any hobbies I could find from some serious Facebook and LinkedIn stalking. "Who do you have first?"

"UChicago," she says. For the first time, a flicker of nerves passes across her face before disappearing again behind her shield of makeup.

"Did you talk to your mom about it already?" I ask, sliding the portfolio as carefully as possible back into my backpack so as not to wrinkle any of the résumés. JoJo pulls into her favorite spot by the doors.

"No." She taps the off button and the engine silences. "I figured there was no point, not until I know if they pick me. Don't want to get her hopes up or anything."

"For sure," I say, even though I'm pretty sure JoJo doesn't want to get *her* hopes up. I haven't been as good a friend as I should have. I have no idea how she really feels about any of this, and she clearly hasn't felt comfortable sharing it with me. Though there are things I keep hidden too. Some things you have to work out with yourself before you're ready to share them, even with your best friend.

The junior hall's filled with students in full suits. It smells like genuine leather and starch. A lot of my classmates clean up nicely. Meanwhile, I feel like stuffed kielbasa in this skirt.

Derek emerges from the boys' bathroom. I miss him, and it's affecting me more than I prefer to admit. He would say something nerdy and inspirational to get me through today. He would quote Yoda or Aang. I don't even know if he remembers the interviews are today, though from everyone's attire, I'm sure he can figure it out.

I don't know if it's stubbornness or fear or both that turns me away from him. When I turn back, he's gone.

"Okay," JoJo says, pulling her hair straight and dropping it all behind her shoulders. "Debrief at lunch?"

"No, mine is at lunch."

"Oh, shit, okay. So debrief after school?" Her shoulders tense. Damn. She's really nervous.

"Definitely."

She nods and then turns in the direction of the teachers' lounge, where the interviews are being held. I stand in the hallway alone, waiting for first period. It's the first time I've realized that if JoJo goes to UChicago, she'll be too far away for an emergency weekend sleepover. We'll have separate lives, hers being one she spends with her mother and not me. Maybe I should be doing whatever's necessary to salvage my relationship with Renee too. But JoJo's always known exactly what she wanted. She's always been braver than me.

For once, it would be nice to be brave.

A few hours later, I can't think of anything but the fact that I should have definitely gone with men's deodorant this morning. I'm sweating so much I'm sure the three interviewers across the table can smell me from their seats. Luckily, the lingering stench of burnt lasagna from the earlier lunch period is stronger.

I'm blowing it. I can tell from their tight smiles and the way their eyes drift past me whenever I answer a question. It started with the usual "Tell us about yourself" question, which, if my college essay is any indication, I don't know how to answer. You know when something bad happens and that poopoo energy seeps down to everything after it? That's how this is going. My terrible opening has residually poopooed the whole thing.

I'm not confident, and they read it all over my face. They hear it in my hesitation. But I finally breathe when the last question falls from the woman in the middle. Jennifer Dillon—Brown University class of 2000 and Vice President for Gingham Oil.

"So, Michelle," Jennifer says, "is there anything else you would like us to know about you?"

I gulp. I haven't been great up to now, but this is my last chance. Greg Wonder—Harvard University class of 1986 and tenured professor at Vanderbilt—and Heather Monroe—UCLA class of 1997 and Head of Marketing for Estée Lauder, stare at me with disinterest. But Jennifer is smiling, so I focus on her.

I raise my fist to my mouth and clear my throat. I give my only confident answer of the last forty minutes.

"There is no one who wants this more than me."

Jennifer nods, smiles, and is the only one to make a final note on her notepad.

Gwen and JoJo are standing outside the lounge when I exit. They both have removed their blazers, draping them in the crook of their arms as they lean against the lockers. They're not worried about wrinkles. I guess people like them never are.

"How'd it go?" JoJo asks, jolting up straight as the interviewers leave the room behind me for a break.

"Terrible," I answer. I take my own blazer off and shove it between my thighs, using my free hands to wave air beneath my armpits.

"I'm sure you killed it," Gwen assures me. Reaching between my legs, she yanks my blazer free and tosses it over her own. She interviewed with Sarah Lawrence and BYU. I can't imagine what she would ever do at BYU, but I'm pretty sure she chose it only out of genuine curiosity about Mormons. She would talk an alum's ear off if she ever got the chance.

"No, I definitely didn't. I promise."

"Well," JoJo says, "at least you tried."

"Yeah, at least I did that."

But all I can think is that I am still messing everything up.

CHAPTER TWENTY

"DO Y'ALL EVER THINK ABOUT WHY WE GOTTA FEEL BAD about this stuff?" For a moment, I think Peter's dug into my head and purged out my thoughts. But there's no way he knows I ruined things with Derek or my interview so fantastically. I haven't checked in with him about Monica since Open Mic Night. So now I'm also the worst matchmaker alive.

Peter twists a paper clip into a straight line as he continues. "Our old men screw up, and we end up being the ones who feel like shit about it."

"Well, Peter," Dr. Schwartz says, "why do you *gotta*?" We all give a pathetic attempt at a chuckle.

"I can't not," he says. "What would I say? Hey, Mom,

sorry that guy's a douche, but I'm not him? When I have his face and his voice and his rage? I don't think so. Half the time, I don't even know why my mom told me. I would've been better off not knowing."

"Do you wish you didn't know?" she asks.

"I don't know. I mean, if I didn't, I'd be cool with Scott because I wouldn't know I'm not supposed to be. But then I'd be cool with someone who did this sick thing to my mom. And that would hurt her a lot. And my family got a big mouth, yo. It would've sucked to hear it from someone else. Might've made me think she was even more ashamed of me, hiding it."

It's a weird thing, the truth. It's like we all wish we didn't know it, but if that were the case, there would be one vital unknown about ourselves. If it weren't for Grandma, I wouldn't know, but she felt I deserved an explanation after Renee's final words. Without the truth, Renee would hate me and I wouldn't know why. I may not like it, but at least with the truth in my arsenal, I understand it.

"Have any of you ever tried talking to your mothers about it? I mean beyond that initial conversation. Has anyone checked in, for lack of a better term?" Dr. Schwartz asks.

Han leans forward, his pointer fingers tapping against the pads of each of his other fingers. "My mom came back once. When I was twelve. I saw her in a park. She was wearing a yellow sweater, the button-up kind. Her hair was short like mine, but prettier. She was pretty. My grandma, I remember she was angry. Sent her away. No one ever talked about it. They think I can't handle things. Sometimes they treat me like I'm easy to break. But I'm tough."

"You are tough," Dr. Schwartz agrees.

"Did you want to talk to her?" Monica asks. "Your mother, do you wish you had talked to her?"

"No," Han says, leaning back again, his hands now loose but clutched tight to his sides.

"Why not?" Monica asks.

Han shrugs. "Because she's a stranger. And I don't like strangers."

He says it like it's such a simple thing. And maybe it is. I don't, didn't, want to see Renee, even though for the first time in a decade, she has made it a possibility again. And Han's right—our mothers are strangers. Why go so far to meet someone I don't even know?

Still, there must be a reason she's back now, right? Maybe she *is* dying and wants to reconcile like dying people do. Or maybe she just wants to know me. Maybe she's been beating herself up as much as I have. Maybe she hated me once, but she loves me now, and that's why she's back. Hate and love— how often do they trade places without us ever realizing? So many maybes against one sure thing—she isn't a stranger in a yellow cardigan standing in a park, but has extended an olive branch I need only to grab onto.

"Would you want to?" Han asks Monica.

Monica thinks for a moment, her eyes glistening. "If I did, I don't think I'd talk to her about"—she gestures around the group—"this. I don't think I would want to talk about anything that reminded her why she left me."

"But you wouldn't even have to," Lindell offers. "I've never talked about it with my mom. And I know she loves me. But sometimes she looks at me and, I don't know, it's like she's not seeing *me*. So I worked hard in school to become something she wouldn't be ashamed of anymore. And when I got into Berkeley, it's like I had built enough good to bury the bad. But it's always there beneath the surface, waiting for some huge seismic shift to unearth it again."

Dr. Schwartz leans back and places her palms on the floor. "All right." She stands. She's miniature, barely clearing Lindell's shoulder as he sits in a plush armchair. She seems way too small to carry all the things we talk about here, like Atlas holding up the world.

"Everyone get up," she says, ushering us to stand with her hands. "Right now, come on. Up."

We stand reluctantly. I shake out my legs, numb from their immobility over the last hour.

"Okay." She claps once. "So, we don't talk about religion much, but I grew up in the church. Every Sunday without fail, hell or high water. And one of the first things we did before every sermon was fellowship. You look to your neighbors and introduce yourself, give them a little fun fact. It was my favorite part of church because it was the only time who you were outside of church seemed to matter. There were whole lives outside of those four walls."

She looks at each of us. "The people in this room are your congregation. You exist here, but not only here. This isn't who you are. It's a small piece of a very large story for each of you. So, I want you to turn to your neighbor. Reintroduce yourself. Give a fun fact that has nothing to do with why you're here. And when you're done, I want you to repeat these words until they sink in. I want you to repeat them every single minute of every single day: *I. Am. More.* Now go."

Because of the table in the middle of the room, we split into two groups. Dr. Schwartz joins Han and Lindell. Then there's Monica, Peter, and me.

"Well, this is dumb, but I'm Peter. Duh," he says.

"Hello, Peter," Monica responds, taking the exercise more seriously than I thought anyone would.

He loses his train of thought at her closeness, and I poke him in the ribs to urge him on.

"Right," he says. "Peter, and I like rock music."

I roll my eyes with a groan. "Tell us something we don't know."

He sucks his teeth, but his eyes squint as he thinks. "I have really bad car sickness."

"Really?" Monica and I ask in unison. I've only seen him walking or skateboarding, so it makes sense.

"Yeah." He nods. "When I was a baby, Scott could never get me to stop crying. Never. So he would put me in the car and drive me around. It's supposed to help. But I would just cry louder. Hated cars ever since. Dr. Lincoln"—his solo therapist—"says it's a figment of my imagination. That I wouldn't be able to remember it. I was too young. But I do. I remember being scared."

He goes silent.

"Now your affirmation," Monica urges.

"Oh, come on." He blinks at her.

"Do it." She's stern. For some reason, this matters to her.

"I am more. Whatever." But his head lifts as he speaks.

"Okay, I'm Monica. My last name is recorded as Mustafa, but no one knows for sure. Whoever dropped me off at the fire station misspelled Mufasa on the stuffed lion left with me, but it stuck."

That's how Monica learned about her mom, and how she got here, the details scribbled in a letter left in the stuffed lion's collar. A particularly mean foster parent read it to her in great detail, to break her, not knowing it would lead her to another family—this one.

"Is that your fun fact?" Peter looks horrified.

"No, no. My fun fact." She taps her chin. "I have a metal rod along my spine."

"Whoa, what?" I lean around her as if I can see the metal through her skin and clothing.

"I got a herniated disc when I fell from the second-story banister in my fourth or fifth home and then twisted in the wrong direction trying to get back up."

"You survived a second-story fall and all you have is a metal back?" I ask.

She laughs. "Kind of."

Peter nods as if she's become even more the girl of his dreams. "Shit, I knew you were tough, but not Terminator tough."

She nods, pleased with herself. I can't even handle paper cuts.

"Don't forget your affirmation," Peter reminds her.

"Oh, I am more." Her smile takes over her face. "Your turn, Michie."

I don't have anything as good as that.

"Michie Cooper," I say. "Short for Michelle, my grandmother's middle name. And, I guess, I can quote the entire 2005 *Pride and Prejudice* by heart."

"Nah, that's weak," Peter says. "Tell us something good. Something not so on-brand."

"Are you gatekeeping fun facts now?" I ask. "Besides, car sickness isn't exactly revolutionary." Which is petty, because the story behind the car sickness is what makes it matter.

He rolls his eyes and waves me on. I rack my brain for anything.

"I think my earliest memory is from my infancy," I say finally. It's super weird, so it counts as a fun fact if you ask me. "It's this hallway, like a school hallway, with blue walls. Sky-blue walls. I remember corkboards on the wall, and I'm, well, it at least feels like, I'm in a baby carrier. It's from that vantage point." Monica and Peter give me their full attention. "There's this classroom, with desks. And then there's Renee. A young Renee. And when I was born, I went to a special school with her. So, I figure that must have been what was happening."

They both stay silent, and then Monica shakes her head. "Michie, you can't possibly remember that."

"I'm telling you I do," I argue. "I dream about it all the time."

"So it's a dream?" Monica asks.

"I think it's a memory." I know it sounds crazy, but now that I'm finally being challenged about it, there's something inside of me desperate for it to be true. I like believing that at one time, Renee cared about me so much she couldn't even part from me long enough to go to school without me.

I didn't really follow Dr. Schwartz's instructions that our fun fact have nothing to do with why we're in group, since it's about Renee. But it's something about Renee that brings me joy, so I consider it a cheat code.

"That's hardcore, then," Peter says. "You have, like, the memory of an elephant."

Monica's face scrunches. "Peter!"

"What? Elephants have long memories."

"Whatever." Monica laughs. "Don't forget your affirmation."

"I am more," I say. I don't expect it, but a pit dislodges from my throat as I utter the words. Finally, I can breathe.

I can be more to Grandma if she doesn't have to spend so much time building me up because I made myself small. I can be more to JoJo by being a friend who's open and honest. I'm too messed up to be anything *other* than friends with Derek, even if he's so much more than that to me, but I'm not too messed up to be decent to him. Grandma, JoJo, Derek, even Renee—I can be more for all of them, and I can be more for myself.

I glance over at Dr. Schwartz, and she gives me a knowing smile.

CHAPTER TWENTY-ONE

MICHIE COOPER AT 12:14 P.M.: do you still hate me? for
yes for no
DEREK DE LA ROSA AT 12:22 P.M.:
DEREK DE LA ROSA AT 12:22 P.M.: Though for the record, I
object to having ever hated you

IT'S OUR FIRST PSEUDO-CONVERSATION IN TWELVE DAYS.
Derek's caught up in Spanish, not that he really needed
my help, and I was wrapped up in interview prep and then
interview misery, so postfight it was easy to stop seeing
each other. Easy in the *we had an excuse* way, not in the *I still
thought about hanging out with him every second of the day* way.

Texting him was my first icebreaker, but now I'm using

my free period to search for him all over the school. Following the usual postgroup percolation time, Dr. Schwartz's message has cracked me wide open. I'll never be able to shake what I represent for Renee, but I do feel bad for how I treated Derek. He deserves so much more than a fight in the middle of the night about how bad we are for each other. Even though we *are* bad for each other. Or at least, I'm bad for him.

I find him sitting between the library stacks, crisscross applesauce. I kick his foot before sitting across from him, wrapping my arms around my legs as I pull them to my chest. The Switch in his hand peeks out from behind the book he's pretending to read.

"Hiding out in the library," I say. "Whatever of your reputation?"

He gives me a sad smile. "I like the library. I can hear myself think."

"A penny for your thoughts, then?"

He smirks at the ground and rubs a hand through his curls, which are already disheveled. Dark circles loom beneath his eyes. "Not sure they're worth that much to you." He searches me with piercing eyes, and when he fails to find what he's looking for, drops his gaze back to the Switch.

I scoot across the carpet and sit beside him. Without a word, he detaches the controllers from the Switch and places it on the shelf at eye level. He hands me the red one for the right-side split screen. He goes to the main menu to relinquish Yoshi—my favorite. The silence grows more comfortable the longer we play.

190

"Friends again?" I ask, when the round ends.

"Thought we were stepping back, not hanging out as much."

"We can't hang out as friends?"

He rubs his hand over his face with a deep sigh, his eyes floating up to the ceiling. "Maybe you can," he mutters.

"Is that why you've been avoiding me?"

"I haven't been avoiding you," he objects.

My eyebrow raises in response.

"Okay, I've been avoiding you."

I tap his foot again. "Let's hang out, whatever you want to do."

"Aren't we hanging out right now?" he asks.

"Yes," I concede. "But is this want you want to do?"

A familiar smirk ghosts across his face for the briefest of moments, and my heart clenches. I didn't realize how much I missed it. "You really want to ask me that question?"

Before I can respond, he's already standing, holding his hand out. I grab it and he pulls me up, his hand squeezing around mine. With one hand, he reattaches the Switch controllers and stashes it in his backpack. He leads me to the school gym, my hand still grasped in his. It feels normal and comfortable, and I panic, yanking my hand away as we enter the gym. He lets it go one finger at a time, lingering. My face burns, and I can only imagine what shade of rose is creeping up to my temple.

I turn my attention to the empty gym. A rack of basketballs sits off to one side. He reaches for a basketball and bounces it off the hardwood with a loud echo. He pivots and shoots, the ball making a *swoosh* sound in the net. "Your turn."

He tosses the ball to me, and I dodge it.

"Aw, come on." He runs to retrieve the ball.

"I have bad knees." I sit down on the floor and spread my legs out in a V shape. The glossy wood is smooth beneath my fingertips. "They're like the opening notes in 'The Box.' *Squeak-squeak.*"

He drops down in front of me, the soles of his feet against mine. Mine look so short in comparison. He rolls the ball toward me, and I roll it back. I focus on it as it moves back and forth. R.P.E.'s last group session sticks to the front of my mind like flypaper. Reintroduce yourself.

"So," I say, holding the ball still. "We should start over."

"Start over with what?"

"With us."

"If you go into one of your just-friends speeches again, I'm lying on the floor and letting you roll that cart of basket-balls over me."

"Be serious."

"I'm as serious as a heart attack."

I study the freckles across the bridge of his nose, the pout in his lips keeping his mouth from ever really closing. Why is he so damn beautiful? I hate it here.

To buy myself time, I remove my glasses and wipe them off with the bottom hem of my sweatshirt. When I put them back on, they're more smudged than they were before.

"I don't want to not talk. That sucked." I roll the ball back a little too forcefully.

He catches it, considering my words. "Yeah, it did," he says finally.

"Would you believe me if I said I'm trying to protect you?"

"I'm a big boy. I can protect myself."

"I have a lot of crap going on in here," I tap my forehead. "And it's best if I don't drag anyone else into it. That wouldn't be healthy. Or fair."

"But this crap has nothing to do with us?"

"No." I watch his gears turn, preparing to tell me it doesn't matter, then. "But it has to do with me, and it wouldn't be right to let you in halfway. I'm not the person you want to give your heart to. Not like this."

"And I can't decide that for myself?"

"No." Because we both know what he would choose, and I can't unravel everything with Renee—whether I want to or should see her—and try to build something with him. I can't come apart and fall together at the same time.

"Fine, but you owe me."

"Owe you for what?" I ask in amazement. "Sparing you?"

"I have not been spared. But you can make it up to me." He rolls the basketball one last time. I catch it with the tips of my fingers.

"How?" I ask, playing along.

"You have to come to Senior Night in a couple weeks. It's the last game of the season, and we're cooking up something pretty sweet."

"Derek," I groan. I hate sports. He knows I hate sports.

"Nope, it is the only apology I will accept."

"I didn't apologize for anything."

"Well then, here's your chance."

I spin the basketball on the floor. I wasn't lying. This past week 100 percent sucked. Somehow, he wiggled himself so completely into the framework of my life that not having him there felt shaky, uncertain. I don't want to go back to that. "Deal." I sigh.

"Deal." He smiles. "How'd your interview go? For hostess to the stars of Brown University?"

"Awful," I say, passing the ball back to him. "My brain went blank. In fact, my brain trauma-responsed the whole thing away. I can't even remember what the room looked like."

"Maybe you don't remember how well it went, then."

I snort and catch the ball he rolls back to me. "Well, I'll know in about…" I raise my arm to wake my Fitbit. "Four minutes. That's when the emails go out."

"Damn," he says. He looks around the room and pauses. "Wait, the timing of this reconciliation isn't coincidental, is it?"

"Let's just say I wanted to be around a friend."

He smiles and grips the ball with both hands. "I like that," he says more to himself than to me. The soles of his feet press against mine with light pressure, like a hug.

We talk about the past two weeks, but the air in the room feels stuffy as we wait for the email notification. When it finally dings, I think my heart leaves my body and walks across the court.

"Well?" he asks.

I click on my messages. The email sits unopened at the top.

From: 2022 Richmond College Fair Hosting Program Selection Committee

I open it and let out a breath in a slow hiss.

"I didn't get it," I say. The words drop between us, loaded.

He doesn't say he's sorry. I have never appreciated him more. Tears burn behind my eyes, but I don't cry. All the time I spent telling everyone I had no shot doesn't make this moment any less painful. I thought I was prepared for this. He scoots over until he's next to me, and the waxed floor squeaks so loudly I almost want to laugh. Almost. He pulls me into his side, and as a reward for not letting any tears fall, I drop my head on his shoulder instead. I'm always surprised he's so much softer than he looks.

> **JOJO KAPLAN AT 3:43 P.M.:** EEEEEEEEE!!! Pizza with mom every night!!

I close her message without answering. I'm happy for her. I'm just more sad for me.

CHAPTER TWENTY-TWO

AFTER THE HOST ANNOUNCEMENTS, I CONVINCE GRANDMA to let me spend the rest of the week home sick. It's not that I'm not excited for everyone. I am. I just don't want to watch everyone celebrate while I sit out. I'm tired of feeling like an outsider at school. But I spend so much time feeling sorry for myself, my least favorite week of the year—my birthday—comes in like a wrecking ball.

Except maybe it won't be my least favorite this year. Renee is back in the picture, which means I should hear from her for the first time in ten years. I've had hope before, a small piece that gets smaller every year. But this year feels brighter.

JoJo and Derek are standing by my locker Monday

morning. Their heads are bent close together in conversation, and my stomach dips. I can smell a JoJo scheme from a mile away.

"Hey, guys," I say from behind them. JoJo leaps into the air with a shriek and thrusts her hands behind her back. Derek startles but freezes in place, as if I can't see him if he's motionless. I yank on his sweatshirt zipper. "What's going on?"

JoJo draws her hand from behind her back. My favorite Whole Foods cupcake sits in her palm, still in its plastic container. Vanilla with strawberry frosting and strawberry filling. The John Ambrose McClaren of cupcakes.

"Happy birthday week," she says, doing a dancing shimmy in place. Derek holds up a pink unlit candle.

"You got here before we could bribe the janitor to light it for us," he says sheepishly. He thinks the unlit candle is stupid. I think it's lovely. "And pink was all I could find." Right, because, lo and behold, it's also Valentine's Day, which I already made Derek promise to ignore under penalty of death. We're doing pretty well at the *just friends* thing, but I covered my bases with a pinkie swear last week just in case. The universe and its jokes.

"But you still have to make a wish," JoJo instructs. She knows I'm not a big fan of my birthday, but I can tell she thinks enlisting Derek will make me more open to it. Plus, she feels bad about getting the UChicago gig, even though she shouldn't. She's always been better at the whole going-to-college thing.

"It's not even my birthday yet." I drop my larger books to the bottom of the locker so I don't have to carry them around all day. They hit the metal with a clang.

"Oh, come on, Michie," JoJo whines, "have a little birthday spirit." I thought that after telling her about my mom, she'd understand why I usually hate my birthday so much. "Besides, if you give me this, I will not send a singing V-Day candygram to your class."

My mouth drops open, and I shoot a death glare at them both.

"I didn't," Derek promises.

JoJo raises the cupcake in front of my face. The smell of fresh strawberries and sugar wafts through the gaps in the plastic and makes my mouth water. It's exploitation of my weaknesses.

"You fight dirty, Kaplan." I snatch the cupcake from her hand. "If I let you celebrate today, do I get a free pass on Thursday?"

She puts a finger to her chin and taps, contemplating. "Not a chance in hell."

I drop my head back and groan.

Derek lifts the candle again, that shy and charming smile that turns me to molten lava cake taking residence on his face. I should be charging that thing rent for all the emotional real estate it's occupying.

"Make it a good one," he orders with mock sternness. "And no wishing for more wishes. That's cheating and I only have one candle."

I wrinkle my nose and close my eyes, puckering my lips to blow.

"Oh," JoJo adds, "and no wishing for us to go away until Friday."

Derek nods in agreement. "You can only wish for things we can actually do."

"You can't leave me alone for one week?" I ask.

"Well...," he considers, "I can't, no."

A startled *oop* leaves JoJo's lips, and her smile is so wide you'd think it's her birthday instead of mine.

I already have a wish. It's the same one I've been wishing since I was seven years old. I close my eyes and blow out the imaginary flame, feeling more hopeful than ever it'll come true.

JoJo keeps the rest of the week low-key, for her at least. There's a different cupcake Tuesday and Wednesday mornings (devil's food cake and red velvet, respectively), and only a few balloons have to die when I find them tied to my locker. But her enthusiasm is hard for anyone with a heart to not appreciate.

By Thursday morning, I'm convinced my birthday may not be so terrible.

My bedroom door bangs open and Grandma backs into my room, a plate of Eggos and Neapolitan ice cream balanced in her hands. It's a tradition started at my first birthday sleepover with some of the kids from the complex. The friendships ended when I switched schools, but the breakfast is forever.

Grandma sings the Stevie Wonder "Happy Birthday," funky and loud, and gives me one of my birthday cards. I always get two—one for granddaughter and one for daughter, since she pulls double duty. The other I'll get later tonight with a present or two. I scoop a big bite of waffle and ice cream into my mouth, moaning at the sweet and crispy flavor bomb.

I untangle myself from the blankets and hug her tight around the neck.

She gives me a noisy kiss on my forehead, her signature gold lipstick rubbing off. I may leave it there for the rest of the day.

"Lunch is in the fridge," she says. "Love you."

"Times infinity," I smile, my mouth full of ice cream.

As she leaves, I'm not even annoyed she left my door open.

"Red Lobster at five thirty," she calls at the last minute, before the front door slams shut behind her. Red Lobster is our go-to destination for all birthdays and celebrations. I get to spend major bank on an Ultimate Feast and keel over at the end of the night from unlimited Cheddar Bay Biscuits and sweet tea. My stomach growls in anticipation, even though it's still hours away.

For the first day in a long while, I trade my faded jeans for a dress and stockings. The stockings are a little tight on my stomach, but it's still too cold to go out without them. I spend so long getting ready, wrangling my curls into a tame wash-and-go instead of my usual day-old high bun, that I almost miss the bus.

Derek's standing outside my APUSH class when I come bolting toward him to make it there on time. His mouth parts as he drags his eyes from my boots to the top of my lower-than-usual neckline. A lopsided grin spreads across his face before he checks his watch, shaking out of the reverie.

"Hap-happy birthday," he stutters, putting his fist to his mouth to clear his throat.

"Thank you."

"Um." He yanks on his ear and looks behind him into the classroom. JoJo is watching us, a breakfast bar held halfway to her mouth. "Here."

He hands me a piece of computer paper folded in half hamburger-style. It has *Happy Birthday* written in block letters across the front, with *(and belated Valentine's Day)* written in miniscule writing at the bottom. Cheater.

I chuckle at the makeshift card. "I can tell you made it yourself."

"Shut up," he laughs.

I move to open it, but he grabs my wrist.

"Don't," he blurts. "I mean don't read it now."

"Why not?"

"Just don't." He looks like I've caught him with his pants around his ankles. "I'll see you in Spanish."

He turns and flees down the hall, but he'll be late for

sure. I barely manage to turn into the classroom myself before the bell rings. JoJo watches me sit, a smug smirk on her lips, but she says nothing.

I drag the note under my desk to open it without anyone noticing. It's short, in Derek's messy scribbled cursive.

Happy birthday. You look beautiful. I hope you get everything you want and more. A crude heart is drawn in a corner.

I gulp and stare at the words. I read them again and again, scared they'll change at any moment. Terrified that I've imagined them.

JoJo stares holes into the side of my neck, but I fold the card closed and slide it under my notebook. I want to keep it for myself. When the bell announces the end of class, I'm out of the room before she can stop me.

I beeline through the swarm of students. People offer *Happy birthday*s, but I acknowledge them only with a quick wave as I stay on my path. I have one coherent thought—I need to find him.

He's standing by his locker. Tom speaks animatedly behind him, but he disappears when he sees me.

I hold the card up as I approach. It's wrinkled in the middle from where I've gripped it too tight. Derek only has time to give half a shrug before I crush myself to his chest. His arms snake around me, tight and secure. My emotions are in turmoil—friends, not friends—but I push the battle away for now and press my head to his chest where his heart thumps off rhythm. He is safe and brighter than the sun, and I want to, need to, be wrapped around someone who wants to be wrapped around me. His arms tighten, and I hold on until I've lost sense of everything but him.

And as dangerous as it is, this feels a lot like love and being loved back.

CHAPTER TWENTY-THREE

GRANDMA'S SITTING IN THE CAR AT THE BUS STOP. UNLIKE most birthdays, it's been a pretty great day. I don't even mind the happy-birthday snaps I get, which usually annoy me as an all-day constant reminder.

"Maybe we'll have room for dessert this year," she says as I buckle myself in.

"Yeah, maybe." The dinner itself is going to push it. I would feel way too guilty ordering dessert after an already expensive meal.

But as we pull into the Red Lobster parking lot and my phone remains dry, the doubt starts to creep back in. This is the first year Renee has reached out since I was seven, and, seventeen hours into my birthday, still no word from her. I remember when we used to play hooky from school and get our nails done before dinner, and now I can't even get a *happy birthday* text. Why am I always waiting for something that never happens?

"Actually, I'm not feeling so great," I say as Grandma turns the car off. "Can we go home? Act like it's a normal day?" I try to rein in the unhappiness, but it's building in my stomach.

"It's not a normal day," she says. She pulls the keys from the ignition. "It's your birthday."

"Who cares?" I know one person who definitely doesn't. Waiting to hear from Renee is never easy, but this is the first time I've allowed myself to hope, the first time she has given me a reason to. For once, my birthday wish didn't seem useless. Until now. And it's crushing, being let down again. I hate how much it bothers me.

"I care," she answers, her voice raised. She never raises her voice, and I'm shocked into silence. "You're not the only person who gets to celebrate you being here another year. So, get out of the car. Now."

She gets out without another word. I take a deep breath. She's not the only one surprised I made it this year. Not after The Incident. This is the least I can do after everything I put her through. So, I do what she says and get out of the car.

I've eaten four baskets of biscuits and am working my way through my last crab leg when the check comes to the table.

I'm so full my stomach is pressing up into my lungs. But thank God for carbs and their ability to make your brain too cloudy to grasp onto the tendrils of sadness spiraling out. Endorphins are pumping, and I'm in a much better mood now than I was when we walked in. We even ordered dessert.

Plus, there are still five birthday hours left. She'll call. She will.

I carry my gifts—a Barnes & Noble gift card and a guitar lesson book—into the apartment. The landline phone is inside the junk drawer, where Grandma must have stashed it before she left the house. There are no missed calls or messages. A text pings on my cell.

JOJO KAPLAN AT 7:17 P.M.: 20 minutes. D got the goods.

I walk back to my room and collapse on the bed. I should change into something warmer, but I don't have the energy. This is the first time Derek will be in my home, but Renee preoccupies my mind enough to keep me from panicking about it.

Pulling myself to the edge of the bed, I reach under my nightstand and drag out a small box. It's wooden and intricately carved with a doll-sized padlock on its clasp that now hangs open because I lost the key years ago.

I remove the clasp and lift the top open. Sitting at the top is a torn piece of white cloth, Minnie Mouse drawn in blue ink on the fabric. *To Michelle*, it says on the top right corner. I lift the cloth and it glides across my fingertips. I place it on the bed in slow motion, scared any sudden move-ment will turn it to dust. It's not that old but feels fragile.

A stack of folded papers are at the bottom of the box. They're all letters on lined notebook paper, flower patterns doodled around the edges. My name loops through petals and vines. I unfold each letter and read them to myself. The paper is soft after years of handling, fragile along the creases. I know all the words by heart.

There are four letters in all.

The last one is smeared and barely legible, and the tears falling now explain why. I can read only a few words, but the last four are still bold and beautiful, indestructible against the pain that has washed over them.

Happy birthday. Love, Mommy

The handwritten year in the bottom corner says *2012*. It was my seventh birthday and the last letter I ever got.

I don't hear Grandma come into my room. She sits next to me on the bed, the mattress dipping under our combined weight. She sighs and removes the box from my lap, piling in the letters and the Minnie Mouse drawing before snapping it shut. Pulling me into her, I lay my head on her chest, and she ignores the tears and the snot that stain one of her few nice shirts.

"I just want her to care." I hiccup. My throat is dry. "How could she want to see me, but still not care enough to say happy birthday?"

I wonder if this, among everything else, is my fault. My punishment for saying no. Maybe I deserve every ounce of pain I get. Maybe this is all my family history will ever be—tearstained letters in a broken lockbox.

"Is she mad at me?" I whisper. "For not going to see her?"

"Oh, no," Grandma says, rocking me back and forth. "I promise. This is not because of you. I *promise*."

We both stay silent. I'm not sure I believe her. Grandma pulls away from me, using her palm to wipe my nose. I try to pull my face away, but she persists.

"Michie, I need to tell you—" she begins, but I raise my hand to stop her.

"No more," I say. "I don't want to think about her anymore."

"So you're done?" It's not condescending or annoyed. She wants to know if she can let me out of the house like this. Me, broken and melted down to scraps. Her, hoping there's enough of me left to weld back together.

I nod against her chest.

"Okay. Then JoJo's downstairs," she tells me. "And a friend."

I stay silent. Earlier today, I was ready to fold and accept whatever fate has in store for us. I had almost recklessly dropped the *L* word. But doesn't my current emotional state signal to her that I should avoid any and all decisions involving other people's feelings? You don't feed emotional black holes. They'll eat until they're satisfied, devouring entire galaxies. I need him in my galaxy.

"Do you like him?" she presses.

I shrug.

"I know you don't believe me when I say it," she says, standing up from the bed, "but you are deserving of love. I love you very much. JoJo loves you. Other people could love you too, if you let them."

"Loving people is how you get hurt." I loved Renee, and she broke my heart. I was friends with the neighborhood kids, and they shunned me. Fewer people means fewer chances of getting hurt.

"You're damn right," she says. "You will break every piece of yourself loving someone deeply. But you'll pull yourself back together too. It's scary and terrifying and out of control. But you don't have to be afraid of it. You're worthy of love, Michie. But it's on you to figure out who's worthy in return. You get to decide. Only you. This is your life."

She leaves the room, keeping the door cracked so she can hear when I've moved from this spot. But before she gets far, she peeks her head back in.

"Five minutes to clean yourself up, or I'm letting JoJo loose in here."

For the first time all day, I laugh.

Derek's hanging from the monkey bars, his arms extended and locked at the elbows as he swings back and forth. Even with his knees bent at ninety-degree angles, his toes drag along the ground.

The apartment complex playground is poorly equipped, but it has the essentials. A swing set with a broken chain, a bright yellow plastic slide protruding from the rickety wooden jungle gym, and one set of monkey bars. The gravel has been replaced with a thick layer of black rubber mulch. It's amazing how miniature everything is. You never feel yourself outgrow things. One day, you're just too big for your old life.

JoJo is cradling a dozen-sized box of Krispy Kreme donuts. The goods. Between the three of us, we've stuffed down nine of them on the walk from my building, the hot glaze hardening in the chilly night air. My belly is still warm with it.

I wipe my mouth with the back of my hand, and hard crumbles of glaze fall. As I move my hand, the motion-sensitive face of my Fitbit lights up. 11:37 p.m.

"So what happens at midnight?" Derek asks, lurching himself in an arc off the last monkey bar and landing knees-first in the rubber.

Nerves crawl over my skin. I don't want to explain it. Not tonight, not ever.

"Nothing," JoJo says with no explanation.

In a way, she's answered his question. Nothing happens. Nothing ever happens. Silence stretches through the night air.

"Presents time," JoJo exclaims. She jumps down from the jungle gym and places the Krispy Kreme box on the ground.

It flies open with the wind, but she leaves it, digging into her purse until she rips out an inconspicuous white envelope.

"No presents," I groan, though it's a rule she ignores every single year.

JoJo loves giving gifts even more than she enjoys receiving them. It's her love language.

"Too bad," she sings, waving the envelope like a winning lottery ticket.

The jungle gym shudders as Derek climbs up to take JoJo's spot. The creaking wood was not designed for this.

She places the envelope in my lap. I lift it and shake it by my ear, but there's nothing to hear. It feels empty. I slide my finger under the taped-close flap, and it pops open with no resistance.

Inside is a piece of paper folded into thirds. An SAT admissions ticket.

"What's this?" I already took the SAT and she knows it.

"This," she says, reaching to pluck the ticket at its top corner, "is Brown."

She floats her hands in front of her face in a ta-da motion.

"What?" She has to be joking. I look over at Derek to confirm the absurdity of it, but a conspiratorial smile peeks through his attempt at a neutral expression. "Did you know about this?"

He raises a gloved hand to his mouth to hide his growing grin.

JoJo looks like she's solved world hunger she's so pleased with herself.

"Are you kidding?"

"Nope. Happy birthday!" She can't reach the rest of my body, so she pulls my dangling legs into a tight hug.

"JoJo, this is for three weeks from now," I say, noticing the date at the top. Mid-March. Of this year. "Are you crazy?"

I hate to sound ungrateful, but she can't be serious. No one signs up for the SAT with three weeks' notice. It's like setting money on fire. I don't even want to think about how much it cost her to do this so late. I know it's way more than I'd ever be comfortable with.

"Yeah, I know. But that's fine." She breathes into her hands to warm them and then stuffs them up the front of her shirt to thaw.

"That's fine?" My voice rises.

"You've been studying. You're ready."

"JoJo, I haven't studied a single thing." I can't even say I haven't studied since October, because I'd gone into that one cold as well. If my score comes out worse, I'll be shafted.

"Of course you've been studying," she presses. "What's the definition of *trepidation*?"

It's a word very fitting to my current emotional state.

"JoJo, that's one word. Out of like a million words."

She glares at me now.

"Michie, I'm ranked second in our class. Do you really think I need you to test me on vocabulary words and mathematical equations? I have a 4.6 GPA."

I think back to the random things she's made me quiz her on. Linear equations, unit conversions, polynomials, vocabulary, graph interpretation. On, and on, and on. Things she should have known in her sleep. And I learned all of it. Friendship osmosis.

"JoJo," I say, "what was your SAT score?"

Her smile is smug, aware that I'm starting to understand what she's done: "1575."

I blanch. That's damn near perfect.

Derek chuckles beside me as the realization dawns in waves.

"But why?"

"Because we both know you need to retake it if you want a shot at Brown. And you've been too afraid of failing. But you're not going to fail because you're ready this time. You don't need to host a stupid college fair. You've got this on your own. And if you're not going to take the things you deserve, then hell, you'll get by with a little help from your overbearing friends."

My chest bursts open and I stagger off the jungle gym. My arms wrap around her, and I squeeze until neither of us can breathe. I can't even protest the decision she's made on my behalf. I am so, so grateful.

"You think I'm ready?" My lips shiver from the cold and the adrenaline.

"I wouldn't have done it if I didn't think you were ready." She takes a stray piece of hair that's blown itself free and wraps it around her ponytail to keep it in place.

I laugh, grabbing her hand and pulling her down to the ground. We sink into the rubber mulch, still carrying the heat of the day. I tilt my head backward. Derek's upside down as he stands by the jungle gym.

"What are you waiting for?" I tease, patting the empty space beside me.

He lowers himself down and lengthens out, his legs extending far past ours as our heads line up. We resemble starfish as we stare up at the night sky.

"Best birthday ever," I whisper. The wind picks up the words, and they dance around us until they get carried away.

Renee opened the door, and I may not have answered it yet, but I didn't close it either. It's been ten years. I get to think about it. I get to take my time. She wouldn't hold it against me.

I turn my head toward JoJo, my ear flat against the foam, and reach for her hand, squeezing hard. "She called." It'll be there when I get home. I know it.

She smiles sadly and pulls my hand to her chest.

It's almost one in the morning when I get home. Grandma's light glows from beneath her bedroom door, the television set to low volume so she can hear me come in. I call out goodnight and slip into my room. I'm clutching the mail from the kitchen table and the house phone.

I sit on my bed and sort through the envelopes. A card from Great Aunt Clara with twenty bucks. A Victoria's Secret birthday coupon. A bunch of Grandma's credit card statements. The water bill. I drop everything in a pile on the floor.

The buttons on the phone beep loudly as I click through to the voice mail. One from Taran singing "Happy Birthday" and giving me the weekend off. One from a telemarketer. Nothing else.

I double-check my cell phone. No new texts appear on the lock screen. No missed calls. No emails. No tweets. No snaps. No Facebook messages. No IG DMs. Nothing.

In through the nose and out through the mouth, I breathe. Hot tears burn behind my eyes. Footsteps stop outside my door. Then silence. It's just me, alone.

I get off the bed, grabbing the box of letters still sitting on the mattress, and drop it into the trash can by my door. The guitar next to it falls to the floor with a discordant wail as the strings hit the carpet. I leave it there.

I made the right choice. I made the right choice when I was five years old and I left with Grandma. I made the right choice when she asked to see me and I refused. She only knows how to hurt. I open my closet door and sit down on the cleared floor. I shut the door to block out the moonlight, lean back against the wall, and let the tears fall.

The next morning, my eyelids are swollen shut with puffiness. The light through my window is too bright as I stumble from the closet. The dropped mail is gone, the phone gone, and the box of letters tossed in the trash is beneath my nightstand once more. The guitar is standing upright against the wall. The trash can is empty.

And I'm seventeen.

CHAPTER TWENTY-FOUR

"I HAVE A VERY SERIOUS QUESTION," DEREK ASKS WHEN he drops in front of me. The library is busier than usual as the SAT draws closer, but he doesn't bother lowering his voice. There's no point since Wexler lets him get away with anything.

"Should I be scared?" I ask. Is he going to ask me out? For real? Without the rest of the basketball team? Am I going to say yes if he does?

"If you were choreographing a promiscuous, but classy, striptease..."

"I'm sorry, what?" I splutter with a laugh.

"Hear me out. Striptease. Are you with me?"

"Not at all, but continue." I cap my pen and place it on the table. Our library sessions started back up again post-apology, but we've stopped the pretense of me helping him with his Spanish.

"Would you choose a classic like Ginuwine, go with some rock, or go outside the box with something from *The Phantom of the Opera*?"

I laugh so loud it echoes over the library. Wexler stands up to give me the death glare of all death glares. But the current collapse of my lungs will kill me long before she can.

"What," I breathe, "the absolute hell...are you stripping to...from *The Phantom of the Opera*?"

"We could jazz something up," he responds.

"Please," I wheeze. I wave my hand in front of me to get him to stop talking. I think I might've cracked a rib.

"Michie, I'm being serious." His eyebrows knit together, and I realize he isn't kidding.

I take deep breaths until my lungs do their job again. "May I ask what the"—I giggle—"striptease is for?"

"No," he says.

"Okay, well, you can never go wrong with Ginuwine. Though good execution of a *Phantom of the Opera* striptease may be too good to pass up."

"Great." He knocks his knuckles twice on the table before standing back up.

"Wait, that's really it?" I ask.

"That's it." He turns to leave before pulling a 180 to

face me again. "You're coming to Senior Night next week, right?

"Um…"

"Michie, you promised."

"Derek," I groan.

"Cooper." His dimples become even more pronounced as he smiles. I don't know if he has control over it, but he always pulls those dimples out at the perfect time because I can't say no to them.

"Fine," I grumble.

"You won't regret it," he sings as he backs away.

But I don't believe him.

I should already be asleep Friday night when my phone goes off. But I'm not, because I got sucked into a *Property Brothers* binge-watch, so I'm awake for the implosion.

> **PETER DONOGHUE AT 11:53 P.M.:** the nxt time I ask for help
> pls turn me away
> **MICHIE COOPER AT 11:55 P.M.:** what's going on?
> **PETER DONOGHUE AT 11:55 P.M.:** nothings goin on thats the prob
> **MICHIE COOPER AT 11:56 P.M.:** i don't understand.
> **PETER DONOGHUE AT 11:57 P.M.:** in not so many words Mo
> very kindly told me to kick rocks so thats embarrassing

I lift myself from my bed, shock catapulting me upward. What?

MICHIE COOPER AT 11:58 P.M.: are you sure? what did she say?

PETER DONOGHUE AT 11:58 P.M.: she said exactly what i just told u literally kick rocks

PETER DONOGHUE AT 11:58 P.M.: its fine i just want to drop it im only telling u cuz i dont know what plans ur cooking up, but drop em

This can't be right. They were so cute at Open Mic Night. And they haven't even gone to Coco and Hazel yet. I haven't pulled out all the stops. *Clueless* did not prepare me for any breakdowns in the operation other than being called a virgin who can't drive, which is true.

MICHIE COOPER AT 11:59 P.M.: I don't understand. She likes you. She told me.

PETER DONOGHUE AT 12:00 A.M.: well whatever she told u aint true no more so thats dead night tho

I reread the text chain. It doesn't make sense. I know she likes him. She told me. I mean, she didn't *tell me* tell me, but she basically told me. Right?

MICHIE COOPER AT 12:01 A.M.: hey what happened with Peter?

MONICA MUSTAFA AT 12:10 A.M.: Drop it Michie.

MICHIE COOPER AT 12:10 A.M.: monica . . .

MONICA MUSTAFA AT 12:11 A.M.: I'm serious. Stay out of it. Please.

MICHIE COOPER AT 12:12 A.M.: can we just talk for a second? what happened?

My last message fails to say *delivered*. She blocked me.

"What the actual fuck?" I mutter, dropping my phone beside me on the bed. "What. The Actual. Fuck?"

Maybe I was wrong and the R.P.E. kids really are incapable of love. The knowledge of that feels like being dropped in the middle of the ocean with an anchor around my waist, where I sink faster than I can swim.

CHAPTER TWENTY-FIVE

MONICA KEEPS ME BLOCKED FOR THE REST OF THE WEEK-
end, and it isn't until Tuesday morning that she finally
unblocks me and responds, telling me to back off. Peter
isn't much better. I'm not exactly sure how I screwed things
up so royally. And because of Senior Night, I won't even be
at group tonight to talk to them about it. Which feels like
an excellent excuse to renege on the whole basketball thing
and go to group instead.

At least it feels like an excellent excuse, until I walk into
school. The linoleum floors are covered an inch thick with
confetti. Green and gold balloons line the hallways. The
school hallways look like the inside of a fun house, but without the creepy mirrors. The cheerleaders are all in uniform,

and a critical mass of students are donning school T-shirts or, at the very least, the school colors. I managed to dig out a forest-green sweater from the back of my closet.

It is Lizzo-concert-level school spirit, which is exactly what I need. Who can be miserable around so much cheer? It's pure serotonin.

Gwen is standing by a water fountain, cornered by a group of students helping one another paint thick black lines under their eyes. She holds her DSLR camera up to her eye as she scans the crowd for photo opportunities. I don't see a flash as I approach her, but I hear the shutter double-click with each press of her finger.

"Yearbook duty?" I ask, nodding toward the camera. I place my empty water bottle under the fountain's automatic nozzle and it fills, the electronic motor groaning. The number of plastic bottles saved from its use ticks up once and then twice.

"Last basketball game of the season gets a full two-page spread," she explains. She points her lens toward a group of players buzzing around the vending machines. "Besides, we're pretty good this year." She winks. Derek.

A loud, whooping cheer sounds from the other end of the hall. A familiar head of curly brown hair peeks out above the crowd. Derek fist-bumps his way through the sea of students, Tom beaming close by his side. They're both seniors, and this is the last moment it will be this way. My legs turn to gelatin at the thought of Derek being gone soon.

A cheerleading-uniform-clad senior hangs off his neck

like a wet towel, her long ponytail draped over his shoulder. They look so *right* together. Long limbs and athletic builds and angular features. She's toned where I'm soft. Brit holds on to Tom's arm less possessively as she waves at the crowd like royalty.

When he sees us, Derek untangles himself and jogs down the rest of the hall. The cheerleader sends me a glare before turning away. Derek's usual dark-denim jeans, video game tee, and Vans have been exchanged for crisp khaki pants, dress shoes, a button-up shirt, and a sport jacket. A navy tie hangs loose around his neck. It's the Miles Morales look I never knew I needed.

Gwen snaps eight photos of his approach in quick succession before leaning over to me. "Can a lesbian think one boy beautiful?"

"Sure," I respond. Gwen has been with her girlfriend, Bridget, for two years, but it's not like she doesn't have eyes, and Derek is beautiful in a Louvre painting kind of way. Even people who don't like art can appreciate it. And if I can have a girl crush on Chloe Bailey, she can have a boy crush on Derek.

"Well," she whispers. "Yum, then." She puts her camera strap back around her neck, before following the rest of the team down the hall as Derek sidles up to me.

He reaches around me, pulling my full water bottle from underneath the fountain. But instead of pulling away immediately, he stays close by my side.

"Not that I don't already know the answer," he says over

the crowd, "but you wouldn't happen to be coming to the game tonight, would you?" He nods down at my sweater, noticing I have put in some effort in joining the festivities.

"What game?" I joke. His smile drops. "I'm kidding." I shove him lightly. He grabs my hand, not releasing it.

"It's a big deal, Senior Night," he explains. "So, it's cool that you'll be there." He works his earlobe through his fingers with his free hand.

"What's Senior Night again?" He's explained it a hundred times, but I like listening to him talk about basketball even if I don't like the sport itself. I give a tug of my hand, but he tugs back. He waves to a passing student with me still attached like I'm a marionette.

"Last home game for the seniors. We lost the games we needed to make the playoffs, so this year, it's also the last game of the season. The last one we'll ever play."

"Until college."

"Only for some of us. Half the team didn't even get picked up for college ball." His voice drags melancholic. Derek's already committed to Duke after being on one of the best teams in California, but for a lot of his teammates, this is it. The whole thing seems depressing. If they all love the game half as much as Derek, it must be devastating.

"That's kind of sad," I say.

"Yeah, it is."

"Well," I say, to lighten the mood, "it better be like the basketball scenes in *Space Jam*, or I'm going to be super disappointed."

"The McKray High team satisfies the alien requirement." He smiles, and it's like the flu—infectious, except you want to catch it.

"Cool."

"Cool, it's a date," he says.

"It's a date."

And if smiles could sing, Derek's would be an aria.

At lunch, I find JoJo in the library at the table I usually share with Derek. I drop my massive softcover edition of *Les Misérables* on the table with a thud. The cafeteria is closed to set up for the team's spaghetti dinner, so everyone is eating lunch here.

"Please tell me you're going to the game," I whisper from across the table. I'm excited to see Derek play, but I'm not excited about the idea of sitting by myself. And I need someone to explain to me what's happening, since the only dribble I know is the one I wake up covered in.

"Of course I'm going," she says. "It's the last major game of the year. Unless you count soccer, which I don't. Or lacrosse, which I definitely don't. And if we win, there's going to be a huge party after."

"It's Tuesday."

"And?"

"We have school tomorrow."

"And? It's not like any of the teachers are going to expect us to be coherent tomorrow. It's Senior Night. You should ask your grandma if you can sleep over."

"So I can go to a party? Are you whacked?"

"Michie, you are an adult in less than a year." I've been seventeen for about thirty seconds, but okay. "Do what the rest of us do." She slides her laptop into her backpack and stands, straightening her forest-green midi dress, and places both palms on the table. "Lie."

But I don't have to. The second I text Grandma about the game, she urges me to stay until the end and crash at JoJo's. One doesn't get much of a rebellious streak when your parental unit would rather you break a law for once than spend another night at home.

But the moment I walk into the gym, fifteen minutes before the game is due to start, I wish I'd never agreed to come.

Lee High's gym is so loud my teeth grind together. And this is the sound when nothing is even happening. The teams are still in their jackets, shooting balls lazily at their respective hoops. The noise bottlenecks in the entrance and peters off to an echo the farther you get into the gym.

Derek makes a shot from a small line on the court. His head jerks like he's been stung, and he glances over his shoulder. I wave.

"Hey," he shouts from the center of the court. Rows of eyes pivot toward me.

He jogs over to us before we climb the steps, grabbing a red-and-white basketball from a chair on his way over. I've never seen him in his uniform. It's a shiny forest green with gold lettering. It hangs a little too loose in the shorts but tight in the shoulders. Derek isn't usually an awkward person, but right now he's holding himself with a heightened level of confidence. My mouth dries.

I try not to show discomfort at the scrutiny directed at the back of my head. "I thought there'd be more theatrics for Senior Night." I move my hands in spirit fingers. "I see not one streamer."

"Oh, there's a whole thing. Don't worry," he says, nodding at a couple who I assume are his parents. They're sitting on the bottom row of the bleachers with a long line of Eurocentrically beautiful middle-aged men and women. His mom has a curly 'fro, styled in a DevaCut that frames her face. Unlike the other moms, dressed in shift dresses and heels, she's in denim jeans and a sweater pulled up to her elbows. His dad, a Latino man pulling a very convincing Eugenio Derbez, whispers into her ear. He grasps her hand in both of his on his lap. My heart squeezes at the syrupy sweetness of it. No wonder Derek is so *heart-eyes* all the time. I'll never have that to look up to.

"Oh, hey," Derek says as JoJo and I turn to grab a seat. He pulls the basketball from under his arm. His name is handwritten in Sharpie along one of the lines. "Hold on to this?"

JoJo chokes on a laugh, but turns it into a cough.

"Um, sure?" I grab the ball and wonder why he didn't leave it in the locker room or give it to his parents, sitting five feet away. What am I supposed to do with it?

"Thanks." He races back to the court, where Tom and Mac smack him on the back encouragingly. He must be nervous for the last game of his high school career.

"Let's go." JoJo puts her arm around my neck and pulls me up the stands. Brit waves us into her row, and everyone shifts to make space. A girl I don't recognize with straw-blonde hair looks at the ball and clicks her teeth. Brit also has one in her lap.

"You'd think they had somewhere to stash these," I say, gesturing to her basketball before shoving Derek's under the space behind my feet.

"Hmm?" Brit leans into me.

"Never mind," I mutter. She probably has to do this all the time, and it's way too loud anyway to carry on a conversation.

Suddenly she stands, screaming with her hands high over her head, the ball still clutched between them.

The court is now clear of people, and both teams huddle by their seats. Lights scan the room like beacons. The crowd does a wave back and forth. I find myself jumping and cheering as well, overtaken by the energy of the room. JoJo and Brit teach me the cheers through the first half, and I channel my inner East Compton Clover.

We're in the lead by over twenty points, more than half of those belonging to Derek. He moves like he's dancing, the other players stumbling over a step-ball-change he's already mastered. Every time he makes a shot, the crowd erupts. But it's the moment right before the ball leaves his fingertips that's my favorite. There's a pregnant pause, a collective held breath, like right after a violinist finishes a solo or a prima ballerina takes a bow. It's so stunning that your brain moves in slow motion. Like we're all watching something special happen.

"He is on fire," JoJo yells into my ear as he sinks another shot.

"I know," I scream back. People cast me looks of approval with each basket, like he's mine and they're thanking me for sharing him tonight. Pride grows in my chest. He *is* mine.

The first half ends. Everyone in the stands sits as a unit, the excitement buzzing like a fly against glass. I'm covered in sweat and a little delirious.

"It's like he knows someone's watching or something," Brit teases.

"He's always this good," I reply, not that I've ever seen him play. But he's going to Duke next year, and even I know how hard that is to do.

"No, he's not," JoJo says, wiping perspiration, and a little foundation, off her forehead with the inside of her wrist. "I mean, he's really good, don't get me wrong, but this is different."

"Yeah," Brit agrees, "this is a show."

The crowd silences as one of the junior players runs to the center of the court with a wireless microphone in his hand. The coach stands up, confused, urging him back to the bench. The junior taps on the mic twice, making the speakers spit out screeching feedback. I flinch under the assault, but he recovers.

"Welcome to Senior Night," he croons, his southern accent deep and even. "It means a lot to us that you all are here tonight." He points at the line of guys standing up from their seats. "Each of them has given a lot, not only this season, but for four years now to this team and to this school. Some even a limb or two." Laughter spreads through the stands at his dig at Andrew Kim, the point guard Derek replaced, now wearing a boot.

The group of girls around me shift their focus to Brit's postgame party. Apparently, more alcohol is needed for a victory.

"I'll text my brother," an athletic brunette suggests, whipping out her Android to send a text. "And his girlfriend." I try to remember her name. Jamie?

"Oh, oh," Brit interrupts, waving her hand around to quiet the group. They snap to attention immediately and lean forward in their seats. Maybe-Jamie abandons her text mid-sentence. The player at the mic, whose name is Lawrence, is going to call out the seniors one at a time, JoJo tells me.

"Sanjeev 'Young Jeevy' Patel," he calls. If I thought the crowd was loud before, I was dead wrong.

Everyone rises in a synchronized wave, clapping and cheering until their palms turn red. The radio-edit version of the latest 21 Savage single blasts from the loudspeakers, the bass shaking the stands. The coach has turned a shocking shade of purple as he yells for everyone to sit down, but the players still on the bench cajole him back to his seat.

I stand up on the bleachers to see over the mass of heads. Sanjeev's tall and deep-skinned with jet-black hair that falls just below his ears. A man that looks like a bearded older version of him, his dad, I assume, walks with him, his hand on Sanjeev's shoulder. Girls scream themselves hoarse.

Mac is next, and he swoops across the court to Post Malone. His parents are hype too, with arms held out like they're flying. The guys in the stands are as loud as the girls, all screaming themselves into a frenzy.

Then Andrew, and I wonder what he can do on crutches. But as soon as Nipsey's verse drops on "Victory Lap," he tosses one crutch away and his dad lifts him into his arms. Andrew's leg dangles as he pumps the other crutch in the air. His other arm is around his dad's shoulders. His tiny Korean mom follows behind them with the thrown crutch, shaking her head in laughter. When they get to the center of the court, Andrew's placed back on the floor. His mom hands him the crutch so he can stand.

Tom comes out to a new Megan Thee Stallion single, and the opening hook bounces around the walls. *Real hot girl shit.* Brit's scream is so piercing I'm worried she'll break a hole into the space time continuum. She raps the first verse flawlessly at the top of her lungs and waves his basketball in the air. Tom holds his mom's hand as they make their way across the court. His dad walks beside them, with his arm extended across both of their backs.

When he finally turns around, he searches the crowd until he finds Brit, who has lost her mind as she jumps up and down on the rickety plastic. He blows her a kiss, and she yells "I love you" into the void of noise. There's no way he can hear her, but he smiles like he can.

Two seniors I don't recognize come next, and I get the feeling most of the crowd doesn't know them either. But the fanfare doesn't die down even a little bit.

"And lastly, this season's leading scorer..." Lawrence pauses, allowing the crowd to lose its mind. He feeds off the hysteria. "Derek de la Rosa." He drags out *Rosa* until his voice is swallowed by the eruption in the stands.

I can barely hear his intro music, but then the speakers slice through the cheers and the iconic *Space Jam* anthem, Seal's "Fly Like an Eagle," blasts out louder than any song before it.

I throw my head back with unabashed laughter that pulls deep from my belly. He promised *Space Jam*, and he delivers. Every mouth sings along, the long *fly*, a booming chorus. Derek's arms are around his parents' shoulders, both smaller than him. He and Tom fist-bump behind the unknown seniors when Derek stops at the end of the line. His mom reaches up to hold his hand draped over her shoulder.

All seven players stand and soak in the excitement as the cheering goes on and on and on. A few try to inconspicuously wipe tears from their eyes. Tom lets them fall freely.

Cheerleaders bring each of the seniors a bouquet of

roses. I've never seen anyone give a guy flowers, but it should happen more often because each of them smiles brightly. Derek hands his to his mom. She cradles them and puts her hand on his cheek.

The cheers finally die down, and the team walks their parents back to the bleachers but remain standing, watching Lawrence expectantly.

"Now our boys here have a surprise they've prepared for you all tonight." He gives the stands a suggestive wink.

The crowd explodes again in anticipation.

"A select few of you were given a basketball by a member of the team earlier tonight." I glance down at Brit's, still on her lap. A nervous tingle starts at the bottom of my spine. "If you got one, could you please make your way down to center court?"

My stomach drops to my toes. Shit.

Brit pops up and runs down the stands. I use my foot to push Derek's basketball as far out of sight as possible. Four additional girls, and one guy, scattered all over the gym stand up as well and join Brit on the court, red-and-white basketballs in their hands. Everyone scans the stands. My nightmare of public vomiting is about to occur.

"There's one more of you out there," Lawrence teases. "Don't be shy."

Oh my God. Please no. I squeeze my eyes shut, knowing I'm making this ten times harder the longer I hide here. When my eyes open, Derek's staring at me with wide eyes.

JoJo finally realizes what's happening and shoves her elbow between my ribs.

"Ow," I yelp, rubbing the bones. But she's already reaching behind my feet for the basketball. When it's in her hands, she shoves it into my chest and lifts me by the sweater.

"Go," she commands, shoving me down the steps. I almost trip over my feet but catch myself on a random shoulder with my free hand, the basketball clutched in the other.

Every eye in the room is staring at me. I glare at Derek like I can kill him right here and now with my gaze, but he just laughs.

As I make my way to the group, seven metal folding chairs are set down in the center of the gym, staggered in rows. I find Derek again, but he smiles at me with a thumbs up. Too bad he's too far away to murder.

"Hey, girl," Brit trills, touching my hand clinging to the basketball for dear life.

"If you all could take a seat," Lawrence asks into the microphone.

I hesitate before sitting down to the left of Brit. She stores the ball between the legs of her chair, trapping it in place.

Collin Wakefield, the lone guy in our group, sits next to me and urges me to do the same with my basketball. "So it's not in the way," he advises. In the way of what? How am I the only person with no clue what's going on? But he has a kind smile to pair with his hazel eyes and gaged ear piercings, so I follow his instructions.

My lap is now empty, so I take the free moment to rub my sweat-soaked hands against my pants legs.

The lights go down, and we're sitting in pitch black. Anticipation slinks through the room, and I almost black out from the hyper focus of trying to parse out any familiar sounds. But all I make out are wolf whistles.

When the lights come back on, Derek is standing two inches in front of me. I jerk backward, and my grip tightens on the edge of my seat.

Don't, I mouth, my brain catching up. He smirks. "Don't you dare," I threaten aloud.

He puts his hand to his ear as if he can't hear me.

The music starts pumping through the room. The whoops and hollers crash like a tsunami from the stands as Ginuwine's "Pony" fills the space. The team begins a coordinated dance around our chairs that is all hips and arms. The screaming is deafening as they shimmy and shake. Derek drops to his knees in front of me, leaning backward like Patrick Swayze in *Dirty Dancing*. His eyes stay on mine in strict concentration. I cover my face with my hands before doubling over in hysterical laughter. My abdominal muscles whine in protest. It's so embarrassing, and I love every second.

The smile spreads deeper into Derek's face, and he gets even more lost in the music.

The guys jump up to their feet, coming close enough to straddle our legs. I keep my eyes straight forward, somewhere around Derek's navel, not sure where else to look.

They all lean down in unison. To my right, Tom is kissing Brit sweetly on the lips. To my left, Mac is making out with Collin, their hands everywhere. Derek looks me straight in the eyes with a smirk. He's mine, and I am so, so his.

He pecks me on the tip of my nose, lingering for a breath before moving away.

The team regroups in front of us, linking arms and closing out the song in a line of hip thrusts and jazz hands. The cheers continue over the music. The whole thing is hysterically brilliant.

The music ends. I'm hot in unfamiliar places when Derek makes his way over to help me out of my chair. My legs are gelatin, so when he jerks me forward, I fall to his chest. His arm is slung around my waist.

"Hi," he mutters. He's sweaty and my blood flares.

"Hi." I should be upset for being tricked into this very embarrassing public display of affection, but I'm not. All I can do is laugh.

He leads me backward off the court. Their coach looks like he's ready to pass out, he's so angry at the halftime-show striptease. When I detach myself from Derek, my legs stumble, boneless. I realize I've forgotten my basketball.

"Oh," I turn, pointing back at it under my chair.

"I'll grab it," he assures me, before rejoining the team.

I make my way back up the stands in a daze, fanning my hands in front of my face. I sit down, the girls around my seat giggling. Every sound that was so abrasive moments ago now goes straight into one ear and out the other, my brain unable to latch onto a single thing. I'm wrecked.

"Mm-hmm," JoJo hums.

We sputter a laugh until the buzzer rings for the second half to begin.

CHAPTER TWENTY-SIX

"FLY, FLY INTO THE FUTURE," JOJO SINGS, BELTING THE notes into the air until her voice gives. She sticks her head out of the back seat window, hair whipping around her face. She holds her diet lemonade out of the car, resting it against the window. I'm counting down the seconds until it splatters against the side of the Audi.

Derek beats his hands against the steering wheel with the music. I turn my head to face him. The smile I've been donning since I first started watching him play is still carved into my face, unshakable.

"It was an inspired choice." I laugh, referring to the song. My basketball is cradled in my lap.

"Well, I did have a muse."

"And how much trouble are you all in?" I ask.

"Oh, we'll be running laps around the school until we throw up." He makes direct eye contact with me, his eyes smiling brightly. "It was worth it though."

JoJo slithers her body back into the car, lemonade still in hand, and leans between the seats. Her breath smells like citrus and syrup.

We were at Brit's victory party for a mere ten minutes before we bailed, opting for Sonic French toast sticks and drinks instead.

"This is me." JoJo points at her large brick house. The driveway is empty, her car left behind in the school parking lot again.

She leans forward between the front seats and twists her head between me and Derek.

"Night night, lovebirds," she sings.

"Oh, honey," I say, placing my hand on her cheek. She's the only one of us who drank at the party, and I make a mental note to make her down some water before she goes to sleep. She turns to lick my hand on her cheek, and I jerk it away. Blowing us both kisses, she slumps back into the back seat to get out of the car.

"Oh." She catches herself before getting out. "Do you mind picking us up tomorrow morning?"

"Yeah, sure," Derek agrees.

"Merci beaucoup." And she's gone. A cold wisp of air

whistles through the open door before she slams it shut behind her.

"Subtle, isn't she?" Derek asks. Sometimes I forget how much space JoJo's personality takes up until she's gone.

"As a nuclear bomb."

He turns the car off, and I gulp down nerves. The hand still resting on the gearshift twitches, brushing my thigh.

"Can I ask you something?"

My stomach folds into itself. I know what's coming and I'm scared. The truth changes things, things I might not want changed. I don't respond, so he continues.

"Your mess? Is it about your mom?"

I shift, squeezing impossible dents into the ball I'm clutching like a lifeline.

"I'm not trying to pry. You told me about your siblings and you talk about your Grandma a lot, but you never talk about your mom."

"Yeah," I mutter, running my fingers over the bumpy surface of the basketball. I turn to stare out of my window.

"You're good at keeping secrets, Michie, but your eyes? They're terrible. It's like you're trying to tell me something but the picture's blurry. But you asked me to trust you, and now I'm asking you to trust me."

I work my lip between my teeth.

"Is this about what happened at lunch that day?" he asks. "About that girl, Trisha?"

"Trish," I correct.

"Trish." I can feel him watching me, but I don't turn my

240

head. "Did you…" He pauses to find the words. "Get one? An abortion? And she didn't approve?"

I can't help it. I laugh. Because that reality wouldn't be so bad, all things considered.

"I don't think you can ask people that," I say. "For future reference." Now or never. "I didn't have one. I should have been one."

I hear his sharp intake of breath. My skin is on fire, and my chest is rising and falling way too fast. Anxiety builds up like a torpedo but I focus on steady breathing.

"When I was five, my grandma moved to Virginia. We lived in Houston, me, my… Renee, and my grandma, but my grandma wanted a change. So they gave me the choice—stay with Renee or go with Grandma. And I went." I pause, sorting through things I've never even shared at R.P.E. "There was always this disconnect with Renee. She never felt like my mother. She used to visit on my birthdays, until I turned seven. She came to visit, and we were all sitting in the car at a gas station. ExxonMobil. I was being a brat; I don't even remember what about."

I turn back to the window again, the heat of tears behind my eyes. I've never said these words before. "As she got out of the car to pump the gas, she said, *I should have killed you when I had the chance.*"

Derek's hand reaches for mine, gripping it tight in his. I expect him not to believe me, to tell me I'm exaggerating, to assure me I must have heard her wrong.

"She said she didn't mean it after. But I saw it in her eyes, heard it in her voice. She meant it. It was freeing for her to finally let it out." As freeing as purging it now. Pain never wants to be confined. It yearns to be set free.

I release one hand from our tangled hold and pull at a frayed rip in my jeans.

"I guess I always knew how hard it was for her, being my mom."

"Why? I mean, that's...why would she say something like that?"

I turn to face him, tracing the outline of his shadowed face. How far do I want to go? But I can't shove the monster back into the closet now. I squeeze my eyes shut. My body is humming with fear.

"My mom," I begin, stalling out. "Sorry, I haven't told this to anyone outside of my therapy group, except JoJo. And that was pretty recent."

Derek reaches over and grabs my knee, squeezing it as reassurance pours into me. It's subtle, but it gives me the strength to continue.

"She was raped when she was fifteen. Six months later, there I was." Born three months early into a life I shouldn't have. So early, I shouldn't have made it. I've been fighting for breath my entire life.

The words are birthed into the world. I hope they find it a warmer place than I did.

"What it must feel like, to look at this thing that reminds you of everything stolen from you—it must be sickening, to know what I am, where I came from, to see him in me.

242

And then everyone agreeing kids like me, the ones conceived from the ashes of so much pain, so much evil, shouldn't be here. I hate it. No woman should have to go through it. My mother, she shouldn't have had to. And sometimes I think everyone would be happier if she *had* gotten rid of me when she had the chance. But then other times, I feel like I deserved the chance. And that makes me feel like shit, like I'm a selfish monster."

The pain of that truth is what keeps me awake at night.

"I thought if she could love me back, it would prove I had been worth it. But she doesn't. I am her albatross. She never finished high school; she never went to college even though she was smart and driven enough. And it's all because of me. I took everything from her."

"You didn't take anything," he objects. "He did, whoever he is."

"I am him." It's so deeply true that it chokes me. I am as much him as I am her, maybe more. Original sin personified.

"Michie," he starts, but I rip my hands from his.

"I don't need you to change my mind. I've lived with this my entire life. It's a part of me I don't get to reason away. She gets to hate me. And she gets to hate him. And I get to hate him. But I don't get to hate her. Because despite everything, I'm here. She gave that to me when she didn't have to. When the whole world told her it was okay to wipe herself clean of me."

"I don't think you're being fair to yourself," he whispers. "I told you about my grandpa, and you said it wasn't my fault.

And if you believe that, how could you ever think this is your fault? This happened to you."

I stay silent, trying to make out shapes through the cloudiness of my tears. The pain goes deeper than anything he can say here and now. But for the first time in ten years, everyone I care about knows the truth. I'm free from this secret's burden. This isn't R.P.E., where everyone shares the same pain, where our secrets exist only in the four walls of Dr. Schwartz's office. This is real life. My real life, and its two tracks finally come together. It feels good to be one complete person instead of a life made up of disparate parts.

He reaches over and wipes a tear from my cheek with the pad of his thumb.

"Thank you," I whisper. "For listening. For not judging." I muster everything inside of myself to give him a smile before slipping out of the car.

"Hey, Mich," he calls, before the door slams shut.

"Yeah," I say, pulling a sweater over my wrist to dry my eyes.

He looks at me, his fingers tapping on the gearshift. His mouth opens, but there's indecision in his eyes. "Try to get some sleep."

I enter JoJo's foyer and close the door behind me, locking both the top and bottom locks like I do at home, though it matters so much less here. I slide down to the floor, pulling my phone out of my pocket. I scroll to a number I've never used, reserved for emergencies. I tap on it and listen to the ring.

"Hello?"

"Hi, Dr. Schwartz," I say, pulling my knees up and burying my face between them.

"Michie?" Her voice snaps as it bends under concern. "Is everything okay?"

I realize it's after midnight.

"Oh yeah, I'm sorry," I mutter, speaking quickly in a panic. "I called because…" The words stick in my throat. "I called because I wanted to talk about Renee, but it's late. I'm so sorry. I'll stop by tomorrow."

"No, it's fine, Michie. Thank you for calling me." She says it as if I'm the one doing her a favor. "What's going on?"

"I'm just—" I pause. "I'm so tired." She doesn't respond, urging me on with her silence. "There are people, a person, who could care about me, who does care about me, and I can't let him. Not completely."

"Why can't you?" she asks.

Why can't I? Wanting love feels like too much to ask for in a life that's already given me more than I deserve. How can I expect love from anyone when my own mother can't love me? I mean, moms are the easy ones, and I can't even get that.

"He's good," I whisper.

"Michie," she begins, "I speak with a lot of kids, some in your situation and some not. And do you know what you have that a lot of kids struggle with?"

I don't answer. I have no idea.

"Heart, Michie. You have so much heart. Everyone loves

245

you the minute they meet you. You project so much kindness into the world, and you do it without expecting any of it in return. There aren't a lot of people like that. You are so much more than you allow yourself to see." I hear the shuffle of the phone on her end. I hope I didn't get her out of bed. "Do you remember when I visited you in the hospital last summer? What we talked about?"

Honestly, I've blocked out as much of it as I could. I thought that was the whole point. I remember hating her then, for not letting me die.

"We talked about your grandmother."

I lift my head. "What?"

"Your grandmother. You told me what happened with the pills and why you took them. Your grandma was at work, and you were home alone, and being alone felt ... *heavier* ... than usual."

I do remember. I remember the bottle of pills on my nightstand. The way I convinced myself that if one pill could make me happy for a minute, two would make me happy for two minutes, and all of them would make me eternally blissful. I knew that meant dying. I wanted that at the time. I don't anymore, but I did then. It seemed easier, to be happy forever somewhere that wasn't here, where the pain resided. I don't even remember what triggered the whole thing. I don't remember what made me sadder than usual, sad enough to finally do it. You can hurt only so much before you need to unload it.

"But you called me. Scared. And you lifted *yourself* from the fog. You didn't even need me. You did that, and do you remember why?" This time she doesn't wait for me to answer. "You said, *She can't lose someone else she loves.* You saved your own life because even then, you knew you mattered to someone and you didn't want to hurt her. And I thought it was beautiful, wanting to live for your grandmother. But Michie, you need to want it for yourself. And not just living, but *really* living, thriving."

A silent tear slips down my face and settles onto my lip as I listen to her. "Michie, I don't understand how you feel. I don't understand how any of you kids manage it. You're all stronger than I could ever hope to be. You believe she hates you because you think she should, that you deserve it, that you're bad. But you aren't. You're allowed to feel pain, for how Renee's treated you and for the things she's said. You're allowed to miss her. Sometimes we miss the things that hurt us, even when we shouldn't. And that's okay. But you're good, Michie. You are so, so good."

"More," I whisper, more to myself than to her.

"So much more," she repeats. We sit on the phone in silence. No one has ever told me I'm good. They've told me I'm loved and I'm deserving and I'm too hard on myself. But not good. I didn't know I needed anyone to. But I did. And maybe Renee does too. She doesn't know I'm good. But I can tell her. I can show her. And if she sees that I'm good, maybe she'll want to be a part of my life again.

JoJo moves across the floor above me.

"Are you okay? Do I need to call someone?" Dr. Schwartz asks.

"I'm okay," I say, and I mean it. I am okay, or I will be. Because I've decided.

"You've come too far to stop now. So keep going," she says before hanging up.

"I will."

"Call me back if you want to talk again. I'm here, always."

"I know." I nod, even though she can't see me.

"Have a good night, Michie."

I hang up first and stare down at the phone. I dial another number, this one by heart.

"You get in safe?" Grandma asks.

"Yeah, we're home," I say. I blurt out the rest before I can change my mind. "I want to see Renee."

She is silent for a moment, and I hear her bed rustle beneath her as she sits up.

"Are you sure?"

"I'm sure."

"Okay," she says.

"Okay."

CHAPTER TWENTY-SEVEN

I CLOSE MY LAPTOP ON THE CAFÉ COUNTER. IN THE WEEK since I decided to see Renee, I've finally made progress on my scholarship essay.

JoJo sits at the counter with an open SAT vocabulary book she's been putting me through like a drill sergeant. Even though the café is empty, I ask her to watch the counter while I handle some business. Or, you know, go meddle some more.

Peter is sitting quietly in the reading nook, staring through a stained-glass pane of the front window. He got here pretty quick after I sent him a 9-1-1 text, which he knew was bullshit because he's been sitting quietly. He must still be upset about Monica, because *sitting quietly* aren't two words I would have used to describe him before today.

"Hey, Petey," I sing, dropping down beside him.

"No," he says with a shake of his head.

"Yeah, I know." I drag my hand through his already messed up hair, but only because I know he secretly likes it.

"So, where's the fire?" he asks. "I was in the middle of a game."

"Aw, you went offline for me?" I ask.

"Michie." He twists away from my hand. His eyes bulge as the front door swings open. "Michie." He says it with more apprehension now. "What did you do?"

I turn around to find Monica approaching us. I shouldn't be surprised since I invited them both here, but part of me still is. Like, wow, people do stuff without making a big fuss about it even when they know you're up to something. You love to see it.

"Hey," she says, standing in front of us.

"Take a seat," I say, moving from the cushions so she can sit. I drag a chair up in front of them. They sit with an awkward amount of distance between them. "So thanks for both coming today." I sound like a Maury introduction.

"Why are we here, Michie?" I lean away from Peter to avoid any fire he breathes. Despite Monica being the more annoyed one via text, Peter for sure carries the torch in person.

"I screwed up, and it's not important how, but somewhere along the way I overstepped my boundaries. I was trying to help because I thought you liked each other, and that was unfair because I inferred things Monica never said, which led to both of you getting hurt, and I feel awful about it." I take a deep breath, having spoken in one long unending sentence. "I love you both and want us to go back to being friends."

Monica raises her hand, like she does in group. It's so normal I almost laugh. But I don't. Because I can keep it together once in a while. And I don't want either of them to murder me.

"You didn't misinterpret anything," Monica says so quietly I can barely hear her. But I get confirmation when Peter falls out of the window seat. Monica turns to look at him. "I did like you. Do like you."

"You told me to kick rocks," Peter says.

"I know." Monica sighs. "I thought you were better off. I mean, my life is a mess. I'm probably getting kicked out of the first home I've ever loved in a month when I turn eighteen, and then what? No one needs all those extra problems."

"Wait," Peter says, "you think I care about any of that?"

Monica shrugs in response.

"I don't. I mean, yeah, our lives are fucked up. If they weren't, none of us would have ever met. We'd be, like, normies."

Peter reaches for her hand, and after the most pregnant pause in history, her fingers close around his. She smiles behind a curtain of now-pink hair since the red has faded.

"Well, now that my job here is done," I say, slapping my

thighs before standing. "Unless you want me to stick around and—"

"Goodbye, Michie," Peter and Monica say in unison.

Okay, I see how it is. You pull off one monumental matchup, and suddenly you're chopped liver. I glance back at them as I return to the counter, where JoJo is now making her way through the candy dish. It's kind of wild. All three of us came from the same place, and somehow, it's so much easier to find them deserving of each other than I ever found myself deserving of Derek.

"All sorted?" JoJo asks around a Twizzler.

"Yup. I should open a matchmaking business," I answer.

"No, you should not."

"Ouch," I say, swiping the candy dish from beneath her nose. I would have been better at it if she were a more engaged Dionne, but I keep that to myself since I sort of volunteered her for the role.

"At least you worked it out and learned something all at the same time."

"And what exactly did I learn?" I ask.

JoJo stands up and makes her way to the bookshelf. "You learned that people meant to be together don't need intervention." She raises an eyebrow at me. "It'll happen."

"Okay, Dr. Phil," I laugh. "Queen Meddler lecturing me on meddling. The irony."

She pulls a battered copy of *Red Rising* from the shelf, followed by a *Buffy* graphic novel omnibus. Peter and Monica wave as they pull their rain jackets over their heads and make their way out into the storm.

Sip and Serendipity is quiet as heavy rain pounds down. Hail comes down in sharp pellets, hitting the ground with a constant knocking. I place JoJo's peppermint-tangerine hot chocolate in front of her, and she scoops a fingerful of whipped cream off the top and stuffs it into her mouth.

"So, you never told me what happened the other night with Lover Boy." She dips another Twizzler into her hot chocolate.

"What are you talking about?" I gape at her. "I told you."

"No, you told me what you talked about. I want to know"—she winks at me—"what *happened*. You were in his car forever. Two plus two equals tongue."

"JoJo, ew."

She groans, her eyes rolling so far back, she must be able to see her own brain.

"At least admit you want to see him naked."

"Are you going to grow up anytime soon?" I ask.

"No thanks," she shrugs. "God, you two are so boring."

"I'll have you know, we held hands for, like, twenty minutes." I wince. I don't think that helps my case.

"You held hands? Slow down, tiger," she exclaims, clutching at her chest. "God, you managed to find the one teenage boy on the planet with the patience of Job. When I saw him in Calc the next day, he still looked like he was walking on cotton candy. And when I asked him the same question I'm asking you now, the poor boy got redder than a chili pepper. So?"

"Nothing happened," I say in slow motion.

She drops her forehead to the counter. "I give you the perfect opening, and you both squander it. What am I even doing here?"

"Didn't you just say people meant to be together don't require intervention?"

"They do when one is a saboteur!" She looks exasperated. "Tell me something interesting, at least."

I pull out the register till to close it down before my shift ends. Normally I'd do it in the back office, but the café's empty, and I'm a little worried JoJo will eat every piece of candy in the jar if I leave her here.

I do have one thing I still haven't told her. But if I want her to come with me, then I need to. Now.

"I'm going to see Renee."

JoJo chokes on hot chocolate. "Renee, like your mother, Renee?"

"The one and only. She reached out, and I went back and forth on it for a while, but it's time."

"Wow," she sputters, wheezing to clear hot chocolate from her throat. "Are you ready for that?"

"I guess I was waiting for the right time, but there'll never be one. So I might as well...jump."

She leaps off the stool and is around the counter in an instant, pulling me into a back-breaking hug.

"I'm so proud of you it hurts." She speaks into my hair as she squeezes even tighter. My ribs groan, but I don't move away. Only a hug like this can break you and glue you back together at the same time.

She pulls away, but her hands stay planted on my shoulders. "Where is she now?"

"Still in Houston," I respond, my hands recounting the singles in the till.

JoJo whistles. "So not a day trip."

"Not a day trip," I agree.

"When are you going? Spring break? Summer?"

"Next Tuesday." I slam the till closed as an exclamation point on the plan. Its ring echoes around the empty café.

"Next Tuesday, as in..." She counts off the days on her fingers. "Nine days from now? Why?"

"I need to go before the SAT." Which is in exactly thirteen days.

"Because?"

"I phoned in the first test because I took it thinking the outcome didn't matter—whatever happened would be more than I deserved. I mean college? What right did I have to any of the things Renee couldn't do because of me? At least that *was* my thinking."

"Keep going. I'll get there."

"I don't want to go into the test again with all this crap in the way, all this baggage." Monica and Peter are climbing their way out from beneath theirs. I need to do the same.

"I'm ready this time, thanks to you, and I want to do well. That not-good-enough feeling already sabotaged my first try and my interview. But if I see Renee before the test…"

"It's like lightening the load," she finishes.

"Right, exactly. Plus, in the triple whammy of reasons, I owe Milligan a new essay. This Renee thing is like a Zadie Smith novel, but someone ripped out the last chapter. I need to know how it ends before I can figure out what the rest of the book meant."

"Okay." JoJo nods. "But what if it doesn't go well—not that I think it won't—but what if it doesn't, and you're even more messed up?"

Which is something I've thought about. It's all I've thought about.

"Then I guess I have nothing to lose. Either it goes well, and I come back ready to kick some ass, or I get emotionally body slammed and bomb the test the same way I would have anyway."

She tilts her head to the side like she does when someone's made a good point. "But why Tuesday? Why not this weekend?"

"Because you have a run-through for the college fair this weekend," I say. "And I need you to go with me."

"Go with you to Houston in nine days?"

JoJo hasn't missed a single day of school in her entire life. It's a tall ask, so I'll allow myself only a modicum of disappointment if she says no. She dips her finger in the chocolate sauce settled at the bottom of her empty mug.

"For how long?"

"Leave Tuesday, come back Friday. SAT Saturday."

The seconds stretch as the silence extends around us.

"Okay," she decides. "But only if we study on the plane."

"You're not even going to think about it?"

"I thought about it. That was a solid three minutes of hard-core thinking."

She pulls her phone from her purse and starts typing. When she lays it on the counter, it's open to a flight-scanner app, zipping through dozens of sites to find the best deals. "I assume you haven't gotten your ticket yet?"

"No," I admit. "I didn't want to go alone if you said no." Though the truth is, I thought she or Grandma would talk me out of this, since it is a little nuts. But neither has, and now I'm both stuck and liberated by the decision.

"And you're positive you want to go? No doubts?"

I have nothing but doubts. But I'm still positive, so I nod. She picks the phone back up, navigating through the pages. My phone vibrates in my apron, but I ignore it.

"Your grandma too?" she asks, still tapping on her phone screen.

"No."

JoJo finger hovers over the screen. "I'm doing it. Stop me if you dare."

"Doing what?" I crane my neck to see her screen. Expedia.

She turns the screen back to her and presses a button. "Done, then."

My phone vibrates again. Reality settles in. "Wait, did you just get tickets?" Part of me kind of thought it was all performative, like she was testing to see if I was serious.

"Yup. Three tickets booked for next Tuesday. Well, two tickets. I forwarded the link to Derek to get his own. I don't know his birthday. Or middle name. American Airlines. They have the best movies." She drops her phone to the bottom of her purse. I stop midreach for my own.

"What do you mean, Derek?" I squeak. "And Emmanuel. His middle name's Emmanuel." After his grandfather.

"Derek wants to come, so he's coming," she says. She wipes her mouth with a cloth napkin and tosses it down on the counter, carrying her dirty mug to the large, dented metal sink. She nods at the till. "You done?"

I put the till back in the register and slam the drawer closed. "How could he want to come? He doesn't even know about it. I just told you thirty seconds ago."

She taps her waist and points to my apron, my phone bulky in the front pocket. I rip it off and slide my phone out. The raise-to-wake triggers, and there is a series of unread messages from the group chat. JoJo posted the flight itinerary with a question mark and *Michie Mom Mission* in parentheses. Derek responded with a thumbs-up emoji. It had all gone down in less than five minutes.

"You're scary sometimes."

"So they say." She pushes the door open with her back. I lock it as fast as I can, hail pelting down my neck.

In the safety of her car, from the hail if not her driving, I look at the flight details and almost drop my phone.

"Six hundred dollars?" I blanch. "Each? Are you crazy?" Mooching off her streaming services and accepting some clothes every once in a while is way different from spending a rent payment. "There is no way I can let you pay that."

"It's already done." She taps her forehead like a mastermind. "Dad's platinum. Don't worry; he won't even notice." She sets the heater to high and clicks on both seat warmers. "Besides, what do you expect? We're flying halfway across the country in less than two weeks. And my private jet is booked, on account that it doesn't exist. It's not like we have a cheaper option."

My stomach sinks. "It's too much. Way too much. And it's not your responsibility. Grandma and I already talked about splitting it. Her extra shifts plus my extra tips."

"Well, now neither of you need to do that. It's not like y'all don't work hard enough already. And it's a necessary purchase. I can practically write it off," she says. "Besides, I owe you way more than that."

"Okay, David Rose, what are you talking about? When have I ever loaned you six hundred bucks? When have I ever loaned you *twenty* bucks?"

"Not literally," she says. "But in essence. The good friend IOU. Consider it payment for all the food and lodging I've used at your house since we were thirteen. With interest."

I stare at her. "JoJo, we do that because we love you, not because you owe us anything."

"I shall show my appreciation however I deem fit. And getting you to Houston is what I deem fit. Can you look up Airbnb spots in Houston?" she asks, pulling out.

She picks my phone up off my lap and puts it back in my hands, pushing it toward my face. She glances over and sees my stricken facade. "Okay, don't panic. I'm only being heavy-handed because I know you. And if one of us doesn't do it, you'll paralyze yourself into inaction. But if you want me to stop and let you feel it out, then say the word."

Breaths rise from my chest in broken hiccups.

"In through the nose, out through the mouth," she instructs, demonstrating, and I follow her lead. It's the only thing that always works. The nurse taught her that when she came to visit me in the hospital, how to help me. She tried so hard to make my life feel normal afterward. I don't know what I ever did to deserve her. "My parents suck *today*, but ten years is a long time. You have the chance at something better. I want that for you."

This is why I needed her to go. She'll make sure it happens, even if I can't.

She taps the phone in my frozen hands. "Airbnb," she urges.

But I stare down at the blank screen, unmoving.

"What if she doesn't actually want to see me?" I whisper, giving a voice to the core of my fear. "What if I get there and she turns me away?"

"Then it's her loss," JoJo says, reaching over to squeeze

my shoulder. "But this isn't about what she wants. It's about what you want. And if you get there and she turns you away, then at least you know there's nothing more you could've done. And then we turn around and come back to our lives."

Two hours later, Derek, JoJo, and I are all crashed in her den theater with *Black Widow* on the screen.

Derek stretches out his legs, even though he's already taking up two oversized seats on the sectional. He manages to keep his shoulder pressed against my hip, his head resting on my upper arm. It's like wearing a weighted blanket, except he smells like warm spices. His hand dangles in the popcorn bowl in my lap, a responsibility I have taken on by sitting in the middle.

JoJo wipes her hands on her jeans, now covered with butter stains. She's focused on her phone, orchestrating a doctor's note to get her out of school next week.

"What sounds more believable?" she asks. "Bronchitis or measles?"

"Measles? Is this the 1800s?" He laughs.

"I'll have you know," she retorts. "Measles weren't declared eliminated until 2000. And they're the comeback kid of the anti-vax movement."

"Now you've started her," I mutter, turning my attention back to the screen. It's like a battle of the brains.

JoJo settles for bronchitis after Derek reminds her that

she's already been vaccinated for measles, unless she wants to create a new strain and cause the next disease crisis.

"Don't you remember the bird flu and Ebola reactions? Coronavirus? My mom wouldn't let me play in leagues for a year." He rolls his eyes, and it's such a rare movement of his facial muscles that it looks painful.

Grandma already called the school and told them I would be out for a family thing. Derek's a second-semester senior three months from graduation, and basketball season is over, so no one cares anymore whether or not he's there.

"Okay, okay," she concedes. "How does this sound?" She clears her throat like a politician, smoothing her hair from her forehead. "Dr. Hamil—he likes to be called *doctor*; it's how you win him over," she interrupts herself to explain. "Okay. Dr. Hamil, Joanna—my mom would use my full name, right?" she interrupts herself again.

"JoJo, read the damn thing and we'll tell you how it sounds." I knock her leg with my foot.

"Duh, okay." She clears her throat again, and I wonder if we'll ever hear the letter. "Dr. Hamil, Joanna is ill with bronchitis, which may be a rare case of the measles. She will not be in attendance this week as we explore the best options for her health. I would appreciate her teachers making allowances upon her return. Veronica Kaplan née Khoury."

Derek doubles over with laughter as she finishes. "Are you trying to convey that you're dying a slow death or out for a few days? Because one of those, you have achieved."

"Whatever, it's perfect." She prints it through her Wi-Fi.

"Did you ever talk to your mom about moving to Chicago?" I ask.

"Not yet," she replies. "I was going to, but then I thought I should wait until after the fair. I mean, I might hate it."

"Fair," I say, "but you could also love it."

"And if I do, then I'll talk to her about it. Promise." She leaps off the couch to grab the letter from the printer in her mom's office.

Derek and I watch her ascend the stairs, her footsteps soundless on the carpet.

He drops his head back against my arm, dragging a handful of popcorn into his mouth. I listen to his teeth work against the half-popped kernels.

"Is it weird to be so scared?" I ask. He reaches his arm across my legs to grab my hand.

"It'd be weird if you weren't scared."

"This could go terribly, couldn't it?"

"It could. But it might not. It might be great."

I doubt that very much. But I appreciate his optimism.

"And even if it sucks," he continues, "you can't control if she hurts you. But you can control if she breaks you."

Derek turns his head upward to me, and his freckles stand out like rest stops on the road map of his every emotion. He lifts himself up and swings his legs around until his feet are on the floor. He moves the popcorn bowl and wraps his arm around my shoulders, pulling me down to his lap. His fingers lace into the curls at the base of my neck.

I faintly hear JoJo storm back down the stairs and the couch cushions dip as she plops back down. She grabs my curled-up legs and pulls them onto her lap. I doze off, feeling complete peace from the tip of my head to the tips of my toes.

CHAPTER TWENTY-EIGHT

I'M FIRST IN THE ROOM FOR GROUP ON TUESDAY, ONE week out from when JoJo, Derek, and I board a plane to Houston.

"Michie," Dr. Schwartz says, looking at the large clock hanging above the door. "You're early." She sounds surprised.

"Yeah, the bus was early. Or, well, it was on time for once."

"Well, I'm happy to see you. Have a seat anywhere, of course."

I drop onto my usual spot on the couch. I missed last session for Derek's basketball game, and the cushions have forgotten my shape in the interim.

"I actually wanted to speak with you," she says, approaching and sitting beside me on the couch. "Now seems as good a time as any."

My muscles tighten. Other than our phone call, I haven't spoken to her one-on-one, in person, since The Incident.

"I wanted to check in. See if you're feeling better since our last chat." She's sitting too close, but it'll be rude if I scoot away.

"I'm okay. Good, actually. Sorry I called you so late."

"You can call me anytime you need to," she says. "But that's great." I smile and she relaxes. "That's really great, Michie." She reaches to squeeze my shoulder.

"Ayo," Peter announces himself as he walks in the room, Monica following close behind. Her fingers are linked between his as they squeeze together on the couch.

I look at them with what I'm sure is the goofiest, most ecstatic grin.

"Hey, Mich," Monica says. She smiles so wide I imagine she'll never be able to wriggle her face from its impression.

"Hi, guys." I look pointedly down at their hands. "I'm happy for y'all."

"You're the one who told me to get my head out of my ass," Peter says.

"I didn't quite put it that way."

He rolls his eyes. Monica mouths a *thank you* and squeezes his hand. This room holds so many of our tears; it's high time it held our joy.

The rest of the group trickles in, settling into their usual places. Dr. Schwartz takes her place on the floor.

"It's wonderful to have the full group this week." She catches my eye. "Who wants to start?"

I raise my hand. Her eyebrows raise. In seven months, I have never volunteered.

"Yes, Michie, go ahead." She folds her hands in her lap.

"I—" I pause. The people in this room know how much Renee has affected me, so they're the scariest to tell. "I'm going to see Renee, my mom."

There's an audible holding of breaths. Peter stills beside me. Dr. Schwartz's face is unreadable. Everyone weighs the words, trying them on for size.

"When? Where?" Monica is the first to speak.

"Next week. In Houston."

"Wow," she says. "That's huge. Congratulations." She smiles. I don't know what I expected. How could I ever think these people wouldn't be happy for me?

"That is huge," Dr. Schwartz agrees.

"Are you scared?" Han asks.

"Yeah," I admit. "I'm scared."

"Of what?" Dr. Schwartz prods.

I shift on the couch. "I don't know. All this time I thought she didn't know me, and that makes it easier for her not to want me. But what if she knows me, and she still doesn't want me? What happens then?"

Everyone is silent, thinking about the correct answer, if there even is one.

"Who cares?" Peter finally says. "It's not important, is it? You're gonna be the same person. You're still gonna be funny as hell. You're still gonna read too many books and listen to too much rap, instead of the heavy metal you should listen to." We all laugh. "Nothing's gonna change. Might as well go to Houston, rock out with your—" Dr. Schwartz clears her throat. Peter rolls his eyes. "Just go do your thing, Cooper, and if she accepts that, then cool, and if she doesn't, well, we still got your back."

Before I can stop myself, I pull him into my side, wrapping him in a tight hug.

"That was very well put, Peter," Dr. Schwartz says. "Thank you."

"That's all you, Doc," he says, his voice muffled as he wrenches himself from my grip. "What's that you're always saying, life is about choices? Well, I choose to not let our parents tell us who we are. How about we tell them for a change?"

"Or show them," Monica says, squeezing his hand.

In her silence, I've let Renee tell me a lot. That I'm the problem. That existing is my fault. That I'm both too little and too much. Too small yet larger than life. Peter's right. I might as well do my thing.

The rest of the group shares their updates. Some good mixed with some bad. Peter and Monica get a hard time for dating, the kind of ridicule that can be delivered only by friends who are over the moon for you.

"Man, y'all are like my baby brother and sister," Lindell says. "Shit's weird."

Dr. Schwartz doesn't tell him to watch his language.

She's too busy laughing alongside us. Sometimes I wonder what it's like for her, seeing us grow from the lost kids we were to the adults we're becoming. Who knows where we'd all be if we still thought we were in this thing alone? I remember when I thought I was the only one. It seems silly now, but when you believe something like that, it's easy to think you're expendable. I mean, you're just one person. But there are more of us, and it's not until I see our worth as a group that I began to realize that the only way a group has value is if each of its parts have value. And I am one of those parts. We all are, and Dr. Schwartz brought us together. I don't know if anyone up there is keeping score, but I can count five lives she's saved.

To send me off with good vibes for my trip, Monica proposes a group hug at the end of our session. Han joins by placing his hand on my shoulder. They all wish me luck as they empty from the room. I wave at Dr. Schwartz. I don't know who I'll be when I see her again.

I turn and slam into a body.

Oof. I use the wall for balance. "Sorry, that was my bad."

"No, that was me."

I look up. Trish Peterson is standing in front of me, wide-eyed. She could be a mom right now. But she's not. She looks brighter than the last time I saw her. More alive. More at peace.

"We have to stop meeting this way," she says with a soft laugh.

"Right," I say, attempting to step around her.

She moves in front of me.

"You go to Lee, right?" she asks.

"Yeah," I say. "Junior."

"Right. I think we had gym freshman year. Ms. Harper?"

"Yeah, wow, what a weird class."

She laughs again. "Ugh, yeah. Remember that CPR class? Those little babies freaked me out." She pauses as if someone has played her words back to her. She looks down at her feet, and I see the subtle shake of her hands.

"Well, it was nice to see you," I say, moving to step around her again. She lets me this time.

"Hey, actually," she says. I pause and turn back to her. "Do you..." She points at Dr. Schwartz's door with a thumb. "Do you see her? Dr. Schwartz?"

I don't know what to say. It's actually a deeply personal question to ask someone. I can admit I'm in therapy; plenty of people are and more should be. But I don't know if she knows what type of therapist Dr. Schwartz is or if she cares Dr. Schwartz spends half her time trying to convince kids like me, kids who could've been Trish's baby, kids who feel like they should have been, that they matter.

"I just—" She speaks like she's nervous. "I've been trying people out. My OB recommended her for my—" She looks at me and then remembers that I probably already know. The good ol' high school rumor mill. "Situation. I wasn't trying to pry or anything. Is she any good?"

Part of me wants to lie. The petty part that wants Dr. Schwartz to stay on our team, the R.P.E. kids' team. But I can't judge Trish for her choices, even if they chill me to the core. It's no use to think about what her baby would have become. All that matters now is what Trish will become. I turn to the now-closed door. Five lives. It could be six.

I look back at Trish. She wants someone to talk to. Needs someone to talk to. I know that feeling. Some battles can't be fought alone.

"Yeah, Dr. Schwartz is the best," I say.

She smiles, straightening her shoulders. Her knuckles rap against the wood. I move to leave the building but stop at the door.

"Hey, Trish?"

"Yeah?" She smooths her hair behind an ear.

"Are you okay?" I shove aside the *how could you*s. It's none of my business.

She considers my question. "No," she admits.

"You will be." I walk out of the building as Dr. Schwartz's door swings open.

CHAPTER TWENTY-NINE

"TWO QUESTIONS." DEREK BOMBARDS ME BEFORE I'VE made it five steps into the building, matching his long strides to my shorter ones.

"Yes, you still need a light sweater in Houston. And no, I will not get on any mechanical bulls," I reply. I meant to answer both in the group chat this morning, but I was too busy listening to JoJo's fake coughs on FaceTime to determine which one sounded the most contagious. Twenty-four hours until we board our plane and it's Shenanigans City.

"Thank you. But I was going to ask if you like chicken tikka masala? My mom's on this whole Indian cuisine kick."

"Um, yes?" I twist around to face him, unsure why I need

to have an opinion on his mom's culinary interests. "Why? And that's only one question."

"Because my second question is if you'll have dinner at my house tonight?"

"Like with your parents?" I don't know how to do parents.

"And my little sister," he confirms. "Though as you'll soon find out, that isn't particularly comforting."

"Do I have a choice?"

"The parentals are insisting." A sheepish expression settles into his worry lines. "It's their one condition for letting me go to Houston without adult supervision. The whole *We should meet this girl you're flying across the country with* thing. Especially since I've told them the fate of the free world depends on this trip."

I suck my teeth. Technically, we have adult supervision. Him, since he's already eighteen. But I doubt that will sell our case.

"Um, yeah, I guess." Meeting his parents feels serious, real. If they don't like me, will he listen to them?

"Cool. Meet at my car after Calc." He gives a small wave before rushing off to first period.

As soon as he's out of sight, I call JoJo, praying she's still at school, but it goes straight to voice mail. The automatic voice message she's never bothered to change tells me her inbox is full. I text Grandma to tell her I'll be home late. I haven't spent much time with her in the last couple of months, and I had hoped we could hang out tonight watching Food Network over pizza. I try texting JoJo this time.

MICHIE COOPER AT 8:01 A.M.: EMERGENCY CALL BACK.

JOJO KAPLAN AT 8:02 A.M.: Nurse's office. Laryngitis.

MICHIE COOPER AT 8:02 A.M.: what happened to bronchitis?

JOJO KAPLAN AT 8:02 A.M.: Yeah, laryngitis brought on by hacking cough from bronchitis.

MICHIE COOPER AT 8:02 A.M.: oh my god.

MICHIE COOPER AT 8:02 A.M.: derek invited me to dinner with his parents…

I visualize her spit take. The typing dots flash on the screen and then disappear. There are few things that make Joanna Gertrude Kaplan speechless.

JOJO KAPLAN AT 8:03 A.M.: Woah

MICHIE COOPER AT 8:03 A.M.: HELP ME

JOJO KAPLAN AT 8:04 A.M.: Relax. His parents seem super nice and normal.

JOJO KAPLAN AT 8:04 A.M.: Nurse coming back. Be chill.

By English, I have come up with twenty-two reasons why this is a terrible idea, and twenty-one of them are keyboard smashes.

Gwen slams her books down on the desk in front of me. I reach the eraser end of my pencil forward and poke her in the back.

"You know, in some countries that's assault," she argues

as she spins around, throwing her arm over the back of her chair.

"In some countries, it's a love tap. Have you met Bridget's parents?" I ask.

"Maritza and Leonard? Yeah, why?"

"What do you guys talk about?"

"Normal stuff," she answers. "College, work, home ownership. I don't know." She takes in my shell-shocked expression. "I assume you're meeting Derek's parents, since y'all are thirty-two seconds from sending your save the dates."

I huff in objection.

She laughs. "I'm sorry, but the two of you always look like you want to crawl into each other's skin. And he stamped his name on that ass at Senior Night. It's not exactly a leap."

I mentally object to having an ass that is stampable by a guy, but her point is taken.

Mr. Milligan attempts to call the class to order.

"The boy is in love with you," she says quickly, trying to get it all out before Mr. Milligan starts. "You'd have to wish dishonor on his entire family and his cow for Derek to ever stop having stars in his eyes around you. Answer some questions about your hobbies, don't insult the food, and you'll be fine."

What is up with rich people and hobbies? Jesus Christ.

Derek is standing beside his car like he promised, drumming his fingers on the hood to the music always in his head.

"Sorry I'm late," I apologize.

"No worries. My mom sent me a long list of stuff to get for the trip if you don't mind a Target stop. We have a couple hours until dinner."

"I never mind a Target stop," I answer. "Plus, Target is a cheaper serotonin boost than therapy and I could definitely use some of that before dinner."

We spend the next two hours in Target grabbing random items from every aisle. I stuff a brand-new honey leave-in conditioner I want to try, a cropped sweatshirt in pink tie-dye, and a marble-print planner I will probably never open into my backpack when we get back to the car. He sets a plastic bag filled with empty airplane-approved bottles, body wash, and mini toothpaste down by my feet.

As we make our way to his house, the yards start to spread out until neighborhoods cease to exist and houses take up entire streets, corner to corner. His face is scarlet. We've moved from the rich to the disgustingly wealthy part of Richmond.

"Derek," I ask, "what do your parents do?" How have I never asked this question before? The houses are now set so far back I can't see them past their winding driveways.

"My dad owns a tech company," he says. "My mom's a surgeon."

I've never met a Black female surgeon. That's pretty cool.

"What kind of surgeon? What kind of tech company?"

The fact that they moved here from San Francisco makes sense.

"Cardiothoracic," he answers. "And a small one." He glances in his rearview mirror for all the cars that aren't there.

I narrow my eyes at him and he twitches.

"PignusUltra," he sighs.

I take out my phone and plug the name into Google. A blurry photo of his dad pops up on the main page, followed by a Wikipedia description. My eyes scan the company's blurb.

> PignusUltra is a security operating system recently acquired by the US Department of Defense in one of the largest government contracts in the country's history. It is currently the most advanced artificial intelligence system on the market and has been deemed by the Fortress Cyber Security Awards to be the future of artificial intelligence and military operations. Dr. Carlos de la Rosa, the founder and CEO of PignusUltra, was recently awarded the Millennium Technology Prize, the world's most prestigious technology award.

I stare at the words in disbelief.

"Small," I shriek. "Your dad is Tony Stark." Why the hell is this guy in freaking public school?

"It's not a big deal," he replies.

But I can't respond. My mouth hangs open as we pull up to a steel gate at the end of his driveway, bookended by stone walls that wrap around the property.

It swings open, revealing a long, cobbled path that draws into a wide circle at the end. There's a fountain. A goddamn fountain. My apartment building could fit inside the house at least ten times with room to spare. I never knew people who looked like us could have so much.

"Are you kidding me?" I sputter. "Oh, you are so dead."

I look down at my ripped jeans and dirty Converses, blue Sharpie flowers etched into the hard white plastic of the toes. I am going into the house of one of the most powerful men in the country, probably the world, in a sweatshirt with the Golden Girls and *Stay Golden* ironed on.

"You have to take me home, right now."

"It'll be fine," he urges as he climbs out of the car.

I stay seated, grasping my seat belt like a life raft. He walks around the car in three strides and opens my door.

"Come on." He holds his hand out.

"No." I cross my arms in defiance. There is no way I'm meeting his parents at the Afro-Latino Stark Enterprise with sneakers that have holes in them, jeans that have holes in them, and a sweatshirt that will have holes in it if I raise my arms. Hard, hard pass.

"You're being ridiculous," he says.

"If you're the richest person in the country, it should come up at some point."

"You never asked me what my parents do. And you're so weird about money. I didn't want you snatching at another reason to not do this." He wiggles his finger between the two of us. "Besides, I'm not rich. My parents are. And we're not even close to the richest. Jeff Bezos and his ex-wife share that crown." If that's supposed to be comforting, it isn't. Jeff Bezos's toilet paper is worth more than my entire existence.

He leans into the car and unbuckles my seat belt. He grabs my hands and pulls me out. "Are you going to make me carry you in?"

"This is kidnapping," I object, as he reaches back in the car to grab my backpack and the Target bag from the floorboard.

"You got in the car of your own volition." He puts my backpack on his back, the plastic bag around his wrist, and grabs my hand, pulling me with a firm grip toward the front doors. Plural.

"These jeans are missing a pocket," I moan as he slides his key into the locked door. "And this is a three-day-old twist out."

He smirks but continues on unhindered, pushing through the front door. I imagined a dungeon-type foyer for the, pretty much, security head of the world, but it's cozier than I anticipated. The setting sun spreads an orange glow through colossal bay windows spanning the length of the house. It smells like curry and herbs, and sweet laughter travels from the next room. He drops the bags on a pile by the front door.

I follow his lead and remove my sneakers. At least they won't see the Sharpie flowers.

"Mamá," he calls. The laughter pauses.

A small figure moving like a dart slams into Derek. Derek squats and wraps his arms around the girl. His sister, I presume. She's willowy knobbiness that hasn't grown into her limbs, but she shares his scattered freckles. Her head burrows into his neck.

He stands, but keeps his arm around her shoulders. She's almost as tall as I am, though that isn't a hard thing to accomplish.

"Juliet, meet Michie. Michie, my little sister, Juliet."

Juliet shoots her hand out toward me like a small politician. "Hi, Michie," she says, giving my hand two firm pumps.

Derek's mom circles around the large bookcases separating the foyer from the rest of the house, and it's the most nervous I have ever been in my life. She wipes her hands on her jeans.

"Hi there." Her curly hair is pulled up into a pineapple, and she has a dish towel over her shoulder, feet bare. "You're early."

I'm pulled into a tight hug. She smells like vanilla with the undertones of turmeric. Is this how all moms smell? I like it.

She hugs Derek next, standing on the tips of her toes to wrap her arms around his neck and kiss him on the cheek.

"Mom, this is Michie." He wiggles out of her grasp.

She has the kindest face I've ever seen. "I remember, from the game." She puts her arm on my back, higher up than Derek does, but with the same light push to direct me through the house. The floor plan opens up to a bright kitchen and dining area, with crisp white cabinets and a large island in the center.

"Are you guys hungry?" she asks, pulling a package of Double Stuf Oreo cookies from the pantry. The name-brand kind. Juliet rips into the bag before it even hits the countertop. I stare at them in disbelief. "Those are the right ones?" She looks at Derek for confirmation.

Derek has told me a hundred times they never have junk food at home. She'd gotten my favorite cookies, the fancy version, for a dinner I found out about five hours ago.

"Yeah, thanks, Mom," Derek answers, sitting down on a bar stool at the island. I pull myself up beside him, though it takes more of a leap. Everything here seems set up for tall people, though Mrs. De la Rosa is tiny.

"Great." She turns her attention back to the stove to stir. Two separate ovens have timers going.

Juliet sits down on my other side. "What cabin are you in?" she asks around a mouthful of cookies. Her fingers are already covered with Oreo dust. I'm waiting for their mom to scold her about table manners or something, but she never does.

"Oh, uh, Poseidon," I respond, remembering she's a huge Percy Jackson fan too.

She nods, accepting that answer. "I'm Ares."

"I like Ares," I lie.

"Of course you do," she says, as if it's an honor to be in her Ares demigod presence. She points at Derek while reaching for another cookie. "He's Demeter."

We both chuckle.

"Do I want to know why that's funny?" he asks. He's split an Oreo open and is eating the inside filling.

"It means you're a loser." Her eyes roll as she places her fingers, shaped in an *L*, against her forehead. Definitely an Ares.

"Mija," Mrs. De la Rosa scolds. I didn't know she also speaks Spanish, but it makes sense. Juliet turns her focus to the cookies stacked in her hands.

"It means you're nurturing," I explain. His eyes brighten, and his expression flattens into one I can't decipher. I blush crimson, having no idea where that came from. I have never felt protective of him before, and I certainly don't need to against his own sister.

"Doesn't seem like a loser to me," his mom adds, giving me a knowing smile.

"Um, may I use your bathroom?" I ask. Grandma would kill me if she knew I started eating before washing my hands. It's the nurse in her.

"Oh, of course," she says. "Derek can give you a tour after." She removes the Oreo bag from the countertop, glancing at the stack Juliet has in front of her. "Your dad will be home in twenty minutes," she tells him as he gets up to lead me out.

I splash water onto my face in the bathroom. I stare at my reflection and take deep breaths. Derek is standing outside of the door when I open it. I pray he didn't overhear the pep talk I gave myself in there.

The house is three stories plus a den. The entire top floor is for guests, and the family's bedrooms are on the second. The main floor has the standard living room, kitchen, and dining room, except they're all huge. Plus, there's that extra living room that doesn't get used. Rich people, I swear. A massive emptied and covered pool takes up most of the backyard. A basketball hoop stands to the far right on a paved area, and beyond it the lawn stretches out endlessly. I bet there's a koi pond. They seem like koi-pond people. The den holds a movie room and a huge film collection organized in order of influence on the industry, starting with *Psycho*. None of the steps creak when you put weight on them.

The vastness of his house is overwhelming. But his room is the most surprising.

It's clean, like hospital-corner meticulous. Not that he's a messy person, but I thought boys were supposed to be gross in a cute way. The desk is mostly clear, but comic books and graphic novels are scattered across the top. Limited-edition action figures still in their boxes line his windowsill. Shelves nailed up close to the ceiling hold statues of little gold trophy men with basketballs and medals of all sizes. A collection of autographed baseballs covers one whole shelf of his bookcase.

The room smells like him. Sandalwood and the subtlety of cardamom. I find Old Spice deodorant on his dresser.

The book from the first time we met, *We Have Always Lived in the Castle*, sits on his nightstand. Its cover is still creased in the middle from having been folded in half. I lift it and turn to the dog-eared page. One sentence is underlined in pencil, slightly crooked like I've seen him do many times before.

Slowly the pattern of our days grew, and shaped itself into a happy life.

I trace the words with a finger. I feel him watching me, and I close the book and place it back on the nightstand. There's something intimate about reading the exact same words you know spoke to someone else.

A guitar leans against a corner, music books stacked haphazardly in front of it. I strum my finger over the strings.

"I didn't know you played," I say, strumming a note, if you could call it that.

"Not as well as you." He laughs, and I wish he would never stop.

The flight itinerary and his tickets are printed out on his desk. I grab them and collapse onto the edge of his bed.

"I can't believe we're going," I mutter, mostly to myself.

He sits down beside me, our knees grazing. "I'm proud of you. If I had the chance to do things differently—" He pauses with a gulp.

His face is so close I can connect the constellations of his freckles. Instinctively, I flip my hand over and he folds his into it. His thumb traces my knuckles against the bed. My nerves leap like jumping beans. I glance back up at him and his head lowers, his lips parting.

"Dinner," his mom calls up the stairs. I jump away from him. He leaps off the bed like it's lava.

"We should—" he starts, gesturing toward the hall.

"Yes," I blurt.

He ushers me back downstairs. His mom gives us a conspiratorial glance as we stumble back into the kitchen. Derek's hands are in his front pockets. I wonder if they're shaking as much as mine.

"Papi," a deep voice from behind us rings out. Where Derek's mom is birdsong, his dad is wolf howl. Mr. De la Rosa has the same face as Derek, with a few extra laugh lines and wiser eyes.

He pulls Derek into a bear hug, and a boyish grin spreads across Derek's face. Juliet joins them, only tall enough to wrap herself around their torsos.

"Michie, I assume," he says, pulling away from his children and holding a hand out to me.

"It's nice to meet you, Mr. De la Rosa." I shake his hand, the same two-pumper Juliet had given me, before he pulls me into the same crushing hug. Air leaves my chest in a wheeze.

"Carlos," he bellows into my ear. "Call me Carlos."

"Okay," Derek's mom says. "Don't break her." But she's laughing. He releases me and kisses her on the lips, his hand grazing her deep mocha skin. Two parents, unapologetically in love.

"Dinner," she whispers, their lips still touching.

"Please," Juliet groans as she bounces over to the dining room table.

A large dish of chicken tikka masala sits in the center of their dining room table, surrounded by salad and naan. It's the kind of meal I've seen only in Hallmark movies.

I sit across from Juliet with Derek at my side and their parents at either end. Everything on the table glitters iridescent. His mom says a quick grace, thanking God for friends, family, and food.

"So," Carlos begins. "Houston." He slaps a sizable portion on his plate, ignoring the salad. "Have to say we were a little surprised."

"It was pretty quickly planned," I agree, accepting the naan basket from Derek.

"Have you been?" The breath from his nose sways his mustache hair.

"Um, not in a while." I'm scared to eat, not wanting to be caught midchew.

"Derek says you're going to see some family?" his mom says, a statement in the form of a question. I'm not sure how much he's told them. I'm hoping not a lot. I don't want them to think I'm complicated.

"Yes, ma'am." I look at Derek, but his face is more guarded than usual. How much of a fight had they put up about the trip?

"Can't say we're thrilled, sending our teenage son on

an overnight trip to Texas with his girlfriend." His dad laughs. It clamors around the room and rattles off the silverware.

It's the first time I've heard that. *His* girlfriend. I like it.

"But he came into my office, like a man, said he wouldn't ask if it wasn't important," he adds, no longer laughing, but serious as a stroke. "He's a good kid. Doesn't ask for much. We trust him."

Everyone around the table is silent. A piece of naan hangs out of Juliet's mouth, forgotten.

Derek's avoiding eye contact like I'm Medusa. I know he's thinking about his grandfather.

Carlos stares at me. I inhale and hold it.

"So." He leans toward me. "Don't take advantage of our son in that Airbnb, or my wife will never let me forget it."

Derek squeezes his eyes shut, and secondhand embarrassment washes over me. But there's a hint of a smile.

Carlos's face breaks into a wide grin. His deep laugh carries around the room as he slaps the table. Derek's mom joins, her laugh like a symphony with just the strings and no bass. He carries the percussion in his belly. Derek's shoulders uncoil, and he laughs too. Third degree over, I guess? I finally exhale, only mildly still on edge. Mark this down as a dad thing I don't understand. At all, which makes sense since I've never had one. But Derek relaxes, so I do too.

He reaches for my hand under the table, and I give it to him.

∞

I pick up the empty pie pan from the table. Caramelized apples are stuck to the bottom, despite Derek and his dad fork wrestling over every leftover scrap. They're upstairs now, helping Juliet finish a three-dimensional model of the solar system.

I carry the pan to the sink, where Derek's mom is elbow deep in dish soap, the sleeves of her cashmere sweater futilely rolled up. She smiles as I place the dish and glasses clutched in my fingers on the counter.

"Derek says you live with your grandmother," she says, grabbing one of the glasses and dipping it into the soapy water. She scrubs her lipstick off the lip of the glass before sliding it into the dishwasher.

"My whole life," I respond, not sure what to do now that the table's cleared. I look around for some way to use my hands that won't involve further fraying my jeans.

She nods. "But she's not going to Houston with you all?" Again she poses it as a question, her tone clipped.

"No, she has to work. She's an aide at the clinic and, well, flu season." The truth is, Grandma doesn't want to go, but that isn't anyone's business. Not even mine.

She turns off the water, dragging a dry dish towel over her wet forearms. She's silent as she sizes me up, the only sound coming from the glugging water moving down the drain.

"I think you're really sweet, Michie. But this whole

trip, it's against my better judgment," she says. "I'm not exactly keen on my eighteen-year-old son flying a thousand miles away on his own with his…with you. Carlos is more optimistic."

"I understand." I can't exactly disagree. This plan is absurd.

"He asked us to trust him, and so we're loosening the leash this time, seeing what he does with it. He's not the same angry, withdrawn teenager he was in San Francisco. The family was a bit of a mess. We didn't handle much the way we should have, and that hurt him. I think a large part of this happier version of my son has to do with you. So, this is us saying thank you." She smiles, but it doesn't reach her eyes.

She chuckles nervously, fanning out the bottom of her sweater. "God, he'd be so mortified if he knew we were having this conversation."

It feels more like being talked at than having a conversation. But I would want my mom to protect me the way Mrs. De la Rosa is protecting Derek right now.

"I don't want him following you to the ends of the earth just to get left out in the cold. Because he would," she adds, "follow you."

"I wouldn't ask him to," I say, my body trembling. She hates me.

"I know." She nods. "But we both know you wouldn't have to."

"You ready?" Derek says suddenly from behind me, his eyebrows raised at us.

"She's ready," his mom responds, reaching to squeeze my shoulders before walking around me. She stands on her toes and kisses him on the cheek. "Come right home after. Goodnight, Michie." She smiles at me before heading up the staircase, her bare feet padding against the hardwood.

It's the most surreal interaction I've ever been a part of.

I follow him out, slipping into my sneakers at the door. Derek's neighborhood is so unlike mine, quiet and still. You can see the stars, not drowned out by bright downtown lights. He doesn't turn on any music as he drives me home, the car silent most of the way.

"Hey," I say, facing him.

"Hey." He smiles but keeps his eyes trained on the street ahead.

"Thanks for dinner. Your family's sweet."

"They like you a lot," he assures me. "Juliet wouldn't stop talking about you."

He squeezes my fingers wrapped in his. I've grown so used to how they fit together. His heartbeat hums under the surface, and mine matches his tempo.

"Your mom really loves you," I tell him.

He studies my face as we wait at a red light. "What did she say?"

"If I break your heart, I die." I laugh.

He doesn't. "Yeah. She was kind of worried about me in California. Like I said, I was angry at the world and took it out on everyone. When I wouldn't go to my grandfather's funeral, she thought I was one step away from juvie or

290

something. Being here has helped though." He smiles at me now, but it's small, flickering. "Watching you do this, I wish I had the strength. Every Sunday, I tell myself I'll get some flowers, drive down to the cemetery, and tell him I'm sorry. Facing it is the hardest part."

"And what happens? On Sundays?"

"I wake up, I get the flowers, and then nothing."

I hum in assent and close my eyes.

When the car comes to a stop in front of my building, I've already dozed off. I moan defiantly as he pulls his hand away, the wind whistling as his door snaps open. I push the heels of my hands into my eye sockets, rubbing them to wake myself up. He pulls my door open and I nearly fall out of it, caught only by my seat belt. I unbuckle and grab onto his shirt, pulling myself out of the car.

"This is what my family calls apple-pie wasted." He laughs, leading me to the front door. I'm hanging from him like a sloth. "Happens to my dad once a week."

"So good," I moan, and I don't even usually like pie.

He chuckles as he removes my keys out of my back pocket. I grab them from his hand before he can use them.

"So." Old nerves set back in.

He steps closer. My breath hitches. "So."

His hand moves to my face, and the pad of his thumb runs along my jaw. He traces his finger to my mouth, pulling down my lower lip. I shift to my toes, lifting my face up toward his.

"Can I kiss you?" he whispers. He's so close I can feel the heat radiating from his skin.

I hum unintelligible words. My eyes flutter closed a breath before our lips collide and my insides turn to vapor. It's slow, and I want it to extend into forever. He still tastes like baked apples. I slide my hands beneath his sweater, feeling the warmth of his skin and the flex of his back muscles as he pulls me closer. A deep groan rises from his chest, and it rumbles beneath my fingertips.

He pulls away and kisses me again, this one quick and fleeting. His lips curve upward against mine in a smile, his teeth grazing my lip.

"Tomorrow," he says, removing his hands from my face. They leave my skin scorched as he retreats to his car. I enter my building in a haze. His car engine starts again and disappears gradually until it's just a memory.

Somehow, I make it into my apartment. I don't know how, since I exist outside of my body. I jump at the sound of a sharp knock on the door.

"Long time, no…" I say, expecting to find Derek on the other side. But it's Morgan Williams. She looks so small standing in her pajamas—it's been months since I've seen her out of the puffy winter coat she wears to the bus stop. "Hi."

"Hey," she says, in the awkward exchange of pleasantries between two people who don't speak. "This was in our box." She holds up a large envelope—misplaced mail.

"Oh, thank you." I grab the envelope, and we stand staring at each other. "How's, um, life?" Smooth. Real smooth.

"It's good." She nods. "Getting ready for college. Kind of checked out."

"Oh," I say. I didn't know she was going to college, even though I shouldn't be surprised. Morgan was always smart, much smarter than me. "Where are you headed?"

"Penn," she answers.

"State?"

"UPenn." Oh. Oh, wow. Her tone is as if she has had to make the correction several times before.

Well, cheers to me for assuming and putting a foot in my mouth. Again, much smarter than me. An unsettling feeling grips me, the sudden realization that where we come from doesn't have to hold us back. Morgan never left, and now she's going to an Ivy. You don't need to leave this place to make it. I don't know why I ever told myself that I did. I don't know why this place made me feel weak when all it ever did was make me strong.

"That's amazing, Morgan," I say.

She smiles and nods. "Yeah, it is. I was going to go to UVA, but Penn, you know." Okay, flex, but I respect it. "I'm actually helping out with the fair this weekend at the Convention Center. You should stop by our table. I know Lee is hosting this year."

I'm still up in the air if I'm even going, to be honest. It would be nice to take a look at the schools, but a taste of bitterness still sits on my tongue. "We'll see."

She nods. "Well, I have to go."

"Of course," I say. "But good luck. You're going to kill it."

"Thanks, Michie." And she's gone, shutting her own door behind her. I wish I had let myself love this place, these people, more.

I shut my own door and creep farther into the apartment. Grandma's light is still on. Always awake until I get home. I peek my head into her room.

"Have a nice time?" she asks, a crossword puzzle book open on her lap. I make my way over to her bed and lie down beside her. She brushes my curls back from my forehead. "Want to sleep in here tonight?"

I haven't done that in years, but the thought of getting up makes my bones hurt.

"I didn't pack yet," I mumble.

"We'll do it tomorrow morning."

She turns off the light, and I kick off my sneakers. We don't address the Renee-shaped elephant in the room.

"I love you," I whisper into the dark.

She smooths a hand in my hair and pulls the comforter over me. "Times infinity."

CHAPTER THIRTY

THE AIRPORT IS PRETTY SUBDUED. I GUESS FEW PEOPLE travel through the Richmond airport on a random Tuesday in March. Derek's parents picked JoJo up this morning since she was on their way. They're all standing in a group by the automatic check-in stands. I Ubered so Grandma wouldn't need to get the beginning of her shift covered this morning. This trip is already a money pit.

Derek's mom gives me a hug. This time my arms wrap around her. I could get used to mom hugs. "I was hoping to meet your grandmother before you all left, give her our contact information."

"Oh," I respond. "I can send it to her." She spells out their address and their phone number as I text it to Grandma. I give her our house number and Grandma's cell in exchange. She texts Grandma immediately. I have a feeling they'll be in constant contact until we get home.

"Ready to rock and roll?" JoJo waves our printed tickets in front of my face. Derek has two copies, both tucked into the front cover of his passport.

"You're bringing that?" I ask him, flicking the passport with my fingers. I don't even have one of those.

"Sure. What if we end up in Mexico by accident?"

His mom's smile clinches as his dad slaps him on the back with a guffaw, a noise I thought existed only in books.

"Let's not keep the kids," he says. "Text us when you land." He squeezes Derek's shoulder.

"Call," his mom corrects, hugging him tight. "When you board. And when you get to the Airbnb. And—"

"Good God, woman," Carlos groans, before pulling her away. A large family with lopsided suitcases blocks them from view.

Derek eats a peanut butter Clif Bar as we shuffle through the security line. JoJo transfers some of her liquid items to my near empty ziplock bag containing toothpaste and leave-in conditioner.

"You know it's only four days, right? And two of those we're flying?" She's packed enough toiletries for a summer abroad.

"Do you know what happens to your face in four days

without proper skin care?" She stares at my face with concern. She squeezes in one last beeswax serum. A small container of mud mask lies in her hand. "Do you think this qualifies as a liquid?"

"Yes," Derek and I respond in unison. She grimaces at the tiny clear bag on the conveyor belt as if it's betrayed her. The plastic is already stretching, close to splitting open. She drops the container to the bottom of her large purse and shakes it down below a mountain of crap.

"We'll see how it goes."

I step into the metal detector, my arms up over my head like I'm a murder suspect. It spins back and forth before spitting me out. The bulbous TSA agent eyes the computer screen image as my head flashes red.

He nods to a female agent, bulky in her oversized navy cargo pants and button-up.

"I got to pat your hair," she mumbles, pointing to my high bun. Because if I were a terrorist, right next to my brain is the first place I would hide explosives. Her pudgy fingers squeeze my hair. She waves me to the side, all clear.

Derek is wearing basketball shorts, Nike slides with socks, and an N.W.A T-shirt, expert attire of one who travels often and efficiently. He ducks into the scanner and comes out. The agent slithers his eyes over Derek in a predatorial glance. Then he waves him on with a grunt.

I don't get those looks as often as he does, because the boy who attacked Renee looks more like the white TSA agent and less like Derek. I rub the sides of my temples. Now is not the time to be plagued by thoughts on how I benefit from the race of my mother's rapist.

JoJo's last. Her hair is also in a high bun, but neater and more deliberate than mine. It's still winter, and her pale skin looks more Caucasian white than lighter-complexion Persian. But still, she walks through the scanner with bated breath. She's told me about her "random" additional screenings too many times to count. The TSA agent's lips pull upward into a perverse smile as he waves her through.

"Have a good day, miss," he says in a nasal voice.

She grabs her bags from the end of the conveyor belt and releases a breath. Both she and her mud mask have made it through unscathed.

Derek pulls another Clif Bar from his bag, revealing a side pocket chock full of them. JoJo and I watch with disgust on our faces.

"What?" he asks, midbite, noticing our noses pinched upward in revulsion.

"You're eating those for fun?" I ask. I don't care what anyone says. Clif Bars taste like sandpaper.

"Yeah, they're great." He shoves half of the bar in his mouth, this one blueberry crisp.

"If you say so." JoJo turns away as if the mere sight of it offends her.

The gate flashes with an hour delay as storm clouds move overhead.

"That's a sign, right? We should go home?" See Renee at your own risk, the skies seem to open up and say.

JoJo rolls her eyes and places a piece of spearmint gum on her tongue. "Chill or be chilled. It's just rain." Lightning snaps behind her head.

When we board, I have the window seat, JoJo has the center, and Derek has the aisle, which is a mercy since his legs are longer than the entire row.

"Can we switch?" JoJo asks him. "Small bladder," she says as explanation.

"It's a three-hour flight," I scold, and eye Derek's legs with empathetic discomfort.

But he shrugs and settles in next to me. "Yeah, sure."

Over his head, JoJo winks. I scowl. Surely her manipulation need not come at the high price of torture. But deep down, I'm excited I get to spend the next few hours cuddled beside him.

The pilot comes over the speakers, announcing the flight conditions and expected landing time. He informs us the seat belt sign will be on for most of the trip because of weather and possible turbulence. My fingers dig into the seat divider.

"I have something for you," Derek says, digging into his Clif Bar–filled pocket. He pulls out a smooth gray stone.

"What is it?" I ask, rubbing my finger over its glassy surface.

"This is a lucky talisman. For flying."

JoJo leans over. "It's a rock."

Derek glares at her. "A lucky rock."

I close my fingers around it and grab his hand, squeezing tight.

Derek puts one of his AirPods in my ear, and we watch a movie downloaded to his laptop. He skims his lips over my knuckles with a quick kiss before holding my hand in his lap.

Halfway through the flight, while JoJo's asleep, we split her complimentary pretzels. He pulls a ziplock bag of Oreos out of his bag. God bless this boy.

JoJo never once gets up to use the bathroom.

Walking out into the Houston humidity, I strip off the two sweaters I threw on while airborne. In addition to planes being small, they are also super cold. My curls frizz by the second as I tie the sweaters around my waist.

An employee from the shady and totally not legit Rent-A-Hoopty succumbs to JoJo sweet-talking him into giving us an old hatchback from the seventies despite our ages. We dump our bags into the trunk, and I jump into the back seat before Derek objects. But he releases a long sigh of relief when he pushes his seat all the way back and stretches out his legs.

Country music blasts through the speakers when JoJo turns the key in the ignition. Derek reaches to change it, but she slaps his hand away.

"Leave it," I call from the back seat. If this trip goes

horribly, I want to be able to recall as many good memories as possible.

"If you don't sing along to losing your cowboy hat and your woman on Route 66, were you even in Houston?" JoJo asks, turning the radio as loud as it will go and rolling the windows all the way down to let in the breeze.

"Route 66 isn't anywhere near Houston." Derek hangs his arm out of the open window. "You'd have to drive, like, nine hours from here to get anywhere near it."

As much as JoJo knows, she's total crap at geography. Book smarts do not translate to street smarts. I lean my head against the window with a sudden stomachache.

JoJo glances at me in the rearview mirror. "I support you doing this a hundred percent," she says. "But I'll also support you if you change your mind. If you wake up tomorrow and you're not ready, then okay. So we spend two days at the space center instead of one. No biggie."

"Or no days at the space center," Derek suggests, eyeing JoJo with disdain. "There's this sick comic book store that could take two days easy."

"Get over it," she says. "The space center is happening."

Derek shakes his head in exasperation. He's more of a *pew-pew*-space fan than a *real*-space fan.

Our Airbnb is close to a taco stand, where we grab dinner, which pleases Derek to no end. He plans to get breakfast, lunch, and dinner there every day until we leave.

The key to the small guesthouse is supposed to be beneath a potted plant. But there are about two dozen potted plants. We begin flipping them over, and after we've over-turned nearly all of them, I start to panic.

"Guys, this is a definite sign," I say.

"You don't even believe in astrology, and now you're Madame Zeroni? There are no signs." JoJo flips over the second-to-last plant, which has a gold key taped to the bottom. She holds it up. "See?"

I groan as I follow her in. For ninety bucks a night, the house is amazing. An overstuffed couch in front of a fireplace gives it a cottage feel and, despite the small space, it fits two bedrooms comfortably. JoJo and I throw our bags in one of the rooms while Derek takes the other.

Since we expect tomorrow to be a long day, we go to bed early. But sleep evades me well into the middle of the night. As JoJo snores to my left, I stare up at the ceiling as the moon sends dancing light beams through the window shades. I slip from beneath the covers and tiptoe out of the room. The air-conditioning purrs through the living room.

My phone is charging in the kitchen, and the backlight shocks me as it turns on. I call the only person I wish were here.

"Hi, pudding pop," Grandma mumbles drowsily. It's a nickname she hasn't called me since I was a little girl, and a lost comfort washes over me. "How's Houston?"

"Great tacos," I joke. I pull a frayed string at the bottom of my nightshirt, a large Disney World tee I stole from Grandma years ago. Not that either of us has ever been to Disney World.

"I'm sure." She grows silent.

"I don't want to do this anymore," I confess. A pipe in the house creaks.

"You don't have to," she urges. "But you should."

"Why?"

"Because you need to face it. If you walk away, in ten years you'll think that things might be different if you had done this now. But whatever happens, Michie, you still deserve good things."

"When'd you get so wise?" I ask.

"I learned it from my tough-as-nails granddaughter," she says. "Get some rest, okay?"

"I love you," I say.

"Times infinity," she responds.

The call beeps to an end, and I attach it back to the charging dock. I lean against the counter and rub my hands over my face.

I blow out a deep breath and notice Derek's door ajar. I knock before pushing it open after no response. It groans on its hinges.

"Are you awake?" I speak into the dark. His room faces away from the moonlight, and the shades are closed tight. The pitch dark is tangible as I push through it.

"Yeah." A figure rises straight up in the shadows.

"Can I?" I motion to the bed with shadow hands. My body aches to be closer.

"Yeah, come here." The sound of rustling sheets fills the quiet room as he moves to one side of the bed. I climb from the foot up and settle in next to him, our kneecaps touching as I face him. I'm close enough now to see the outline of his body, as my eyes adjust. He props his head up with one hand. "What's going on?"

"Can't sleep."

"I didn't think you would. Stayed up just in case."

Of course he did.

"I'm sorry," I whisper, trying to train my eyes where I expect his face to be.

"For what?"

"For pushing you away," I respond. "At first. Treating you like you didn't matter."

"You were going through stuff," he reasons. Instinctively, he reaches forward and places a hand on my hip. Sometimes it's scary how well he knows the shape of me. "And you never treated me like I didn't matter. You just didn't treat me like I'm the only thing that mattered. That's a good thing."

"Still, I'm sorry."

"Then I forgive you." His breath warms my face, smelling like spearmint toothpaste and I'm pretty sure another Clif Bar.

"You shouldn't."

"Well, I do. That's what you do with people you love; you forgive them."

I swallow around his words as if they've come from my own mouth. "What if you can't forgive them? What if everything's too broken?"

He pulls his hand away, and I feel bare, until he slides

his arm around my waist and pulls me closer. I fold into his chest, his pulse hard and steady against my cheek.

"Then you don't," he whispers. "And that's okay too."

He kisses me on the forehead. I fall asleep to the soft *bum-bum* of his heartbeat. So this is what it is to feel safe.

CHAPTER THIRTY-ONE

THE UNFAMILIAR SOUND OF EARLY MORNING LAWN MOW-
ers drags me out of sleep.

My face is burrowed into Derek's chest. He has pulled
me into a bear hug, both arms wrapped tight around me, his
face buried in my curls. Spidery long legs hang off the end
of the bed, the sheets tangled around his feet and spilling to
the floor.

He rouses with a full body twitch but doesn't wake up.
His eyes flicker behind shut eyelids. Rolling onto his back,
he pulls me with him. My head rises and falls with his deep
breaths.

I can almost forget today's the day as I match my breathing to his. Almost. My arm is trapped between our bodies

and I can't check my Fitbit for the time, but it feels early. The smell of coffee beans wafts through the bedroom door I left open last night.

I attempt to shimmy myself down toward the end of the bed, but his grip tightens, and I release a small yelp. His eyes fly open at the sound, his head slamming against the headboard with a loud thud. Whistling from the kitchen stops.

"Shit," he groans, releasing me immediately. "Sorry," he grumbles in a sleepy voice as he rubs his head.

"No problem." My voice is husky as I lift myself up onto my butt. If I'm being honest, it's the best night's sleep I've had in weeks.

His eyes are still droopy with sleep, and his hair lies flat on one side. His shorts have ridden up and reveal much of his upper thigh. I follow the muscle with my eyes until it disappears beneath fabric.

"Coffee," I announce, jumping out of bed. I speed walk out of the door.

JoJo is standing at the counter, already wearing another knee-length dress and sandals. Her eyebrows raise as she lifts a large coffee mug to her mouth.

"Good morning," she says, her words doused in accusation.

"Shut up." I reach for another mug and the steaming coffeepot. I don't even like coffee, and caffeine is the last thing I need for the jitters. But I'm desperate for a distraction. The pot shakes in my hands as I pour.

JoJo continues staring in silence.

"What?" I finally ask, putting the pot back. Coffee sprays over the lip and onto the tiled floor.

"I didn't say anything," she says, her mouth turning up at one corner.

I take a too-large gulp, and it burns its way down my esophagus.

She shakes her head and chuckles. "I knew this trip would be fun." She walks around me back toward our room. "Nice pants."

I look down and find my legs bare, remembering that I specifically wore this to sleep last night because it's long enough to cover my butt. Which means I'd slept next to Derek, on top of Derek, all over Derek, pantsless.

Spinning on my heel, I chase her down, grabbing onto the back of her dress.

"Nothing happened," I assert, pulling the tattered shirt down even farther.

"Duh," she says, unfurling the cord from around her hair straightener.

"Good." I sigh. "Wait, what do you mean duh?"

"I mean it took you forty years to even admit this was a thing." She motions her finger between me and the wall separating the rooms. "I didn't think you'd jump him in one night, though your self-control is legend because that boy is a walking sex billboard."

"He's not," I groan, throwing myself down onto the bed.

"You're right. Just the sex, none of the ad."

"I hate you."

"Love you," she sings, closing the bathroom door behind her.

Grandma set everything up for noon, but when the hour rolls around, no one has any sense of urgency. Derek took the car to get breakfast while I showered and brought back everything bagels, because they're my favorite, but I avoid them. Smelling like onions with poppyseeds in my teeth isn't the impression I want to make. A shiver runs down my spine at the thought. It won't be the last time, I tell myself, feigning confidence.

Derek's eyes follow me. My nervous energy is contagious.

Even JoJo's expression grows somber the closer we get to the address plugged into her GPS. A large and mostly empty cul-de-sac spreads out in front of us. Average-sized homes and identical lawns line the street like dollhouses. I clutch my stomach as we head toward Renee's house, my gut doing cartwheels in my lower abdomen. Two cups of coffee and barely any food was not my smartest idea.

"We should get pancakes," I suggest, willing us to reverse.

JoJo stops in the middle of the street and twists around in her seat. "Do you want to go back?"

I look out of the window to the well-manicured yards, American flags and those of various Texas colleges swaying in the breeze. If we go home now, it will be because of fear. And I'm sick of being afraid.

"No," I swallow. "I want to keep going."

JoJo lets off the squeaking brake and sidles up to the curb.

Derek turns to me, his eyes unyielding and focused. "The only person you're fighting in there is this one." He places a finger on the side of my forehead, tucking a stray curl behind my ear. I reach up to squeeze his finger before getting out of the car.

JoJo rolls her window down. "Do you want us to stay or..." She glances around the neighborhood. "We could come back?"

If they leave now, I'll be stranded if I tap out early. But if they stay the entire time, I can run at the first sign of discomfort. I won't have to face anything at all.

"Stay for a little." As in, please don't leave me here alone.

She turns the key, and the car putters as its engine stops.

The walk toward the front door seems longer than it looked from the car. The large brass knocker shaped like a horseshoe is cold beneath my fingers as I tap it against the door. Silence. I rub the sweat on my palms roughly against the denim fabric of my jeans. They turn a slight tinge of blue, the denim's ink bleeding out. When I turn my head back to the car, JoJo waves supportively and Derek gives me a thumbs-up.

I knock harder and it echoes through the house. The door swings open and I instinctively retreat, my heel almost slipping off the step.

She's smaller than I remember, too small for someone who takes up so much space in my mind. Long box braids hang around her head, and her eyes are a much deeper brown than my hazel ones.

310

"Hi," she breathes. I search her face for anything familiar. She looks so different from the decades-old photos
Grandma keeps of her. The baby fat and acne from her teenage years transformed to sharper cheekbones and unblem-
ished skin. She wears her thirty-two years well.

"Are they coming in?" She points at the car.

"Um, no." I wave them away, but JoJo doesn't move as I
follow Renee into the air-conditioned house.

It isn't anything grand, but it's comfortable, with a large
sectional sofa and a coffee table covered with magazines and
nature books. A pair of hiking boots matching the reading material sit in a corner. It smells like Tootie Fruities or
Apple Zings; I suspect from the Wallflower plugged in by the
door.

"This is it," she says, holding her hands out to the room.

We assess each other. Where she's sharp, I'm round.
Where she's long, I'm squat. Her deep brown skin, still
youthful, glows with red undertones. I am a pale gold, worn
down. We are nothing alike. I must look like him, have his
face. How much of him also sits under my skin, in my heart?

"Do you want to sit?" She holds her hand out to the
couch.

"Not really," I answer, with more venom than I intend.
But I don't want to make myself comfortable. Not yet. Not
until I know if I'm safe here without armor.

She nods, clasping her hands together.

"I'm happy you're here, Michie." She attempts a smile,
but it falls.

"Why *am* I here?" I give voice to the question that's been haunting me. Why did she want to see me?

She tilts her head, measuring me with her glance. Confusion settles into her features, and then realization. She holds up a finger before disappearing deeper into the house. She walks with heavy feet, and the floor groans beneath her. At least that's something we have in common—homes that want to share our secrets.

Framed photographs are scattered around the room. They fill in the years after me. Smiling and laughing faces that I don't recognize surround me, except one. It's an old photo of Grandma. She's holding a smaller Renee in her arms and wearing a bright color-blocked pullover.

There are no photos of me. There aren't any photos of my siblings. If all you knew of her life was this one room, you would never believe she has any children at all.

She comes back into the living room, holding an envelope. She removes a folded piece of paper from inside and drops the now empty envelope on the coffee table.

"Grandma," she says, holding up the paper. She doesn't call her Mom, but frames her in how she appears in my life, so there's no mother in the room. "She sent me this essay you wrote for school a while ago. First time I'd heard from her in years."

I know exactly what essay it is. "The Lady of Shalott." The one that gave Mr. Milligan expectations. The one that felt like opening myself up for the first time. She hands it to me. Grandma had typed it onto photo paper, designed with flower vines around the edges. Like the notes I keep in that box beneath my nightstand. Light reflects off its surface as I tilt it toward me.

"Why'd she give this to you?"

"I don't know," she replies. "I called her as soon as I got it, but she didn't say much."

I glance back at the photo of them on her bookcase, prominently displayed in the center.

"And then you asked to see me?"

"No," she says with woe. "She asked if *you* could see me."

Every ball I've been juggling crashes to the floor. I reach my hand out to the wall to steady myself.

Grandma lied to me.

Betrayal, anger, it all floods my mind at once. She made me look like the broken one, the desperate one. My fear that Renee never wanted to see me again is true. A sharp pain shoots through the center of my chest and settles behind my heart. But I keep my face neutral. She hasn't earned any more of my pain.

But God, it hurts.

"I'm happy you're here, though," she repeats. "Please sit."

This time I do, because my legs are not as committed to the pretense of being okay as my mind is. I perch on the edge of the sofa. It's firmer than it looks, uncomfortable.

"Where are the others?" I finally ask, nodding to the photos around the room. I've always assumed I was the only one cast aside. The one forced on her. In her. I'm sad I won't see them today. A hole I didn't know was there widens in my chest. More family, gone.

313

"Thomas lives with his grandparents in New York," she explains. "Yara lives with her dad in Charlotte."

"How convenient for you." I came here with every intention of being kind, but seeing us forgotten sends fire through my veins. She had every reason to throw me away, but not them.

"That's fair," she mumbles. She bites into a thumbnail. It cracks between her teeth.

"Fair?" How dare she. "You think it's fair to throw people away like they're garbage?"

"I didn't throw anyone away," she objects, shaking her head. "I did what was best for them. For you."

"Are you kidding me?" I stand angrily from the couch, gesturing toward all the picture frames where we've been erased.

"So, you came here to judge me," she asks, her eyes bitter. "You think I don't know I've made mistakes?"

"You tell me."

"I never wanted any of this."

"For me to come here? Yeah," I spit, "painfully aware of that one now."

"To be a mother," she says, now standing as well. Her hands are fists at her side.

It stops me dead in my tracks. It's not surprising. I've always known she regretted me. I've never blamed her, knowing what I know. But to know something deep within yourself and to hear it out loud are different beasts, and this one is far more vicious.

Why would Grandma send me here? She had to have known this is how Renee felt.

My stomach twists. I'm going to vomit. My legs move before I know where they're going. The front doorknob is in my hand. Every movement feels detached, like the spasms of another body that doesn't belong to me. My mind can't catch up. I lean over the gardenias and purge the coffee and bit of leftover taco I consumed. I let it all out until the only thing left is stomach acid.

I hear Renee behind me, the unfamiliar hover of her hand on my back, not touching. I start moving again, faster and faster until I slam into the side of our old borrowed car. JoJo's door is half-open, her face stricken. I collapse into the back seat.

"What's wrong?" JoJo asks.

Maybe she's yelling. I can't tell. My ears are ringing, and it's the loudest thing I've ever experienced. I lift my hand to my face. It's wet with tears.

"Drive," I whisper. "Please." My voice cracks. "Please."

Derek gets out of the car and I squeeze my eyes shut, willing everything away. I was right. She doesn't want me. She never wanted me. I wonder if Thomas and Yara blame me, if they know they have no mother because of me. Guilt pushes in waves that leave me exhausted.

My door opens, and a pair of hands catch me from falling sideways out of the car. Derek huddles beside me and shuts the door behind him.

"Drive," he repeats. And finally, the car begins to move.

∞

I was right.

It's the only thought I can muster as I lie curled on the bed. My phone vibrates on the nightstand. I lose track of how many times it buzzes against the wood, pauses, and starts again. Grandma.

Renee probably told her what happened. It hurts to think of Grandma as someone who could lie and hurt me like this. I bet they shared a laugh. Poor, pathetic Michie, look how she yearns. Darkness wraps itself around me. It would be so easy to make it stop, make everything stop. I go back to last summer. Would I be happier if I had quit then?

The door creaks open, letting in a sliver of light from the lit living room. It's silent on the other side.

"Hey," JoJo whispers. She comes to sit beside me. "Do you want food?"

I don't answer, drawing my knees in closer to my chest. She sighs and smooths a hand over my hair. She knows what happened. Both of them do. At least whatever filled the broken sentences I got out before I cried myself into the kind of sleep dreams can't penetrate. Sometimes God has mercy. Sometimes.

"I never told you this, but you're the bravest person I know," she says, continuing to smooth my hair from my face. "I always knew it, but when I visited you in the hospital, that's when I *really* knew there was no one alive braver than Michie Cooper. You inspire me. You're the reason I want to go to Chicago, because if you can put yourself out there after everything, then what excuse do the rest of us have? I know you're hurting right now and you think you're not significant. But you are, Michie. You're as significant as the sun."

She leans down and kisses me on the cheek, pulling the blanket up close to my chin. A tear slips down the side of my face and settles against her fingers.

"We're right outside if you need us," she says. "We're here."

The mattress shifts as she gets up and closes the door with a muted click. Time passes. I stare at a spot on the wall until restless sleep consumes me once more.

CHAPTER THIRTY-TWO

DEREK IS ASLEEP ON THE COUCH WHEN I FINALLY GET UP. From the open door of his room, I make out the lump that is JoJo beneath the covers. He could be home with a family that loves him rather than on the most pointless trip in human history. I make wasting everyone's time an art form.

"Morning."

I jump, not realizing he had opened his eyes. I nod in response and stumble to the kitchen. My legs feel like they're filled with cotton instead of ligament. He follows me wordlessly.

"So yesterday," he starts.

"I don't want to talk about it." I pull the coffee bag from the cabinet and dump too much into a filter. JoJo left my meds on the microwave, and I don't have the energy to be embarrassed by them as I swallow one dry.

Derek takes the coffee bag from my hands and pours some of the coffee back into the bag. He drops the filter into the machine, pressing the start button.

"When are we going to the museum?" I ask. My throat hurts with every word, like I've been screaming for days, years, lifetimes. Haven't I?

"The museum?" JoJo stands behind me. I don't know when she got there. "We didn't think you'd still want to go. We can just chill today."

"No." We came here for two things. Fix things with Renee and go to the space museum. Well, one of those things is never going to happen, but we have a chance at the other. And I have to accomplish something here. "We're going."

"Okay." JoJo swallows, pulling cups from the cupboard. "We're going, then. They open in a half hour." She hands me a full cup of coffee. I don't bother with cream and sugar, drinking it black. It's way too strong, but I invite the overwhelming bitterness. I'm bitter too.

"Thirty minutes." I carry the cup to the bathroom and shower. I'm dressed and ready to go in twenty. Derek is sitting on the front porch of the small guesthouse.

"Love you," he says, and for a moment my back stiffens, until I realize he's hanging up his phone. "My mom." He gives me an apologetic smile. *Mom* is now like yelling *bomb* in an airport. My fight-or-flight response triggers.

JoJo joins us and we walk to the car, the only sound the

crunch of dead grass beneath our feet. They both accept the silence.

The space museum is nearly empty. Not surprising for being the middle of the week.

"What first?" Derek asks, grabbing a map from the welcome desk. I know he'd rather be at the comic book store, and it's only because I know him so well now that I can tell his excitement is feigned. JoJo reads the exhibit list upside down as Derek scans the layout.

"Oh, let's go see *Apollo 17*." She points it out on the map.

"Okay." I don't care where we start or where we stop or even if we get lost in this museum forever and fall under a magic spell that turns us into mannequins. I'd be fine never facing the real world again.

The museum is fun, all things considered, and we hop from one exhibit to another. Luckily there are tons of them. Hours are eaten ravenously by the lights show and the Goddard rocket and the lunar samples vault. We all take pictures at the John F. Kennedy podium. For a while, Renee and Grandma move to a place at the back of my mind that jumps out only when I forget to forget.

Derek points us to a room we haven't seen yet. It's dark, with well-lit items inside large glass containers. I read the description card of the one closest to us. Test ejection seats, one for the commander and one for the pilot. They based the idea on World War II bomber pilots who were able to eject while the rest of their crew was left behind. The commander for the first four-person crewed mission had them removed.

The captain goes down with his ship.

JoJo and Derek move on, but I stare at the seats. Two devices decided who got to survive. But in life, you don't get to eject yourself from a scary situation. You don't get to leave anyone behind. You go down with your ship, even if it means the end of life as you know it.

I ejected yesterday. I feel empty because I am empty. Michie walked into that house, and only the shell of my body walked out. But I can go back and put myself back together. I'll either go down with my ship or I'll save myself.

"You ready?" JoJo asks beside me. They've checked out the rest of the room already. She reads the description card again, thinking she's missed something. But she hasn't. This exhibit means something to me only because I'm the one with a choice—fight or eject.

"I have to go back," I say.

"Where?" She grabs the map from Derek's hands. "The samples room? That one was cool."

I turn away from the exhibit to face them. "To Renee."

JoJo's eyebrows furrow together, realization dawning. "Why?"

"Because I need to understand."

A glint of anger sparks behind JoJo's eyes. The protective kind. The kind that will tear you limb from limb before she lets you hurt someone she loves. "Michie, you've already done enough. She is beyond comprehension."

I shake my head. "It's not about her. It's about me. She took something from me yesterday. I had hope, not a lot,

321

but I had it. And it's gone now. How am I supposed to want a future or, shit, take the SAT in two days, without hope? How am I supposed to write about who I am? What would be the point?" I'm out of breath. "I have to understand, and I have to forgive her. For me. I can't be angry for the rest of my life. I can't hurt for the rest of my life. It will kill me."

I think about how deep I fell last night, of wanting to let the darkness absorb me until I ceased to exist. Because nothing can hurt you when you don't exist. But I don't want another Incident. I want to live. I *want* to live, thrive, just like Dr. Schwartz said I should.

I'm not ejecting. I'm staying strapped into this ride until it lands. And it will land. It has to.

We head out of the museum.

"Wait," Derek says, holding out his arm to block us from the door.

"Oh, so first you didn't even want to come and now you don't want to leave?" JoJo rolls her eyes.

Derek narrows his eyes. "We're going to the gift shop." He grabs both of us by the forearms and pulls us toward the small shop. "We're each getting one thing to remember this trip by. Something good."

Something good. Dr. Schwartz's words ring. *You're good, Michie. You are so, so good.*

We each find one thing. For a moment, I consider life might just be good moments that fill in the fissures the bad ones leave behind. That's how you win, by filling in the cracks until they burst open and let in all the light.

∞

Like déjà vu, we find ourselves parked once again at the curb in front of Renee's house. Her CR-V is still parked in the driveway.

"You should go," I tell JoJo. I'm going to do this on my own. No running this time. No ejecting.

She nods, squeezing the steering wheel with uncharacteristic nervousness. "We'll wait a few minutes," she says. "Just in case." Just in case I'm turned away.

The door swings open faster than yesterday, like she was standing behind it in expectation.

Seeing her now is even more shocking. She looks the same, and I don't understand how she can be so unchanged when I feel so different. But I look the same too. It's hard to know how one event changed someone without living in their skin.

"Hi," she says, sounding surprised. To be fair, I'm pretty surprised I'm here too. "Come in."

I follow her as she shuts the door behind me. I glance out the window. JoJo and Derek are already gone. It's all on me now.

Renee sits on the couch, a deep breath releasing like a popped balloon as she empties into the suede fabric.

"Sit," she says.

I ignore her, standing awkwardly in the middle of the room.

"Michelle, sit," she repeats, now more like a plea than a

directive. "Please." She doesn't call me Michie. It would feel too familiar, too cozy.

We sit in silence, neither of us knowing where to start. Both of us wring our fingers out in our hands. A tic we have in common.

"Do you remember the last thing you said to me? All those years ago?" I ask. *I should have killed you when I had the chance.* I don't waste time with pleasantries. Not today.

"Yes." Her voice is a whisper.

"Did you mean it?"

She sighs. "I don't know." She rubs her palms against the couch cushions, leaving an imprint of her fingers in the material. "When I found out about you, I hadn't told anyone. About any of it. They assumed. . . ." Her shoulders twitch.

"Even Grandma?"

"Especially. I was a wild kid, always getting into trouble, always with the boys. She already had her ideas. When I finally told her, she didn't believe me. Not at first. Thought I was making excuses. I hated it. But eventually, she believed me. She asked me if I wanted to tell the police. But so many months had gone by. It felt too late. I didn't even know if I wanted to. I didn't want them to think the same thing she had thought, that I was lying to cover my ass. That I had"— she gulped—"invited it or something. And I thought that even if I did report it, he would find out about you, and he had rights, you know. I couldn't let him hurt you. I was sure of that, at least."

She wipes tears from her face. "But she promised that if I

kept you, she would help me take care of you. And I thought, finally, we could do something together. We were on the same team. It's like you were a blessing, you know. I needed you to find my way back to her."

It sounds like Grandma, always sacrificing her own life for mine. I try to latch onto my anger toward her, but it's getting harder and harder to hold on to.

"I thought it would make me feel less guilty, keeping you. Like I could make up for all the dumb shit I'd done, and part of me did think it was my fault. When you're a kid, everything feels like your fault, even when it's not. All anyone tells you is how you could've avoided it. If I'd dressed differently or come home earlier, things would be different. I didn't want to punish you if it was my fault. Like if I could do this one thing right, I could fix everything. It was so twisted.

"And then you came, three months early, and no one was ready. Not even you. We sat up all night while you were in surgery, trying to fight for the life I'd almost taken from you when I was scared and angry and hurting. I prayed so hard for another chance. I'd never prayed for anything until that moment, when the doctors were telling us you were too small and too underdeveloped and wouldn't survive the night. All I had to do was get you here in one piece, and I couldn't even do that. I failed you so early. And kept failing, again and again."

Her shoulders shake as she cries.

"I thought I could love you, this thing that was so much

of him, and I did for a while." She reaches for my hand, but I move it away. I'm too raw for contact.

"I had my GED classes, so Grandma came and visited you in the hospital during her lunch break. She never missed a day. All you did when I tried to hold you was cry. But you loved her. It was like she was your actual mother from the very start.

"I remember she left for a conference once. You sat on the bottom of the stairs for a week and would only eat Jell-O and chocolate pudding cups. She had to come home early because I didn't know what to do with you. I thought you'd waste away right there on the steps."

It's a memory I recall vividly. Waking up to find Grandma gone. Feeling abandoned.

"So what happened?" I ask. For the most part, we were all fine and figuring it out. You can't expect a fifteen-year-old with a baby to get it all right.

"I got pregnant." The unspoken fills in the silent spaces of her words. Not like with me. By choices she got to make for herself. "And I thought Grandma would take over again, but she didn't. All this time with you, I never learned how to be a mom. She'd done everything. And I was so resentful of her. But even more of you. She loved you so much.

"So when she moved to Virginia, I refused to go. I was twenty and thought I could start making my own choices. It was a second chance to grow up.

"But we didn't know what to do with you. You were my daughter, but I wasn't your mom, not really. So, I gave you the choice." She laughs. "Ridiculous, isn't it, letting a five-year-old choose who to live with? Grandma thought so at least, but it was like I needed to know, and you chose her with zero hesitation. You didn't even think about it. You already understood so much about how the world worked and how it could hurt you. How I could hurt you."

And it *was* ridiculous, letting me choose. But I know I made the right choice. We both do.

"I thought I'd be angry. But I felt..." She hesitates. "Lighter."

I gulp down bile on a warpath upward. I know she's not saying it to be cruel. She's saying it to free me from the what-ifs of having chosen her.

"I was never supposed to be your mom." Tears are falling freely now, dripping onto her shirt, as she hiccups around the words. "And sometimes I look at my life and think about all the things I could've done if..."

"If I'd never been born," I finish for her.

"I never wanted to hurt you," she says, reaching for my hand again. This time I let her take it. I feel nothing, not comfort or anger. But she needs something, someone to hold on to. "It was painful, being your mom. Being anyone's mom. But I don't regret any of it. Grandma always deserved to love and be loved by you. You've saved her in so many ways, and that saved me."

I chew over her words and brace for their impact. But it doesn't come. Not like yesterday.

I don't know this woman. I don't know what makes her

laugh or cry. She's not a part of me anymore. I came here in search of her love, and didn't find it. And for the first time, that doesn't bring me pain. I am stronger now. Like Grandma, I've grown dragon scales for skin. Impenetrable.

But as I look at her life, I'm not a part of her either. I'm not sure I ever was. I finally understand why she let Grandma take me without ever putting up a fight. I understand why she stopped reaching out after my seventh birthday. She wanted me to live a life free of her, so she could live one free of me. So we both could move on without the weight of each other's pain. She doesn't hate me. But she doesn't love me either. She can't. I am made up of the demons she has spent her life slaying.

Grandma was right. JoJo was right. Derek and Dr. Schwartz. Everyone was right. The monster I had made her into was one of my own design, stitched together by my own fears, my own insecurities, my own self-loathing. I am not unlovable because *she* doesn't love me. I'm standing here because I'm so irrevocably loved.

A soft laugh slips from my lips, and it grows until it's consumed my entire body. I will always be a child conceived from something terrible, but I was born out of love. Her love for her mother, Grandma's love for me.

I got on that plane thinking I had to prove my worth to Renee. But it's not for her to determine. Only I can do that. I gather the guilt into a pile, and I burn it until it's nothing but ash. I take a deep breath. I'm out of shallow water. I'm alive. I'm free.

"Can I give you something?" she asks.

"Sure," I respond. I have nothing to lose, and nothing to gain. She gets up from the couch and disappears from the room. She comes back holding a small box and places it between us. I lift the top, and enveloped cards crammed inside fall out. Each has my name drawn across the front, with a year etched into the bottom corner. I hold one in my hands. It has a familiar weight. I slide the birthday card out of its lime-green envelope.

"I get them every year," she says, taking one out herself. This one even has a stamp on the top corner. "Sometimes I get as far as the post office and...stall. I thought you were happier without me. I didn't want to mess that up for you. If I had known, God, Michie, if I had known." But she doesn't finish, because neither of us know if she would have done anything differently. Maybe the third-best thing she gave me—after life and Grandma—was distance, room to grow.

I place the card back in the box. "Can I keep this?" I ask. "Of course," she says with a smile. "Of course. They're yours."

We stand together, and I let her pull me into a tight hug. It doesn't feel like hugging my mom, but I hope one day it will feel like hugging a friend. I wrap my arms around her tighter.

If this is goodbye, then I'm okay with it. I have a family, and I have a mom. I've had one all along. I walk around the room, moving closer to the photographs. She looks happy in the progression of her life from her early twenties

329

to now. Her eyes get brighter over the years, less burdened. She reminds me of Trish, not okay but getting better over time. I bet my photos will look like this one day too. That's our history, our culture, the story of the Cooper family. We survive.

Renee and I are sitting on the front step when JoJo pulls back into the cul-de-sac. The box of cards is in my lap. It's been only ten minutes since I called her, and one hour since she first drove away.

We stand up. Renee's presence now is less overwhelming. We don't look the same on the outside, but I hope I carry her strength on the inside. JoJo parks the car, and she and Derek consult each other before both getting out. A rush of joy spreads through my body, and I launch myself toward them.

Derek's arms open, catching me midleap as I drop the box on the grass and wrap my arms around his neck. My face buries into his collarbone. I let his familiar scent engulf me as I breathe him in. I find his ear and whisper the words I couldn't say back two nights ago.

"I love you too."

I pull away, his smile brighter than the sun. Standing on my toes, I press my lips against his. He pauses for only a second, caught off guard, before kissing me back. His relief dips into me.

This time I pull away from him, but our noses still touch.

"How do you feel?" he asks.

"Like I just took my first breath," I reply, kissing him again. He holds my face with both hands, pinkie fingers tangling into my hair.

A throat clears behind us. JoJo is staring with a sly smile. I laugh and pull her into us. Renee stands alone in the yard. She's picked up the box of cards. I untangle myself from the hug.

I yank them both up the walkway toward her. She watches them carefully, like a cornered animal. "This is Renee. Renee, this is JoJo and Derek. My best friends."

Derek pulls her into a hug. He feels about her the way his parents felt about me—cautious. But it's the de la Rosa way. The apple didn't fall far from the tree. She pats his back with one hand. I take the box from her.

JoJo has a tight smile on her face. While I've forgiven Renee, JoJo is a lot like Mr. Darcy. Her good opinion once lost is lost forever.

When the silence sets in, it's time to go.

Renee gives me a small smile. "Tell Grandma I say hi?" she asks, shoving her hands into her pockets. We don't hug again.

"I will," I promise. I turn to get in the car and then pause. "Did you ever take me to school with you? When I was little?"

She's surprised at the question, but answers with a nod. "Yeah, I did. A couple of times."

"It's a weird question, but do you remember what color the walls were?"

She looks up at the sky for a moment, digging through memories. "They were blue," she says, smiling at the clouds above her. "Sky blue."

I smile. "Thank you."

She smiles back and then retreats to her front step.

I climb into the back seat of the rental car and settle the box on the floorboard. JoJo pulls away from the curb. I look one last time through the back window and wave. Renee waves back from the yard until we've turned the corner and she's gone.

"Everything good?" JoJo asks, signaling onto the highway and ignoring honks from the other cars. It's so normal for a life so altered.

"Not completely," I answer, leaning back against the seat. "But that's okay."

CHAPTER THIRTY-THREE

GRANDMA PICKS UP ON THE SECOND RING. THE WHEEL spinning on tonight's *Wheel of Fortune* is prominent in the background. She listens to TV louder and louder these days.

"You could've told me, you know," I say. My butt is going numb from the cold bathroom floor. The lights are off, and it's the only place in this home that isn't mine where I can unpack the day and store it all where it fits. "That she didn't ask to see me; you could have told me."

"Would you have gone if I had?"

"No," I admit. I am back in my large Disney World shirt, with an added pair of clean basketball shorts I stole from

Derek's bag. Not that I intend to end up in his bed again. I don't think.

"All right, then." She's silent on her end, and I imagine her trying to solve the puzzle before the contestants.

"But why?" I ask.

"You were so sad," she says. "So unsure of yourself. Your essays, the college fair. It was like you wouldn't even dare to hope. I thought it would help, talking to her."

I lift myself off the floor and shake feeling back into my legs. I'm still a little upset, but the anger, the darkness, is gone. It's easy to forgive her. Everything she did was out of love.

My feet are silent against the floor as I traipse into the living room to turn on the big-screen television, the phone still pressed to my ear. JoJo and Derek are both sitting at the round kitchen table over the large pizza we picked up on the way home, after JoJo and I vetoed Derek's proposal for another round of tacos. A bottle of JoJo's Lactaid sits on the table, though I doubt it will help. She's eaten three slices and had a milkshake. She's tempting fate.

Pulling the remote from between the cushions, I flip to the basic cable stations until *Wheel of Fortune* pops up on the guide. Pat Sajak's voice fills the living room. People, Places, and Things is the category. The trailing contestant catches a bankrupt after having almost solved the entire puzzle. Some of these people have the absolute worst go of it.

"Tough luck," Grandma and I mutter at the same time. We both laugh, the tension releasing from the conversation.

"What did you two talk about?" she asks.

"You."

She grunts.

"You were there from the beginning. Thank you," I say. I don't know if I've ever said it before.

"Thank *you*," she responds. "You're all I've got, kid."

I flip over on the couch onto my stomach, moving my phone to the other ear. "Do you remember when I was little and you went to that conference and left me home alone?"

"You weren't alone," she objects.

"Do you remember?" I press.

"Of course I remember. You were a total brat. Had to come home a week early." She laughs.

"Why did you leave me with her, then?" I don't mean it as an accusation, but pure curiosity. If Renee had been so ill-prepared for motherhood, in her own words, why leave me alone with her? It doesn't fall neatly in place with the over-protective grandmother I know.

"Why not? You were safe. She would never have hurt you," she explains. "And she sat on those stairs for days feeding you cherry Jell-O cups. How many people would have done that? Only your mother."

That word doesn't carry the same pain it used to, nor the same weight. It's just a word, and Renee is just a person, who has punished herself for the same reasons I have for my entire life. But she had protected me when she could, and that's all you can ask of another person—to fight for you when it matters.

"Rome, Italy," Grandma and I yell. The only letters missing are the vowels, and I can't believe none of them have figured it out yet. We solve the puzzle. Together.

"Let me know when you're taking off tomorrow," she instructs.

"I love you," I say, listening to her breath crackle through the phone's poor reception.

"Times infinity," she answers before the call beeps to an end.

JoJo comes over and sits in front of me, leaning back into my stomach. "It's not fair," she says, biting into her slice crust-first. "At one point, all three of us had dysfunctional families." She jabs her finger at herself, Derek, and me. "Yesterday, two of us did." Now she just points at herself and me. "And now, it's just me."

"Aw, JoJo," I say, pulling her down into a hug. Her pizza smacks into the couch cheese first. "Your family's right here, sister." I push her face into the cushions.

She bucks out of my grip. "Oh, no. This family right here's the most dysfunctional one of them all."

I lift my head to look at Derek over the top of the couch. He's double fisting one slice of Hawaiian and one slice of meat lover's from the half-and-half box. He's leaning back in his chair, already in a mozzarella hangover.

"Hot," I joke, though he very much is.

"I do what I can." His eyes sparkle.

"Oh, jeez," JoJo groans. "Take a knee already." She flops back down onto the couch. "If you two become one of those *we* couples—*we* can't make it, *we* would love to, *we* binged *Stranger Things* in one afternoon—I will set your cars on fire."

"I don't have a car," I giggle.

She peers over the couch. "Then I'll set your car on fire twice, De la Rosa."

Derek and I silently agree to let her kick our asses in *Jeopardy!*, and when we all make our bets for Final Jeopardy, I bet it all, confident that I've already won.

CHAPTER THIRTY-FOUR

GRANDMA, DEREK, JOJO, AND I ARE SITTING ON MY LIVING room floor. Open Chinese food containers cover the coffee table. In some ways, it feels as if we've come full circle and are all right back where we started. The same bodies, but filled with different people.

"How was the trip?" Grandma asks, handing us each a cup of orange soda.

All three of us look at one another before breaking into a laugh. What a question for the ages.

"The museum was fun," JoJo says, kicking us off with the easy parts of the trip.

"I hate to say it, I hope I don't sound ridiculous, but it *was* fun," Derek agrees with a nod. He looks pained to admit it.

"Was someone recording that?" JoJo asks, looking around the room. "Can we have that written down and notarized?"

"Okay, don't be dramatic," Derek responds.

"After all the whining, no less." She shakes her head and leans back against the couch.

"I was not whining," he disagrees.

"You whined a little bit," I interject.

"Et tu, Michie." He stares at me wide-eyed, betrayed.

"*Why can't we go to the comic book store?*" JoJo mocks in a deep voice that does no justice for the musical rhythm in which he speaks.

"Ms. C," he says, looking to my grandma for help. "Do you see how they treat me?"

Grandma chuckles, collecting empty cartons from the floor.

"Did you learn something?" she asks.

"I learned about ejection seats." They all stare at me. "They're these seats they wanted to use as a safety precaution so the pilot and commander, but no one else, could get out of a spacecraft about to crash or explode or something. But they got rid of them."

JoJo snorts. "Why on earth would they get rid of them?"

"I guess because they wanted to face things together," I answer.

"And the whole survivor's guilt thing," Derek adds.

"Right. Survivor's guilt." I look over at Grandma. "Sometimes surviving is the hardest part."

She pats a hand to her chest and mouths, *I love you*.

I look past her through my open bedroom door. I can't see them, but I know they're there—the box I brought back from Houston and the one Grandma pulled from the trash on my birthday. They still hold painful memories, but they also hold a lot of hope, each representing years of survival.

I love you too, I mouth back.

Times infinity.

"What's the formula for the Pythagorean theorem?" JoJo asks from the back seat. An old stack of SAT flash cards are in her lap.

My feet are up on Derek's dashboard as we fight the unusually heavy Saturday morning traffic. Everyone is headed in the same direction. It's 7:15 and we all need our butts in our seats, pencils sharpened, in the next thirty minutes. I would have left the house sooner, but it took Derek and I a little too long to grab JoJo after he'd picked me up this morning. He has soft lips; sue me.

The quarter-size ziplock bag Grandma packed for me is overflowing with yellow number-two pencils and erasers. Derek maneuvers through the cars trying to make an illegal U-turn into the middle school parking lot.

JoJo snaps her fingers. "Focus," she shrieks.

"JoJo, anything I don't know by now I'm not going to know in the next"—I check my Fitbit—"twenty-eight minutes." Then I remove the watch as illicit contraband before I forget and take it in with me.

"What do you mean you don't know it?" she asks hysterically. "It's the foundation of the math section." She looks ready to pull out her eyelashes, hair by solitary hair.

"Oh my God," I groan. "Relax. Pythagorean theorem, A squared plus B squared equals C squared." I turn to glare at her. "Happy?"

"I'd be happier if we could do some practice problems," she replies, digging through the stack for examples.

Derek glances at me out of the corner of his eye, and we both attempt not to laugh, lest she kill us both right where we sit. He reaches over and pulls my hand into his lap, right before slamming onto his horn at a group of kids crossing the street like a pack of zombies. I squeeze his fingers.

He parks in front of the doors, earning a scowl from a group of girls huddled together. I grab my phone out of my pocket and drop it in Derek's cupholder.

"You have your admissions ticket?" JoJo asks like a concerned parent, trying to count out everything in my clear bag. "Extra pencils?"

Between her and Grandma, I have a grand total of twelve extra pencils. I can switch out every half column of bubbling and still have pencils untouched.

"Admissions ticket makes it sound so enjoyable, like an amusement park. Why don't they call it horror ticket, or anything else?" I mumble, climbing out of the car.

JoJo nearly forces her entire body through her rolled-down window. "Remember to fill in an answer even if you don't know," she advises. "And erase fully. And don't get spooked if you get a lot of Cs in a row. It's a psychological test designed to freak you out. And…"

"Okay," Derek interjects, moving to roll up her window with her body still in it. She punches the back of his headrest. "You'll do great," he says over her yelping.

I laugh and wave them both away, wondering how they are going to not kill each other over the next few hours. A crowd of on-edge teenagers sweeps me into the building, where my ID is checked and I'm shuttled off to a freezing classroom. I roll my fingers into the bottom hem of the space-museum crewneck sweater that both Derek and JoJo forced me to buy. Who knows if I'll ever be back in Houston to get one another time.

I'm more nervous now than I was the first time I took the SAT, when it felt like just another test on just another Saturday. Now that so many have put in countless hours to get me here, I don't want to let anyone down, most importantly myself. I've been on the sidelines of my own life, but now I'm finally in the game. I smile at the sports reference and laugh at the small smiley faces Derek has drawn on all thirteen of my pencils.

Three hours later, the proctors are collecting our tests, and I have pencil lead all over the inside of my left hand. My brain feels like cold oatmeal. But I feel good. I smile at the girl next to me, wanting to share the feeling of crossing the finish line. But she glowers back before standing to leave the room. I shrug, sliding my rolled ziplock bag into my back pocket.

It's noon now, and the sun sits high at its peak in the sky. Despite everyone starting around the same time, my room was the last one released and the parking lot is now deserted. Only a familiar Audi sits parked at the curb.

Derek and JoJo are leaning against it, sharing a gas station–sized bag of nacho cheese Doritos. JoJo races up the stone stairs to grab my arms.

"So?" she asks. "How was the verbal? I think we drilled the hardest words." Unlike me, JoJo is a big fan of the exam postmortem.

"It was fine." I shrug, leaning next to Derek on the car. He wraps his arm around my shoulders. His fingers are tinted orange.

"Fine?" JoJo asks. "Like you did fine, or the test was fine? Like you don't think you did well?"

I don't know the difference between those iterations of her question, but my brain is too tired to figure it out.

I roll my eyes. "I killed it." I say it to appease her, but it feels true. I *did* kill it.

"Wooh," she yelps, shooting her hands over her head in a full body shimmy. "Take that, Brown; your newest freshman is coming in hot." She waves two middle fingers in the air, earning a disdainful look from a passing dad and his two teenage sons. They look like they've been hit by a semitruck.

Derek chuckles as he pulls me in close, his lips pressing against the back of my head.

"I love you fools," I mumble, as JoJo joins us, sandwiching me between them.

Derek releases us and reaches into the car, turning the key just enough so that the radio starts. "Sweet Victory" blares through the speakers. We all laugh, our voices carried away in the Virginia breeze. Yes, sweet, sweet victory.

CHAPTER THIRTY-FIVE

DEREK DE LA ROSA AT 7:38 A.M.: Busy?

MICHIE COOPER AT 7:45 A.M.: its sunday

DEREK DE LA ROSA AT 7:46 A.M.: Great, so no?

DEREK DE LA ROSA AT 7:46 A.M.: Want to go get some flowers?

DEREK DE LA ROSA AT 7:47 A.M.: I don't want a box of cards I never got to send

I GLANCE DOWN AT THE NEW BOX OF CARDS RENEE GAVE me, a box of missed chances and regret. I get out of bed and get dressed.

The cemetery is empty when we get there, the thick layer of dew starting to lift as we traipse across the wet grass.

Derek is holding a bouquet of blue hydrangeas in one hand, his other clasped around mine. I can feel the tension in his fingers.

We stop at a new gravestone. Emmanuel de la Rosa, his grandfather. The tension turns to trembling as Derek begins to cry.

"I can step away," I offer, so that he can have a moment. I don't know what people do at cemeteries. I don't know anyone who has ever died. People on TV always have long conversations, so I presume he wants his privacy. But when I start to pull away, his hand tightens around mine. So, I step closer and wrap my free arm around his stomach.

We stand there in silence. For minutes, for hours, I can't tell. Whatever conversation Derek has with his grandfather, carried back and forth by the wind, it seems to work. His shoulders relax, unburdened. He stoops down and leans the flowers against the granite. He touches the stone with the tips of his fingers.

"Nos vemos, Abue," he says before standing. He wipes the dirt from his jeans and then reclaims my hand. His is gritty, but I don't mind it. He pulls me closer and wraps his arm around my shoulders as we head back to his car.

"You okay?" I ask him.

He grips the steering wheel until his knuckles turn red and then shakes out his shoulders. "Yeah, I'm…I'm good actually. Thank you for coming." His eyes are wet but focused.

"Of course," I say. I'm honored that he trusted me with this. "Now what?" It's still pretty early.

"Pancakes," he says, "and then we have a college fair to get to."

It takes over half an hour to find free parking near the Convention Center. Derek offered to pay for the garage several times, but on principle, I refused. College is expensive enough. The least they could do was make the fair free.

The building is full of people from all over the city. As Derek and I get our passes for the fair, someone jerks my shoulder backward. I spin around, ready to buck on whoever woke up and chose violence this morning, but Monica and Peter stand behind me, laughter on their lips.

"What are y'all doing here?" I ask, pulling them into a hug.

They reclaim each other's hands as I release them, and my smile is so big I think my face might fall off.

"Decided to check out what all the hoopla is about," Peter says with a shrug.

Monica blushes. "A couple of schools have pretty good game-design programs. I don't know." She shrugs like she feels silly for even daring to dream about it. But Monica loves video games, she's good at them, and she always has cool ideas for new ones. If this room is made for anyone, it's her. She deserves a good life more than anyone I know.

"Mo, that's awesome," I say. "Any of these places would be lucky to have you."

"I don't know," she repeats. "It's been kind of hard to keep my grades up moving around so much."

Peter rolls his eyes. "She's being modest. She's still top ten percent of her graduating class, you believe that?"

"I believe it," Derek says, earning a smile from Monica and an approving nod from Peter.

"I want to check out SCAD's booth," Monica says. "I'd need a portfolio, but I could do community college for a year or two and build one."

Impulsively, I pull her into another hug. She wheezes as I squeeze all the air out of us both.

"I'm so, so proud of you, Monica," I say.

"Yeah, well, I figure if you can do the scariest thing ever, I can too."

Now we're both smiling so wide I bet NASA could pick up our energy signatures.

"Okay, I'll let y'all go, then, but milkshakes later to celebrate?" I offer.

"Celebrate what?" Monica asks. "We haven't gotten in anywhere yet."

"I don't know," I say. "Living."

"Say less," Peter says as he directs Monica away in what I suspect is the direction of SCAD's booth. Monica turns back and gives us a thumbs-up before being swallowed behind a wall of people.

Derek and I continue our search for JoJo, finding her

beaming from the UChicago table in a crewneck sweater with the school logo. I have to admit, she looks bomb in maroon.

"Hey, you two." She looks at our outfits. "What's the occasion?"

Derek and I are still wearing the clothes we wore to the cemetery—khakis and a button-up for him and a cream-colored dress for me. We didn't have to dress up, but it felt respectful.

"Shotgun wedding," I deadpan.

JoJo rolls her eyes and reaches past us to hand a brochure to a waiting family.

"So, how's the hosting going? Getting excited about the school where fun goes to die?"

"Actually, yes." She smiles. "They have an amazing engineering program, and some of the best firms in the country are in the city, so I could get some cool internships. Plus, anything is fun if I'm there."

"You tell no lies," I say, grabbing a brochure.

"You could apply too," she says, getting more excited as the idea grows in her mind. "We could tear up ChiTown."

"I'm not sure anyone from Chicago actually calls it Chi-Town," Derek says.

"Well, I'm not from Chicago."

"Fair point," he assents.

"You should look around though. Every school on the planet is here, it feels like. Brown is by the escalators."

I look at Derek.

He shrugs. "Might as well. We came all this way."

The way he says it takes the pressure off. We're just browsing. Why wouldn't we check out every table, including Brown? We make a beeline through the rows of tables, collecting swag from each school along the way. Beer bottle openers, koozies, key chains, sunglasses. You name it, we grab it. I don't ever turn down a chance at free merch.

"Michie!"

I spin in a circle to find a familiar face shoving her way through bodies to get to us.

"Hey." Morgan's wearing a UPenn hoodie and baseball cap, her braids pulled in a low ponytail. "Showed up after all."

"Yeah, a couple of our friends are hosting," I explain. I introduce Morgan and Derek, slightly better than the Peter introduction, but not by much.

"Well, I wanted to make sure you didn't miss the Penn merch and the application fee waiver." She hands me a small baggie, like the kind you get at the dentist's office.

"I had no idea there were fee waivers here too." Derek steps closer to get out of the way of the crowd. Normally I would feel uncomfortable talking about this around someone like him, but not anymore. Not with him. I smile to myself at how far we've come.

"Oh yeah." Morgan smiles. "That's, like, half the point. Anyway, have a good time. Some of the swag is amazing. Definitely don't miss Tech. They're doing a football-season-pass raffle."

She waves and begins pushing her way back in the direction she came from. Derek takes the small bag from me to hold and begins to urge me in the opposite direction, but I step away.

"Hey, Morgan," I say before she's too far away.

"Hmm?"

I have to yell now to make sure she can hear me over the noise. "We're going to do milkshakes later. Want to come?"

She gives me a thumbs-up before returning to the over-crowded UPenn booth.

We find Brown's table where JoJo directed us. It's sur-rounded by students attempting to impress one of the four representatives sent to recruit us. Lana Zhao, a fellow Lee High junior, stands at the table, passing out Brown-branded hand sanitizer. We exchange awkward hellos. We aren't friends, and her having gotten the coveted Brown spot makes it even weirder.

I collect brochures and two hand sanitizers, ready to hightail it out of there when Jennifer Dillon, the main inter-viewer I bombed in front of, steps up to the table.

"Michie," she says with a soft smile.

"Uh," is all I can offer. I mean, for fuck's sake. How am I going to get into college if I turn into a Cro-Magnon when-ever the opportunity presents itself?

"It's great to see you." She circles around the table to shake my hand. Derek moves away to give us space. "It was a hard decision, but I'm thrilled you're still interested in Brown."

"Um, of course." Like, is she dumb? It's Brown. Did she think I was kidding when I said no one wants it more? Which, I don't know if that's actually true, but, like, damn—if anyone wants it more than me, they're pretty hard-core.

"I was actually going to reach out to you, but here you are." She smiles like she's speaking to a friend and not some random high school junior. "I know this process can be overly competitive and, well, snobbish, to be honest. But if you ever need anything—a tour of the school, an alumna letter of recommendation—please reach out."

She whips out a business card. She must keep them in her bra or something because she pulled it out of thin air, it seems. She grabs a pen from the table and writes down a number and email address.

"This is my personal cell and email," she explains. I can feel eyes watching us. Some curious. Some jealous. This is the woman they're all trying to impress, and she's talking to *me*.

"I'm serious, Michie. You're exactly the person I want to see at Brown, and if you want, I'll help you get there."

I keep staring between her face and the card, wondering if I'm being punked. "I'm sorry, but why? My interview was terrible."

She laughs now. It's high but sweet, like lemon tart. "You have a lot of heart, a lot to offer, and you really want to be here. When you said no one wants it more than you, I believed it."

A man approaches us and places a hand on her lower

back, leaning to whisper in her ear. She nods in response, and he disappears as fast as he showed up.

"I have to go, but please use that," she says. "Just to keep in touch, even if you don't end up at Brown."

"Yes ma'am," I say, still in disbelief as she waves goodbye.

"That was unexpected," I say as Derek rejoins me.

"Was it?" he asks.

"She basically told me I'm Brown material."

"Michie, you're whatever-you-want-to-be material," he says.

"Yeah," I say, putting the business card safely in the back flap of my phone case. "I guess I am."

Sitting on my bedroom floor, I open up the Word document that has plagued me for months. The cursor flashes at me on a page full of disconnected words created by someone equally as incongruent. The early-decision application to Brown isn't due until November, but Mr. Milligan's rewrite is due on Monday. I skim through Brown's scholarship application package and its list of majors. For the first time, I feel deserving. And ready.

I organize photos I pulled from one of Grandma's albums, the ones of just me and her. Despite the possibility of Renee being in my life, when it comes to family, it will always be the two of us. The two of us with our MLK Day movies and Red Lobster birthdays and waffles topped with ice cream. If family is about history and tradition, we have enough to spare. I add the photos JoJo printed at CVS from our trip—the three of us in our NASA sweatshirts, at the comic book store, and at the taco stand we came to love. They're my inspiration.

I press my finger on my laptop's delete button. I erase every word I had hacked together and glance back at the prompt.

Tell us about a place or community you call home.

Grandma. JoJo. Derek. R.P.E. My family.

I stare at the once-again blank page, seeing only possibilities instead of barriers. This time the cursor flashes and I don't feel fear.

I begin to type.

ACKNOWLEDGMENTS

There are so many people to thank for this little book here that started as personal healing and became bigger than I could have ever imagined. *insert Paul Rudd gif* Look at us, who would've thought?! Not me!

First, to my grandmother. I wouldn't be here without you. I wouldn't be fearless without you. I don't think the English language yet contains the words of gratitude necessary, so thank you will have to suffice. You are everything.

To my agent, Pete, thank you for giving this book a chance. I could not have asked for a more relentless advocate, who sometimes believed in Michie and Co. even more than I did. And thank you to Stuti, for being way more organized than me.

To my editor, Alex. I knew the moment I got off the phone with you a hundred years ago now that this story would be safe with and nurtured by you. Thank you for unlocking pieces of Michie I hadn't even known were there.

To everyone at Little, Brown and Poppy who has touched this book with loving hands and gotten it into the hands of readers: Farrin, Annie, Karina, Stef, Marisa, Hannah, Savannah, and Christie. Thank you to all of the assistants who keep the ship afloat. And a huge thank you to

Erick Dávila. You are an ARTISTE and gave me the cover of my dreams. It is The Moment.

To my first readers who helped me iron out the kinks and gave this book wings: Jen, Mia, Amber, and Gabriella. This book may have stayed on the cutting room floor without your constant support.

To Alex and Amanda, my soulmates. I would never have picked up a pen if you two had not told me that I could. I am nothing without you. To Mrs. Johnson, thank you for reading everything unfinished so that I could one day get here. Thank you to the friends who became family who lifted me up: Taj, Dre Dre, Cathy, Ayana, Julie, Daniel, Maya, James, Kai, Monet, and Myah. I love you all more than Cherry Coke.

To Milo, I hope you're chewing the biggest bone up there in Dog Heaven. Thank you for being my best friend.

To Pickles and Pax, thank you for the cuddles and following me around the house. You have no idea how loved it makes me feel. To G, thank you for the milkshakes that got me through deadlines and for the one funny joke you have ever made that still sustains me. *Al dente.*

To sixteen-year-old me, thank you for not giving up. Thank you for listening to that sometimes near-silent voice in your head that promised it would one day be worth it. You gave us a chance and I am forever grateful.

To God, thank you for strength and wisdom. Thank you for listening.

To you, the reader. Thank you for choosing Michie and her friends. I hope you found peace in these pages.

Nohelia Valentin

LANE CLARKE

is an author of young adult contemporary books who was raised in Virginia, aka the greatest place in the world. When she is not binge-watching *One Tree Hill* or *My Wife and Kids*, you can find her experimenting with food recipes or baking cakes (out of the Funfetti box). She works as an attorney in Washington, DC. She invites you to visit her online at laneclarkewrites.com and @lanewriteswords.